# FOREVER
# BOUND

## DEANNA ROY

casey shay press

# Forever Bound

Casey Shay Press
PO Box 160116
Austin, TX 78716
www.caseyshaypress.com

Paperback: ISBN: 9781938150234

Ebook-ISBN: 9781938150289

Library of Congress Control Number: 2015910116

## Other books by Deanna Roy

**Forever Innocent**

Part 1 of the Forever Series

**Forever Loved**

The shattering sequel to Forever Innocent

**Forever Sheltered**

Tina's story with Dr. Darion

**Stella & Dane**

A bad boy romance

**Baby Dust: A Novel about Miscarriage**

Women's fiction on baby loss

**Jinnie Wishmaker**
**Marcus Mender**

an adventure series for 9-12 year olds under the name DD Roy

**Dust Bunnies: Secret Agents**

an iPad story book app for children ages 3-9

Learn more about the author at

www.deannaroy.com

For all the moms so lovingly listed
in the final pages of this book
by fans and readers

•\*´`\*•♥•\*´`\*•

# 1

## JENNY

This face would be in all the tabloids tomorrow. It had to look good.

"I need *something*," I told my friends Tina and Corabelle. They both sat on my bed giving me moral support as I put on makeup for this crazy important night.

Corabelle rose and stood behind me, her fingers lifting my soft pink dreadlocks. "You look beautiful," she said.

"It's not enough," I said.

Maybe I needed more color. I dug through one of my drawers.

"Please tell me you're not going Kardashian on us in front of all those photographers," Tina said.

"Uggh, no," I told her, pulling out a tube of emerald eyeliner. "I have to keep it classy for Frankie."

Frankie was my movie director boyfriend. Well, *pretend* boyfriend. I had been his paid arm candy the past few months to attend premieres and industry parties. But now we were done. He'd fallen in love for real.

And not with me.

Not that it mattered. I didn't love him either. We'd just been having fun. Platonic fun. Normally I didn't do platonic, but Frankie had been an exception.

"You're making yourself crazy," Corabelle said as she adjusted a few stray locks over my ears. "It will be fine."

I watched my friends via the mirror. Corabelle's face was serious, her hands fiddling with my hair like she was solving a puzzle.

Tina flopped back on the bed and stared up at the cascades of colored silk draped from the ceiling. "Girl, this room looks like a Care Bear puked a rainbow," she said.

I turned to her, realizing I might have overdone the decor. But Frankie had given me his credit card, and said my love of color made him happy. So I went nuts. The wallpaper shifted colors like a pastel waterfall. Even the makeup table with its movie-starlet surround of bulbs was a soft pink.

"Well, I can't afford to change it now," I said, and opened the glitter liner.

"He's cutting you off now that he's ditching you?" Tina asked.

"I gave up the credit line yesterday," I said, adding an edge to the wings coming off my eyelids. The deep green liner matched my dress perfectly.

"These guys show no mercy," Tina said.

"Part of the contract," I said with a shrug.

Corabelle continued to smooth my pink dreadlocks. She couldn't get enough of them. "These are really going to make you stand out," she said.

"I hope so," I said. "This is my last chance to get in the

industry before I graduate and have to work someplace boring."

"The photographers are going to love you," Corabelle said. "It's a big movie premiere. It will be a madhouse."

She was right about that. And my public breakup with Frankie was going to turn some heads. Make some people dislike me. Sigh. But I couldn't let anybody know the real deal. I had signed on the dotted line.

Tina hopped off the bed to stand with Corabelle. The three of us were a sight, me with my pink 'do, Corabelle and her long trailing black curls, and tiny impish Tina with her signature short pigtails.

"You are totally going to draw all the clicks, especially once they get a whiff of the scandal," Tina said.

I pressed my hands to my cheeks. "The paparazzi are merciless. They LIVE for getting your bad side."

"You don't have a bad side," Corabelle said gently.

I stared into the mirror, cursing my eyes for being such a dull gray. Half the reason I kept my hair pink was to make up for my boring eyes.

Tina shook her head. "I can't believe you got into this mess."

"It's not a mess," I said. "It was a mutually beneficial arrangement." I dropped the liner back into the drawer and dug around for some lip gloss.

"You're at the end of it, at least," Tina said, sitting back down.

I picked up a sparkling tube and shook it. "Now I have to survive the fallout," I said grimly. Tonight was going to be brutal.

"You will," Corabelle said. "And you'll be free to chase all the teaching assistants and doctors you want." She smiled over at Tina.

"I had forgotten about all the hot docs at the hospital," I said. I hadn't, but they'd been out of reach since Frankie, so I'd pushed them from my mind.

"They don't make good sugar daddies," Tina said. "They're workaholics."

"Why did you go with dreadlocks?" Corabelle asked. She couldn't stop playing with them.

I dotted my lips and tilted my head, watching the thick pink extensions sway against my bare shoulders. "It was my last hair appointment on the director's dime," I said. "I had to make it good."

"I liked Frankie," Corabelle said. "I hate that it has to end with such drama."

I turned around in the chair to face her and Tina. "Thank you both for keeping the secret. Nobody was supposed to know, not even my friends."

Tina tweaked her pigtails. "Not my circus. Not my monkeys."

I walked over to my dresser to choose some earrings. Almost everything in my jewelry chest was from Frankie. I wished it didn't have to end so soon.

But I had to let him go without a fuss, per our agreement when we began our *faux* relationship. In the time we'd been together, I'd gotten more manicures, hair appointments, and skin treatments than a beauty pageant diva.

He'd also bought me an incredible amount of gifts. Clothes. Furniture. A diamond-encrusted Rolex that was worth more than my car.

I'd gone to outrageous parties with famous musicians and movie stars. My name had as many Google hits as a B-list actress even though I was just a lowly undergrad who worked at a coffee shop.

It had been amazing.

But unlike in romance novels, my movie director boyfriend hadn't fallen in love with me. He hadn't even made a move. Everything was just as he'd laid it out in the contract. Event attendance. Fidelity. Charm. Lovesick expressions for the press. Occasional PDA when the photographers were around. We had an optional clause for a mild scandal as a publicity tool, but Frankie decided not to use it while we were together.

For our last night as a couple, he was introducing me around. I didn't really think I had it in me to be an actress, and I liked pizza too much to go for modeling, but a non-talent position in those industries would suit me just fine. Even being on the fringe of the glamour was better than some boring desk job.

I didn't have any other idea of what I was going to do with a liberal arts degree come graduation in June.

Just as I slipped the diamond studs through my earlobes, the doorbell rang. "That's the limo," I said. "Is the dress perfect?" I asked, turning in a tight circle.

"It's gorgeous," Corabelle said.

I smoothed the fabric across my belly. The dress was stretchy and form fitting. You couldn't even wear a thong with it, or it showed. The top was off the shoulders with a tight band running across the front. So no bra really worked. The strapless ones had all seemed too bulky and the little tape-on lifters didn't seem to do much for me.

So I was full commando. If I played strip poker, I'd be a goner in one round.

"I can't believe you're not wearing underwear," Tina said. "Please tell me you're not going to pull a Britney."

"No way. I'm a class act," I said with a laugh. "Not because I *am*. Frankie's contract insisted on it."

Tina snorted. "That must be one heck of a document."

"It is. Was." I tugged the skirt down. It wasn't super short, hitting just above my knee. I didn't think it was a risk. Besides, it was so tight that I could barely separate my knees.

"Call if you need me later," Corabelle said.

I nodded, suddenly feeling my throat get tight. "It'll be hard, giving all this up."

"You going to look for a new sugar daddy?" Tina asked. "Bound to be some at the party."

"No." I picked up my tiny evening bag. "I'm fine with whatever happens. I can return to my man-hopping days."

Corabelle headed for the door. "You'll be back in your element."

I dropped the lip gloss into my purse. "It's been a while since I got to bang a stranger." Or anybody, I thought. Strictly faithful to a platonic boyfriend. It would have been impossible, if the perks hadn't been so fabulous.

I'd gone through a lot of batteries.

Corabelle gave me a quick hug, careful not to disturb my hair or makeup. "Just let me know if you need anything."

The three of us walked through my apartment. I felt a wave of melancholy. I liked Frankie. Even though we'd never so much as made out other than in public, I was sad to see him go.

But also, it was losing this life. I was born for it. I didn't mind the photographers. I didn't care about the gossip. I loved the mingling. The way people worked a room, sizing up who they needed to talk to and who needed to talk to them. The whole hierarchy, shifting and changing, rising and falling along with box office returns and bankability.

The worst part of this whole arrangement was that it had to end.

Maybe a quickie with some rich, hot actor would make me feel better.

Yes. Yes, indeed.

# 2

## CHANCE

I sure picked the wrong road to hitchhike on today.

The wind picked up, and I pressed the neck of my T-shirt over my nose. The dust was unrelenting, like somebody was kicking sand in my face.

My guitar case banged against my thigh as I stumbled, hardly able to see as the desert floor seemed to rise up to the sky. Interstate 15 was only a few feet away, but I could barely make out the asphalt.

Hell, if the drivers were as blind as me, I could get run over any second.

I took a few more steps away from the highway. Nobody would pick me up in this mess. They couldn't even see me.

My feet kept going out of sheer will. I could make out something ahead, some sort of low billboard. I hadn't seen a gas station or another building in a couple miles, so I couldn't really backtrack. Maybe that sign could at least give me a wind break until whatever was going on settled.

For the first time since I left my hometown of Chattanooga, Tennessee, I questioned my decision to quit my dead-end job and take off across the country playing for tips anywhere that would take me.

I'd been doing all right, but this was definitely a low point.

The sign loomed ahead, but the wind was slowing down a little, so I plunged on. I started to worry that maybe I didn't have enough water to last me however long it might take to catch a ride.

This was the hardest stretch of the journey. I left Vegas three hours ago and was aiming for LA. Getting to the ocean sounded like a fitting end to these months of living by the seat of my pants. Once I got there, I'd have to figure out what I was doing next.

I definitely didn't look forward to that.

Headlights pierced the dusty gloom. I shifted my guitar case to my right hand and held up my left. I doubted they could even see me, but it was worth a shot.

The car blew past me, just as I figured, but then the world turned red as brake lights lit up the haze. It was stopping.

I hotfooted it up to the car, an aging boat-sized Buick with half the paint sandblasted off from driving through the desert.

This was the trickiest part of hitchhiking, seeing who was picking you up, figuring out their motives, deciding if you were safe.

The lock popped up and I opened the passenger door and bent down to peer inside.

My whole body relaxed as a grandmotherly woman gazed over at me, her silver hair tied back. She reminded me of Gram. "Hello, ma'am," I said.

"Well, don't let the whole desert in, boy," she said in a smooth friendly voice. "Get yourself settled."

I opened the back door and shoved my guitar case on the seat. The car was immaculate inside, and I winced a little to see all the sand spilling across the green vinyl.

"Nothing a hand-vac won't handle," the woman said. "Come on. I want to get out of this sandstorm."

I jumped back into the front and yanked the door closed. "Much obliged," I said.

The woman dropped the gearshift into drive and stomped on the gas. We zoomed forward, and I fumbled for the seat belt.

She laughed as I shoved the silver buckle into its slot. "Don't worry about me. Been driving some fifty-five years and never an accident yet."

I watched her strong wrinkled hands turn the wheel. She wore a cranberry paisley dress and sturdy brown shoes. But a pink ribbon was tied through her hair, ending in a big bow just above her ear. It held just enough dash to make her seem like a much younger woman.

"I like your bow," I said.

She cupped her hand over it. "No reason not to put on a few little pretties, even at my age." She gave me a wink. "You never know when a handsome beau is going to turn up."

I laughed a little.

"Where are you headed, young man?"

"LA," I said. "Though any distance you can take me, I'd appreciate."

"I'm only going as far as San Bernardino," she said. "But that'll get you past the desert anyway. You could bus in from there easy."

"That's great, thanks," I told her and settled back against the seat. The car was roomy and cool, a relief after the dust outside. "These storms happen often?"

"Oh, yes," she said. "I see one every few runs to Vegas." She peered out the window. "That where you're coming from?"

"I did a stint there," I said. "Sang in a little cafe on the west side."

"So you're a singer," she said. "Planning to change the world in LA? Be a big star?" Her voice held no hint of derision or amusement. Just a plain question.

"No, ma'am. Just going to play around town a little, figure out what's next."

"So you've been doing this a while?"

"Started off in Tennessee, been thumbing it for five months."

"You got family back home?"

My jaw tensed over that question. "Not really."

She nodded, leaning into the steering wheel to stare at the haze. "Sure is a good 'un out there. A boy could get lost in that."

"I appreciate you stopping for me."

She glanced over at me and smiled. "Gotta help a boy live his dream."

We sat in companionable silence for a bit, and I relaxed. I was lucky she had picked me up, as the storm blasted us for twenty more miles.

Hopefully my luck would hold out in California.

Gram dropped me off at a truck stop on the Interstate. I'd learned in the past few months that these were the best places to pick up rides. Truckers didn't mind companions. But she was right. If a ride didn't turn up, I could always catch a bus into town.

I didn't have enough money to spend on a hotel, even a bad one, but maybe I could get away with sleeping on the beach. That was certainly something that I'd never done. Nights could get tricky. Sometimes I rode 24-hour buses just to catch some z's.

I got a cup of coffee at the counter and looked over the customers, seeing if there were any prospects. The drivers were sparse midafternoon. One gruff man with a beard to his chest stared at me with beady eyes. I nursed my coffee for another half hour, then decided maybe I'd take off down the highway.

The doors burst open and a raucous group of four guys tumbled in. The waitress behind the counter paused with her order pad. They didn't take a booth or a table, but piled onto the stools to my right.

"You got some pie?" One of them, a skinny dude with purple sunglasses, slammed his hand on the counter. "I need some old-school pie."

The waitress braced her elbow on the counter, making no move to serve them. "I think you need some old-school manners."

The other guys chorused a "Whoooa" and laughed themselves silly. I suppressed a smirk.

"All right, ma'am," Purple Sunglasses said. "May I please see your list of pies?"

"I got apple, chocolate, and lemon," she said.

"I'll take lemon, thank you," he said, his face poker-straight, like a chastised schoolboy.

She nodded. "Some coffee with that?"

"No, ma'am."

The other three gave her their selections. As soon as she moved past the doors to the back, they took up their loud conversation again.

"We're gonna be late to the gig, man!" one said.

"Nah, no way," the other said.

I couldn't stop staring. They made me think of the Beatles in their '70s phase, all long haired and scruffy, rail thin in polyester pants and colored vests.

Purple Sunglasses caught me looking. "You play guitar?" he asked, tapping his foot against my case.

"I reckon I do," I said.

"A southerner!" another cried out. "Where you from?"

"Tennessee," I answered, feeling wary now. I wasn't interested in being the butt of their jokes.

"That's cool," Purple Sunglasses said. "What brings you to Sunny Cal?"

I shrugged. "Just playing gigs across the country."

"What kind of music?" he asked.

"Probably both kinds," one of the others said. "Country AND Western."

I let the joke roll right off me. It wasn't like I looked country. I wore a Grateful Dead T-shirt and jeans with heavy black boots. It was the accent. I never could seem to lose it. "I mix it up," I said.

"We're the Sonic Kings," he said, gesturing to his friends. "Blues and funk."

"You're playing tonight, I take it?" I asked.

"Yeah, a party for some movie dude."

The waitress brought out the pieces of pie and set them in front of the band.

"Sounds like a sweet gig," I said. "That in LA?"

Purple Shades shoveled pie in his gullet for a minute, then said, "Hollywood, USA." He swallowed. "You need a lift or something?"

"I was headed that direction."

"Right on," he said. "You can hop in our van." He turned to the others. "We got us a roadie."

They followed with a round of "Cool" and "Righteous."

Sweet. I was on my way to LA.

# 3

## JENNY

The evening was going according to plan. I soaked up the glory of walking a red carpet from Frankie's limo to the Chinese Theatre. This movie wasn't one of his, but he got invited to premieres all the time.

Reporters shouted questions as we posed in front of a backdrop plastered with the title of the movie we were about to see. An entire bank of photographers was held back by a red rope. Thousands of fans shouted and cheered behind a metal barricade.

God, this was the life. I swallowed hard over the lump in my throat, grief-stricken that it was ending.

"Why so sad, Pink Princess?" someone shouted.

Frankie glanced over at me, and I straightened my expression. It didn't matter. The gossip sites would speculate over my somberness tomorrow after everything was done.

I smiled and waved.

The reporters called out questions about *Prison Hunt*, Frankie's next film. A crew came forward and interviewed him. I stood behind him, smiling, then carefully stepped away at the right moment. I knew the drill. I wasn't anybody special. Nobody wanted to know anything about some random girl the director brought along. I didn't act or have any sort of career. Which was why Frankie chose me.

Regular Joes who had scored tickets to the premiere walked down the carpet, starstruck and shuffled along by ushers. Tomorrow I would be one of those people, able to gaze at the celebrities only from a distance.

Frankie milked his moment until one of the stars of the current film arrived and the press moved on. Frankie reached for my hand. "Let's go in," he said. "That was a good run."

I nodded, aware of the popping of flashes as we walked the rest of the way into the theater. Once out of range of the photographers, we went through a security check and were escorted to our seats.

My throat tightened again as I surveyed the room. Despite arriving fairly late, it would be an hour or more until the film began. We still had to watch the interviews taking place outside, now showing onscreen. Then the traditional introduction of the cast and speeches about everyone's brilliance and talent.

Frankie was animated, anxious, I knew, for his own premiere next month. I hadn't been around during its filming, as that was concluded over a year ago. I would narrowly miss the shooting schedule of his next movie too.

Rotten luck on that. Not that I could afford to miss that much class. I did have to graduate. Still, I craved the chance to be on a movie set, brought in by the director. That was *access*.

I kept a natural, mildly pleased expression on my face as we were greeted by other industry people arriving at the theater. I desperately wanted to take out my cell phone and get one last selfie among the glitterati, but I knew that was out of line for my position and didn't dare embarrass Frankie, even now.

As the lights finally dimmed, I paid little attention to the film and thought ahead to the after-party. Frankie sat close, his arm draped around me. I wondered who he had fallen in love with. He wasn't for me, really, twice my age and not exactly my type. But he was kind, and funny, and I would miss him.

Now I was getting all blue. I couldn't be photographed that way.

Surely there would be someone at the party who would find me interesting. Maybe not as much as Frankie, but I could live with less.

I just had to find him.

# 4

## CHANCE

The boys from the Sonic Kings were raucous and animated in the two hours it took to get to the gig. Purple Sunglasses, whose real name was Paul, navigated their VW van through an impressive neighborhood of mansions flanked with palm trees.

"You wanna hang with us for the night, Tennessee?" Paul asked. "Free food and booze if you help with setup."

I didn't have any better offers, and who knows, maybe fate would shine on me at the party and I'd figure out my next move.

"Sounds good," I said.

We turned on to a long tree-lined street. I'd seen a lot of things in my expedition across the country, but never anything like this. Enormous mechanized gates stood like sentries over the winding road. You caught little more than glimpses of the homes themselves, as leafed-out bushes blocked the view.

We pulled up to a driveway with its gates thrown wide. Dark had already descended, but the front lawns were brightly lit with floodlights aiming down from the trees.

One of the other band members whistled. "Whooee, look at these digs."

The van coughed and chugged its way around a circle drive where a couple valets were setting up a stand.

"Curbside service," Paul said. "Sweet life."

"How'd you get this gig anyway?" I asked.

"Movie director dude is a friend of a friend. His big premiere downtown is tonight."

A valet opened the side door uncertainly. "You with the caterer?" one asked.

"We're the band!" Paul said with exuberance. "Where do we unload?"

The valet pointed to a side driveway that wound to the back.

"We're in!" Paul said as we circled the house. "We've got a stage and all here."

We pulled up next to a truck where two men were unloading an ice sculpture of a dinosaur. Must be related to the movie, I figured, unable to stop grinning. I never expected the final destination of my trip to be as good as this.

We all clambered to the back and Paul passed me a cymbal box. The grounds outside the van were unreal, as big as a park, immaculate and green. Little white balls of light were strung all over the place, crisscrossing tables with red tablecloths.

"Totally prime," Paul said, surveying the yard. "These people have money to burn."

The stage was just past the pool, which was full of floating flowers. All around, perfectly clipped hedges lined meandering sidewalks.

I could get used to this.

We set the first load on the edge of the stage, and Paul took off to find somebody in charge to ask about power. I headed back to the van for more gear, puffed up and pleased to be here. I didn't care if I was schlepping.

After a few loads from the van to the stage, we had all the gear laid out. Paul sat on the stage, plugging in amps and mikes. The drummer assembled his set.

They didn't seem to need me, so I wandered the scene, dodging caterers with metal bins of food and decorators setting out centerpieces.

Swanky. The paths meandered off away from the lit-up area, still lined with hedges. There was only an occasional light on the walkway this far from the party. I looked up and could actually see the stars. We weren't near the ocean as far as I could tell, but I'd explore that tomorrow. See what LA had to offer, spend a few days, or maybe a week.

Beyond that, I had no idea.

Behind me, I could hear the thump thump thump of a drum, then the diddling of a bass guitar. They must be doing the sound check. I hustled back to the lights and energy of the pre-party setup, eagerness thrumming through my body.

Paul played lead guitar and did vocals. They launched into "Super Fly," and Paul wasn't bad. His voice had a heaviness to it, out of sync with his skinny body in the gold vest and purple shades.

They stopped the song midway and the bass guitarist adjusted his monitor.

Paul looked down at me. "What you got in your repertoire, country boy? Any blues?"

"Hell, yeah," I said. I hopped onstage. "This probably isn't a job for my Seagull, though." My acoustic guitar was back in the van.

Paul handed me his electric one. "Be my guest."

I turned to the others. "I'm sure you know 'Mustang Sally.'"

"Right on," the drummer said, and instantly set a simple beat with the bass and the hi-hat.

I turned to the mike. The tables spread far and wide, encircling the flower-laden pool. It didn't matter that they were empty.

The Fender was light, chilled from the night air. I pressed the steel wire against the fret and banged out the opening notes alongside the drummer, and sang like every table was full.

"Mustang Sally… Mmm hmmmm. Mustang Sally."

The bass guitarist let out a whoop and joined in. Paul danced alongside on the stage.

The clinking of dishes subsided as our sound took over the world around us. Waiters paused, trays of silverware upheld. The girls arranging greenery around the ice dinosaur turned to watch.

I made eye contact with each and every one, belting out the blues like my world began and ended with a girl named Sally to ride.

Paul snagged a mike and filled out the chorus. The bassist leaned in and added edge to the vocals.

We were hot. We rode out the song on a magic carpet, gliding through the night on a sound wave.

I signaled to bring the chorus around once more, and we nailed the finish. The sparse collection of workers whooped and cheered.

"Tennessee, you got it goin' ON," Paul said. "You up for doing a tune or two tonight?"

"Hell, yeah," I said.

This day just kept getting better and better.

# 5

## JENNY

The limo pulled up to a beautiful colonial-style mansion with white pillars and a circle drive. I wanted to admire it, soak in my last bit of life in the fast lane, but my nerves were jangling too hard to pay attention.

"It's been fun," I managed to say.

Frankie looked up from his cell phone. He wasn't the best-looking guy I'd dated, more Danny DeVito than Brad Pitt, but he was kind and generous and easygoing.

"It has indeed," he said.

I choked out a laugh. "I think you've been my longest relationship."

He smiled, his teeth flashing in the dark. "I appreciate you changing your lifestyle for me all these months. I know it wasn't easy. Now you can go after boys to your heart's content."

"Probably not my heart that's most interested right now."

His grin grew wider. "I know that was tough too." He leaned

forward and pressed a light kiss to my cheek. "I look forward to looking at the photos of your next conquest. Make it a real good one. Somebody who'll get you in all the tabloids."

"Did you have someone in mind for tonight?"

Frankie tucked his phone in his pocket. "It's up to you. Someone who will make the gossip sites would be best. Alec will appreciate the recognition that I'm available before he and I go public. He doesn't want to be a home wrecker in the press."

I didn't flinch for a second that Frankie's new love was a boy. I knew Frankie was bi when I met him.

"So you want me to appear to be cheating on you?" I asked, my face hot. "I don't want you to look like a chump."

He squeezed my hand. "It's okay. I'm ready to be seen with Alec. I won't be single long."

"I just...like you. I can't stand the way they trump things up for click bait."

Frankie clasped his other hand over mine. "Don't worry about me. When we get there, I need to meet with some industry people, then I'll introduce you to a few who might be able to help you come summer. Feel free to take my limo home when you like. I'll be here all night and won't need it."

"Okay." My eyes pricked a little. "I'm going to miss you."

The back door of the limo opened. "We've had a good time," he said. "But I think you're really going to miss my credit card."

Well, there was that.

Frankie started to move, but I stopped him with my hand on his arm. "Frankie?"

He paused. "What is it, princess?"

"When we started this arrangement, you said you just wanted

someone who looked the part to attend things with you so you could date discreetly."

"That's right," he said.

"Why did you pick me?"

His gentle hand squeezed mine. "You're genuine," he said. "You think you're a plaything, a pretty bauble to flash in front of people, but inside, you're the real deal."

I let go of him. I hadn't expected him to say anything like that.

We scooted around to the back of the car and ducked outside. "Jenny will buzz you when she needs you," he said to Brandon, his driver.

Brandon nodded and closed the door.

The air was cool and still, a near-perfect early spring night. The circle and lawns were strewn with cars of people who hadn't bothered with the valet. The mansion towered over us like a plantation house. I never got used to the places some of these Hollywood people called home.

Frankie held my hand as we headed up the stone steps. I struggled with the dress since it didn't let my knees go more than a few inches apart. I couldn't afford to blow out a seam at this late hour. I had people to impress.

And a man to seduce in front of the paparazzi.

A doorman opened the front entrance, and we passed into the opulent house. The muffled sound of the band playing outside penetrated the indoors.

Ahead were two curving staircases. Between them was a hall to another part of the house. To the right, two tall white doors were thrown open to reveal what could only be called a parlor, full of elegant sofas and paintings. A few men lounged there, smoking cigars. One of them waved at Frankie and gestured him over.

"You go on back and get a drink," he said to me. "Look things over. I'll be around."

"Of course," I said, my heart skittering. Did he really expect me to find someone to cheat on him with? What if no one was interested in lowly me?

I smoothed my dreadlocks and continued through the house between the stairs. Apparently I made a wrong turn, because I wound up in the industrial-sized kitchen packed with catering staff.

"You need help finding the party?" a handsome man in a black vest asked. His blond hair flopped boyishly over his forehead. College student, I'd guess. Might as well work these rusty flirting skills on him.

"Can you show me the way?" I asked. If the photographers caught me with this one, I could already see the headline: *Pink-maned beauty ditches film mogul for busboy.*

Actually, they probably wouldn't even mention me. It would be all about Frankie, what his heartache might do for the film that was about to come out. Frankie claimed they weren't interested in him, but I knew better. Anything movie related was big.

"I'm Andy," the boy said, and extended an elbow.

"You have time to escort me?" I asked.

"Of course. I have to pass through and collect empties anyway."

I took his arm and he led me out of the kitchen and back to the hall. This time we turned left and wound our way through the house.

"No wonder I got lost!" I said.

"Someone should have taken you back," he said.

We arrived at a sunroom decked with white wicker furniture with bright blue cushions. Tucked in a far corner, a couple sipped from wine glasses and kissed. Judging from the age discrepancy and the blond perfection of the stacked girl, she was probably an actress moving in on someone she thought could get her a part.

It happened. It wasn't as common as people believed, but young new arrivals to Hollywood still felt that was how the movie business worked.

In reality, it was a lot of who you knew. The casting agents were as critical as anybody. Directors and producers didn't always get who they wanted. The A-list stars were often attached to a project before it even got funded. And nobody would risk a twenty-million-dollar production budget on someone untested just because she banged them in a back room. It was ludicrous.

"Here you go," Andy said, reaching to open a back door.

The noise hit me, loud chatter and glass clinking and a band playing a passable rendition of "Tell Me Something Good," not that anybody could compare to Rufus.

Andy let go of my arm and picked up a tray full of dishes from a stand tucked into a dark corner. "Enjoy yourself," he said.

I stood rooted to the ground, taking it all in. I had been to a fair number of parties like this, often in big houses, sometimes in hotels, but the spring weather had only recently turned nice enough again for backyard parties.

Round tables surrounding the pool were full of people. In the middle of each red tablecloth was a centerpiece that matched the set of the movie, a dinosaur flick that hadn't worked for me but was probably going to be very popular.

A few heaters had been set up and I stepped close to one. It wasn't really cold, but my dress was pretty bare and I didn't have a wrap.

A waiter passed with a tray full of wine and I snagged a glass of red. I wouldn't drink much. I had to stay sharp in case I met Mr. Right Now. I had to make sure he was single. And heterosexual. Getting turned down on camera might be a bit more than my poor bruised ego could take tomorrow morning, being suddenly without a boyfriend and potentially going viral on social media.

I knew going into this gig that this moment would come. Now I just had to endure it.

My eyes lit through the crowd, trying to spot anyone I knew well enough to approach to chat up. I felt exposed standing here alone. Although, if someone made a move on me, that might make things easier.

I spotted Tellmund, a friend of Frankie's. He was in his sixties and had aged beautifully, tall and silver haired and broad shouldered. He was definitely not a candidate for breaking my fast, but he probably was in the potential boss category.

I headed for him, but stopped when I spotted a guy leaning against the stage, one elbow up on the platform. Nobody was dancing, at least not yet. This band wasn't drawing a crowd.

The man was watching the band play and drumming his hands on the edge of the stage. He wore jeans and a black T-shirt. He was crazy tanned, and the way his arm muscles moved as he tapped mesmerized me to the core.

I figured he must be part of the band, maybe a friend or someone who loaded equipment. The members of the group itself were very different, dressed like a '70s cover band in vests and colored sunglasses.

But this guy? He was glorious. Dark short-cropped hair. A killer jaw. His chest was nicely sculpted by the T-shirt, and the jeans were a miracle on his butt.

A definite candidate.

I couldn't make my move yet, as Frankie hadn't introduced me to anybody, and I had to work my contacts while I had them. I turned back to head for Tellmund, but he was gone. Across the yard, I spotted one weaselly looking guy dressed in black, holding a camera with a ridiculously long lens. He caught me looking and aimed at me.

I shot him a smile, knowing that I wasn't anything he could sell. Without Frankie in the image, I was nothing. Well, until I wrapped myself around some other noteworthy guy. Then those images would be a hot commodity.

That thought brought me back to the man by the stage. I watched him carefully to see how he took in the singers, if he was actually a boyfriend of one of them, and not going to be interested in me.

At that moment, he turned and looked out at the crowd, and our eyes met.

Holy shit.

He drank in my green dress and pink dreadlocks. His eyebrows shot up when I gave him a shy smile.

I brought my wine to my lips. I hadn't gotten to act this way in ages, so it was fun to shift my body a little, keeping his attention, and watch him over the rim of the glass.

I sensed the click, click, click of the camera even though I couldn't hear or see it. I'd learned from my time with Frankie to sharpen my awareness of being photographed.

Good. They could make a little spread about when Frankie's tart spotted "The Man."

He didn't waver, watching me openly. I felt a little heat rising in me. This would be a piece of cake, really, but I couldn't let him approach me just yet. So I lowered my glass, sent him one more sultry look, and turned to head back into the house.

Hopefully he wouldn't follow. It wasn't time yet!

I hurried through the sunroom, the couple still locked together at the end, and back through the house. I couldn't interrupt Frankie. But I had to avoid that boy until I knew I should approach him. The photographer was on to me already. And I still didn't have any industry introductions I could really use for a job.

Damn, this party had already gotten complicated.

# 6

## CHANCE

Whoa. Who was that girl?

The party was full of women, polished and perfect and snooty in how they appraised me, like they were looking for something, and I wasn't it.

But not this one.

She seemed nervous, a little lost. Her green dress was as fancy as anyone's here, but that hair. I didn't know anybody with pink dreadlocks. She couldn't be an actress expecting to get many parts, unless the hair was for something she was doing right now.

It was wicked gorgeous. I'd never seen anyone like her.

She took off after we made eye contact, which made me think she belonged to somebody with a jealous streak. Probably best if I didn't make any moves. I wasn't invited to this shindig, and I didn't want to get thrown out.

The boys took a break and we chilled out behind the van, within sight of the party but far enough that we weren't noticed.

Paul brought a bottle of wine back and scrounged up some plastic cups. Apparently Paul didn't look trustworthy enough for the caterer to turn over any actual glass. Probably a good call.

Paul stretched out on the lawn. "So many dames at this gig," he said. "But I feel like somebody's going to break my fingers if I so much as look at one."

The others grunted in agreement. I sat back against the van, thinking of the girl I saw.

Paul nudged me with his boot. "Country boy's gone all spacey on us."

I knocked his foot aside. "Been an interesting night."

The keyboardist dumped wine into his cup. "Damn straight. Although we could be a boom box for all anybody's noticed us."

Paul examined a blade of grass with outrageous intensity. "It's money at the end of the day," he said.

"Is this all you guys do?" I asked. "Your full-time deal?"

"Nah," Paul said. "I work at an electronics store." He pointed at the drummer. "Jazz there sacks groceries."

"I change oil," said the bass guitarist. "It's something."

"You do anything?" Paul asked me. "Other than thumb rides?"

"I used to," I said. "But it was killing me, pouring concrete all day. So I left."

"Nobody got in your way?" Jazz asked, passing me a cup.

I took one even though I had no intention of drinking. "Nope."

"My old lady would kick my ass if I took off," Jazz said.

I wasn't sure if he meant a wife, a girlfriend, or his mom, but I didn't ask.

"No old lady in my life," I said, and knew it applied all the way around. I hadn't left a soul who meant anything to me. Not anymore.

Something about that girl made me think she would understand that. Maybe it was the hair. Or how out of place she seemed to feel, looking around like she didn't have a friend in the world.

Of course, she was here. Maybe she had some sugar daddy who kept her in fancy dresses. The role didn't fit her, though, not the way she was standing there, unsure if she belonged.

She'd looked at me, though. That was for certain. Maybe she had somebody. Maybe she didn't. I shouldn't really go searching for her. I might not stay in LA any length of time. Messing with some movie star's girl might cause trouble for the band.

But despite what my head was telling me, my butt got off the ground anyway. "Gonna stretch my legs."

Jazz hooted. "Like hell you are. I saw you making eyes at somebody."

Damn, I was more obvious than I thought.

"Don't go getting us thrown out of the gig," Paul said, then laughed. "We can do that all on our own."

"Not a problem," I said. "I've never been one to cause trouble." Not anymore, at least.

"That makes one of us," Jazz said.

The party didn't seem any different from when we left it, despite the lack of a band. I ditched the wine on a table.

Piped-in music filled in the background behind the buzz of conversation. Must be hidden speakers in the trees. Paul was sort of right. The band being onstage didn't seem to matter. They were all in their own little worlds.

The tables at the center were packed, and clusters of animated people talked with exaggerated gestures, like they were game show hosts. I could see from the body language that everybody had too much to say and not enough patience to hear anybody else.

That pink-haired girl was different, though, and I searched for her. I couldn't see past the edge of the crowd, so I hightailed it to the stage and climbed up, examining a guitar as if I needed to adjust something.

Now that I was above everyone, I could easily scan the whole space. Her pink hair was easy to spot from here. She had her hand on some geezer in a sharp suit. He had to be three times her age. My stomach clenched. Maybe she was his daughter or something.

I looked her way a couple more times, trying not to stare. Another guy came up, short, bald, but friendlier than the other. He draped his arm around her and pulled her in with familiarity.

So she did have someone.

I shook it off. She was just a random girl. By this time tomorrow, she'd be lost in all the memories of faces and places I'd taken in these past months.

The Fender felt good. I wanted to crank out a solo, something dark and brooding, but this wasn't my gig. I set it back in its stand and couldn't help myself, but took one more look into the crowd.

My heart revved up when I saw she was watching me. Her eyes flitted to the guy next to her. He understood or something, as suddenly he was looking at me too. Then he nodded.

I had the weirdest feeling he was giving her some sort of approval. Maybe this was one of those polyamory deals, open relationships. I'd never known anybody like that. Doing somebody else on the sly, sure. Seemed like everybody cheated eventually.

But we were in Cali now. Maybe anything goes. Living large. I figured for one night anyway, it didn't matter. Nobody'd managed to last any longer than that for me. I doubted Little Miss Pink was going to be any different.

But she was heading this way.

# 7

## JENNY

My stomach quivered as I headed toward the stage. Frankie had introduced me to two really strong prospects for a job. I was grateful. If one of them worked out, I could still be part of the business.

Now I just had to make a move on a new man very publicly.

This boy fit all the bills. Sexy. Handsome. Interested.

He was also not connected to any of Frankie's movies, so there wouldn't be any drama as they went into release.

He was, in a word, the perfect score.

The band was winding down a song as I moved through the crowd. The O-Maker, as I had come to think of him while I waited on the go-ahead from Frankie, moved in and out of my vision as I passed through people.

But he was watching me head toward him.

Waiting.

I took my time, wondering if any cameras were close enough to catch me when I got there. I didn't sense any. I couldn't sneak away with this guy and sneak back. We had to be noticed. Captured. Shared.

My stomach fluttered again.

The rest of the band climbed up on the stage. The lead singer shouted at the crowd, his voice distorted enough that I couldn't quite understand him. Some tepid clapping followed.

They lacked something. Charisma. Presence. I wasn't sure. There were people here who could have assessed that, but I didn't care. The O-Maker had everything I was looking for.

Except he was gone again.

I stayed in the middle of the ambivalent crowd, listening to them play a song I'd never heard. Once again, it was passable. I scanned the crowd for the boy, although I wasn't tall enough to see very far.

Frustrated, I pushed past a linebacker-sized actor and saw my target hopping up on the stage. I slowed down. Was he going to sing?

The guy in purple shades motioned him over.

My guy walked over to the mike. "Hello, I'm Chance, and Paul here has kindly invited this Tennessee boy up to do a number."

Chance.

His name was Chance.

"Yeah!" Paul bellowed. He lifted his guitar strap over his head and handed it to Chance.

I made it to the base of the stage, where the crowd had left a gap, the party goers uninterested. I wondered if my boy choice was going to get their attention, or if he would be terrible.

I was rooting for him.

Chance turned to the other band members and nodded his head. The drummer slammed into a driving beat, and Chance spun to the mike, looking out at the crowd. He hadn't noticed me up so close, practically at his feet.

"This is a song I think a lot of you will recognize, a little ditty called 'Let the Good Times Roll.'"

The band crashed into the opening licks, and when Chance started singing, I wanted to laugh out loud with giddiness. His voice was pure magic, deep and edgy.

He moved across the stage like a fury, all energy and muscle. I was so close I could feel the wood floor shifting under his feet. His fingers squeezed the guitar in a steady grip. I was mesmerized by every movement. I could already see how his skilled hands would work on me.

I was hooked.

The band wasn't quite on, as if they hadn't rehearsed this one much, but Chance made up for it. The crowd began to turn to look at the stage, moving along to the beat, taking a ride on Chance's fluid vocals.

I felt myself start to unfurl, to loosen up inside. This would be fine. He'd come off the stage. He'd see me. The attention would be directed at us long enough to make the point. And the way the focus was shifting to this hot sensation, it would be logical that I fell for him. People here would get it.

Headline: Blues-singing rock god seduces movie director's girl at party.

The song rollicked along for another chorus, then Chance brought them to a strong stop with a motion of his hand.

That's when he saw me.

He froze a second, as if he couldn't believe I was so close after he'd searched for me for so long. His smile spread to a wide grin. I'm sure my panties would have gone flying, if I'd been wearing any.

"Thank you," he said to the crowd, which was actually showing some enthusiasm now. But he kept his eyes on me.

I thought the lead singer would take back over, but Chance turned and stepped close to the bass guitarist, asking him something. The guy nodded, and Chance turned back to the mike. "We're gonna bring it down for a second. So grab your woman, if you've got one, because this one is for all of you lovely ladies here tonight."

He looked down at me a second, and I was close enough to see his hesitation, as if maybe this wasn't a good idea. But his gaze went back to the crowd and he seemed satisfied as a few people drew closer together.

The drummer clicked out a simple count, and when Chance played the opening line, I felt my knees go liquid. That song. Whoa, that song. Behind me, I felt the crowd pause, attention trained on this man, as if they were ready to give this guy a chance.

Chance.

He closed his eyes as he prepared for that first line. My breath held. Hell of a standard he was about to compete against. A whole blues legacy.

But here he was.

He belted it out, and my emotion surged so hard, I realized I was seriously a goner after a single phrase. I just let it wash over me.

*When a man loves a woman…*

Chance opened his eyes then, looking at me. I ignored how it was silly to think he was singing anything to me. It was just a song.

A romantic song. We hadn't even met.

But it *felt* like it was for me. I couldn't take my eyes off him. He was so earnest. So intense. His voice was spot on, gravelly in just the right way.

My breathing sped up. I clutched the stage like I might fall if I let go. And falling was something I didn't do, not ever.

I tore my gaze from him to see what was going on behind me. People were closing in and the party focus had shifted. They were listening, hugging the stage. Some of the other women had pushed to the front. Women more beautiful than me, famous, recognizable.

Interested.

I was torn between backing away graciously and fighting for this stranger. *I saw him first*, the toddler in me wanted to shout at them. But I was a grown-up, and this was how the world worked. There was no love at first sight, no soul mates. I knew that better than anyone.

There were just people. People with careers to consider and calculated moves to make. Love could figure into it, sure, but there was no clear path to one predestined person.

Even if I had wanted to go, though, I was pinned by his voice, his command of the microphone and the guitar. The words flowed out of him in a ribbon of sound, so convincing. I couldn't imagine anybody wouldn't fall for this.

I let go of my fear, my feelings of inferiority, and just let the music wash over me. The band kept the background simple, letting Chance come through without their interference. He looked up as the chorus came around again, singing to the sky as if the stars were shining for his song.

I felt cocooned by his voice, safe and loved and happy. This touched a part of me I'd buried a long time ago, back when my life was simple and easy, not burdened by grief or regret. My mother and father were still together, and my baby brother still lived. I could picture the four of us, the boring embodiment of the nuclear family. I thought it was all pedestrian and would kill my muse. Now I knew that it was the safe place I could spring from.

Unconditional love.

The song came back to that.

Chance closed his eyes to the stars, then turned his attention back to the party, eyebrows lifting as if surprised by the sudden arrival of so many fans at his feet. My throat got tight as his gaze took in the women who were under his spell. Gorgeous, talented, available women he'd seen in theaters and on television. The sort of women who could open doors for him if he played things right.

My stomach lurched and I tried to back away, but I was hemmed in by the crowd. Chance held out the microphone and let everyone sing out the famous line, but I didn't. I pressed my hand to my chest, already feeling the ache of losing something I had planned to pursue, someone I wanted.

But then his eyes met mine again. He passed right over the Hollywood elite and rested on me. The crowd turned, following his attention, and internally, I heard the silent click, click, click of a camera capturing the moment.

It had begun.

# 8

## CHANCE

She was here. Right here at the stage.

The crowd was listening to me now, and I could feel their energy lifting me, making me better than I'd ever been before. Good enough to be worthy of *her*.

The song was a risk. I should have kept the tempo fast and the party atmosphere going. But I couldn't do it. I'd never sung that song to anyone in particular before. It seemed like the perfect thing. She was so beautiful, as elusive as an ocean wave, and I had to pull out all the stops to make sure I got her attention.

The crowd roared as I tore my eyes from her and bowed to them. I pulled the strap over my head and handed the Fender back to Paul, who looked truly torn about whether he should take the gig back over or leave it to me.

But no way was I going to stay up there. I'd done what I needed to do. The girl had her eyes locked on me, and I had to talk to her now or I might never get another chance.

I knelt on the stage next to her, so close I could reach out and touch those crazy pink dreadlocks. She watched me a moment, then moved aside so I could swing my feet around and jump down. A swirl of people came up to me asking questions, peppering me with comments and praise. A woman wearing a barely there dress with enough cleavage to hide a developing country tugged on my arm, but I managed to work loose, fighting hard not to lose eye contact with the girl.

She glanced away from me, taking in the other women vying for my attention. I wasn't sure what to do to reassure her. We hadn't even spoken yet.

But I took her hand. Her face popped up in surprise. Her eyes were like quicksilver, lively and pale gray. I flashed with concern that I had screwed up already, but then she squeezed my fingers. I pushed away from the stage and led her out of the throng.

My heart was hammering ninety to nothing. The adrenaline of the song, the crowd, and now touching her — God, I was touching her — threatened to make my chest explode.

We moved through the crowd that seemed to part for us. We were making a scene somehow. I thought about that guy who'd put his arm around her earlier in the night. Would he start something? This didn't look to be a fighting crowd. Their faces were too pretty and probably too important. But they had money. That could mean bodyguards and lawyers.

I glanced down at her.

She didn't seem concerned. I didn't know where I was leading her exactly, but she seemed willing to follow. Behind us, Paul cranked the band into another song. I wondered if I should take her far enough away that we could talk.

We broke free of the thick part of the crowd and into the fringes. Then to the edge of the lights, then along the garden paths I'd explored earlier.

Suddenly she stopped.

"Sorry," I said automatically. "I shouldn't take you from the party." Probably she was worried about being too alone with a total stranger. I should have known—

My brain shut off when her hand grasped the back of my neck and brought me closer. Only when her lips hit mine did I realize what she was doing — what *we* were doing.

Kissing.

Need hit me like a blow to the gut. Her mouth was warm and soft. I buried my hands in those pink dreadlocks, more than ready to get lost in them. Her small body in the green dress fit neatly against mine.

I kept it easy with her at first, but as the kiss lingered, my body thundered with urgency. I pulled her hard against me, feeling every curve.

My tongue slid along her lips. She parted for me, and the warmth of her mouth was mine to possess, take over, taste. I didn't think we could get closer, but somehow we did, and the line where my body ended and hers began started getting blurred as we stood locked together.

A burst of light commanded our attention, and I broke the kiss.

"What the hell?" I growled when I saw some punk with a camera taking off down the path.

Shit. This would probably upset the girl.

But she was laughing. "Well, that's done," she said.

"What?" I asked. What the hell was going on here?

"Come on," she said, tugging on my hand. "They won't follow us into the house."

She led me back toward the party. We wound through the tables. I had a million questions for this girl, but I felt like I was walking through a dream. Maybe all these actors made you feel that way, as though you were on a movie set, acting out a story that wasn't really your life.

I hadn't been inside the house. We arrived at a long room full of white wicker furniture. The whole side was glass so you could look out on the party. Nobody else was in there.

"We can take over the casting couch," the girl said with a laugh, drawing me down on a padded love seat along the far wall.

"You lost me," I said, but I sat down beside her. "This whole thing feels surreal."

"These parties have that effect," she said.

"Did they slip you a Mickey?" I asked.

She laughed again, and this made me relax. The sound was infectious, like a child's giggle, innocent and full of life.

"No," she said. "Or at least I don't think so. It's always possible."

Now that we were settled, I realized we hadn't even gotten through the basics. "What is your name?" I asked her.

"Oh, right," she said, and laughed again. "I snogged you without any introductions." She pushed the mass of pink dreadlocks behind her shoulder. "I'm having trouble getting used to these."

"The hair is new?"

She touched her hands to it. "My hair is always pink, or it has been since I was seventeen. But the dreads were added yesterday."

I picked one up and felt its spongy softness. "Ah, so you didn't grow them."

She sat back against the cushions. "I have the patience of a squirrel," she said. "The eight hours it took for these were already stretching my attention span."

I figured she didn't want to give me her name, so I didn't push. I certainly wasn't going to ask about that guy who had his arm around her earlier. He was probably not important, if she was willing to kiss me like she had. Unless she was causing trouble. Using me.

"So the kiss?" I prodded.

"Oh, that." She looked out the windows. "I've always been a little too impulsive."

Now that was an answer I liked. "So, if you're not going to give me your name, what should I call you?"

She turned back to me, and my throat got tight at the sweet, sultry way her eyes met mine, her lashes long and curled. "My name is Jenny. I'm probably the least important person at this party."

I scooted closer. "Not to me."

She laughed again. "Even the waiters have a purpose here. I'm just..." Her voice faltered. "I *was* just a decoration. Like the tablecloths."

I started to get it. Some guy brought her here to show off, then ignored her for somebody famous. That would explain how lost she looked, and why she panicked when those actresses approached me.

She was used to getting set aside.

I picked up her hand and brushed my fingertips along her palm. She shivered. I liked that. I liked it a lot. I decided to take it a step further and lifted her hand to press my lips against the tender spot of her wrist.

She let out a long slow breath, then she leaned in again. I smiled against her lips as I realized that every damn time, this girl was going to be the one to kiss me first.

# 9

---

## JENNY

Chance tasted of impulse and madness. I'd done what I needed to do, and yet here I was, in the house and away from the photographers, locked on his mouth like I was drowning.

Maybe I was. Months and months of no boys. God. I hadn't gone that long since Kenny Granger gave me my first orgasm, and I learned what all the fuss was about.

Chance's hand clasped my neck beneath the bushel of dreadlocks, kneading my muscles, keeping me relaxed and fluid. The door opened and closed a few times, but it seemed far away on the other end of the long room. It didn't matter anyway. I was supposed to get caught, be seen. Someone might be taking Frankie aside right now.

Chance's fingers began to roam, drifting along my collarbone, across my shoulder, and down my arm to rest on my hip. Just going that far made everything heat up, and I scooted even closer, pressing tightly against him.

His chest was solid. I began learning the planes and edges of him, the round muscles of his biceps, the cut of his shoulder. I wanted to see all that sinew, every inch of it.

Like, right now.

I broke the kiss and moved closer to his ear. "I have a limo outside," I said, then realized that made me sound swankier than I was. "I mean, it's a friend's, but I am supposed to use it to take me home."

He held still a minute, and I suddenly remembered he was with the band.

"We can wait until after the gig," I added hastily. "Do you have another set to sing?"

"No," he said. "I'm just a friend of the band. But I do have to get my gear from their van."

"We don't have to leave the grounds," I said. "I live in San Diego anyway. We could just...stay in the limo."

I'd gone stark raving mad.

*So what?*

Chance grasped my hands. "You sure about this, darlin'? We just met."

His hard body shifted against me, and I revved up even more. "Oh, I'm sure," I said.

I stood, bringing Chance with me. I was so ready to break this fast. More than ready.

We raced back through the house, and I was glad I'd wandered it enough to know the way. Outside, I paused on the steps, looking over the line of limos in the circle drive. They were all black. I had no idea which one was Frankie's, or if Brandon was even here or parked somewhere else.

But one of the sleek cars pulled away from the curb and crept around the circle. I stared closely and recognized the silver handle on the door. "This one," I told Chance, then my stomach burst with butterflies.

Was this a good idea? He could be an axe murderer.

Though I had something of a chaperone with the driver.

Was THAT a good idea? His poor burning ears.

But Brandon was already by the door, opening it for us. If he had an opinion about Chance coming along, he said nothing. He was a professional, and probably, he'd been driving Frankie and Alec for weeks and already knew everything.

"Where to, Miss Jenny?" he asked.

"Just cruise the neighborhood," I said, feeling a blush creep through my cheek. That sounded tawdry out loud.

"Is it far to the beach?" Chance asked.

This amused me. "Really?" I asked.

"I've never been," he said. "I just got into LA today."

"Then to the beach," I told Brandon. "Let's do Dockweiler to avoid the curfews." I turned to Chance. "They have camping at that one, so they allow beach fires."

"I defer to your knowledge of the city," he said.

I checked my phone. "The party will go on for hours. I'll get you back in time to get your gear."

He glanced at the house, as if he was remembering something.

"You need to tell them you're leaving?" I asked.

He shook his head. "It'll be all right."

I ducked inside the limo and slid across the leather seat.

Chance followed, scooting in close. Brandon closed the door. When he got in, the window between the front and the back whirred closed.

Yup, he got it.

Now that we were truly alone, and not all up in each other, I felt a little more nervous about my rash decision to drag him out here.

But he seemed to understand this and took my hand, lazily bending each of my fingers.

"So how long have you known that band?" I asked him.

"About four hours," he said. "I met them at a truck stop outside LA this afternoon."

"Really?" My belly fluttered again. He was a hitchhiker. A drifter. Not even the band knew him. "And they just brought you along and put you onstage?"

"Pretty much," he said. "It's not too unusual. There are places where musicians hang out just to pick up last-minute gigs. When I was on Sixth Street in Austin, a drummer I played with couldn't so much as load his set in his car before someone came running down the street asking if he could sub in on a job."

This was all so new to me. "But don't you have to practice together? Match your style?"

The pale strip lights along the roof cast just enough light for me to see his face. "A decent musician has a deep set list," he said. "This past week I've played everything from George Strait to Meatloaf."

His voice was calm and deep, so I began to relax again. Brandon was here. I wasn't totally at this man's mercy. "Is there anything you won't do?" I asked.

His grip on my hand tightened. "Are you going to suggest something I might say no to?"

I knew a nicer, more wholesome girl would have blushed, but I knew a challenge when I saw it. "I might."

He lifted the back of my hand to his lips. At first he pressed a simple, chaste kiss on my skin.

Then he bit me.

"You crazy boy!" I said, laughing. "I'll get you for that."

"Will you, now?" He grabbed my waist and lifted me onto his lap. "I think I've got you."

He buried his face in my neck and hot need bolted through me like a flash fire. I couldn't help but let out a soft sigh as he nibbled along my jaw. I had completely forgotten what it was like to feel like this with someone. This was the stuff I lived for, right here.

"I want to touch everything," he whispered against my cheek. "You are the most beautiful creature I've ever laid eyes on."

I didn't answer, not trusting my voice. My breath came in rapid huffs.

Very little penetrated the dark windows of the limo, but the street lamps flashed by as we sped through the city. Chance kissed me again, and I closed my eyes, paying attention to his seeking mouth.

His tongue sought mine again, and I forced any worries about him being such a stranger away. It wasn't the first time I'd been impulsive with someone I'd just met. And it probably wouldn't be the last.

I kicked off my killer heels, tired of them dangling. My legs were up on the seat, my butt in his lap. He had a good solid hold on me, one arm around my waist, the other hand roaming along my back, probably noticing my lack of a bra.

He tasted like a dream. In the quiet of the car, I could hear his voice, singing to me from the stage. I wanted to hear it again, and was torn between his kiss and having him perform just for me. The thought of that low rumble close enough to feel as well as hear drew a rush of heat through my core.

I broke away, my hands on each side of his face. "What's your favorite song to sing?" I asked him.

His eyes found mine, amusement dancing. "You sure pick an interesting time to ask questions."

"Plenty of evening left," I said. I ran a finger along his cheek. I could tell he was normally clean shaven, but this late in the evening, his skin was rough with stubble.

He turned his mouth to my hand and kissed my palm. A thrill zipped through me. Maybe I wouldn't ask questions. I was about to lean back in when he said, "When I was little, my Gram would sing me a lullaby, you know the one, about Papa buying a diamond ring."

I couldn't suppress a giggle. "That's your favorite song? A lullaby?"

"Maybe." He frowned. "I guess I should have said something clever, like Johnny Cash, or something romantic just to seduce you."

I touched a finger to his lips. They were firm and soft and warm. "I think you already did that onstage. I like that you were honest."

"I never was much of a liar," he said, and his mouth met mine again.

I let myself fall, drifting along with his kiss, the heat of his body, and his hands, moving again along my back. We would be at the beach soon. Maybe I should slow this down. Take a little time.

Chance lingered, not in any rush, tasting me, nipping at my tongue with his teeth. He made me giddy. I wanted to laugh, to cling to him, to fall apart, all at once. He was everything in a single package. Passionate, silly, romantic, careful.

I hadn't been this swept away by anyone in a long time. If ever.

# 10

## CHANCE

I regretted asking Jenny to take us to the beach. A big ol' interruption was about to come, and I'd heard about getting sand in all the wrong places.

I brought things down a notch even though it took some effort. Jenny was more than I bargained for, a pink goddess in her green dress. I had ascertained she wasn't wearing much under that gown. There wasn't any strap or band breaking the smoothness of her back.

As I tugged on her lower lip with my teeth, the urge to drag her down on that limo seat was hard to keep in check. We'd get there. She was pausing and dodging a little, but since that first crazy kiss at the party, she'd been making her intentions clear.

When I was growing up, my grandpa told me about girls who were tigers. That I ought to give them a wide berth. But I learned pretty quick that those were the ones who interested me the most. I never could say no to a single one.

Every now and again, I'd find out the hard way that one of them had a boyfriend — or a husband. I was better now about getting lost in a hurry if I had to. Not that I wasn't up for a fight. But even a single hard punch to some asshole's jaw could mess up my hand for a week, and when you're playing by the seat of your pants on the road, your fingers are your moneymaker.

These days I tried to make sure the girls in my lap were single. I should've asked Jenny about that guy at the party, but I just hadn't done it.

Jenny sighed against my mouth, then pulled away. "We're probably almost there," she said.

I ran a hand along her bare shoulder. "You going to be cold?"

"Not if you do your job." She snuggled up against my chest.

The limo jolted as we bumped over something. We both looked out the window.

"It's the parking lot for this stretch of beach," Jenny said. "It'll be pretty deserted on a night like this."

I reached down for one of her shoes. "You going to try wearing these?" They looked like little death traps to me, spiked heels and very little to hold them on.

"No, I'll go barefoot in the sand."

The limo rolled to a stop. Outside, I could see the ocean in the moonlight, dark through the tinted windows, endless and shifting.

When the driver opened the door and I got a whiff of the sea air, I felt exhilarated. I tightened my arms around Jenny and ducked outside, keeping her in my arms.

"You gonna carry me the whole time?" she asked.

"Maybe," I said. "You told me to do my job." She didn't weigh a whole heck of a lot, and the effort felt good.

"Well, all right, Mr. Strongman," she said, and wrapped her arms around my neck. "To the shore!"

I stepped off the asphalt of the parking lot and took off across the wide expanse of sand. There were no lights out here, only the moon. Farther down, I could see some structures with lamps on the side, and behind us was the road. But ahead was nothing but water as far as you could see. The moon reflected on its surface, fading from the bright ball into a line of sparkling waves that eventually disappeared into the dark.

I stood, feeling a little dumbstruck.

"You can set me down," Jenny said quietly.

I let her feet fall to the sand. Her dress shimmered in the moonlight, although in the darkness, I could no longer see the color of it or the pink in her hair. She stepped out into the first lap of water on the sand, then squealed. "It's always so cold!" she said.

She turned around to me, her body silhouetted in the form-fitting dress. With the dreadlocks dropping to her shoulders, and the perfect outline of her curves, she was like a mermaid coming on land. My groin tightened so painfully that I wanted to snatch her right there, to hell with the sand.

Jenny ran along the edge of the water in short, abrupt steps, leaving shallow melting footprints. "This silly dress!" she exclaimed, then grasped the fabric of the skirt and jerked it higher to free more of her legs.

I had to clamp down my jaw as her thighs were revealed in the moonlight, smooth and soft. The dress was crazy short now, and the need to touch her again was too strong for me to ignore.

I followed behind her as she skipped along the waves. Then I couldn't take it any longer and swept her back up in my arms.

She squealed and kicked her legs, sending sand flying. But she turned to me and wrapped her arms around my neck. I ducked my head to capture her mouth. Every movie I'd ever seen on the beach had it nailed. This was hands down the most intense place to be with a woman.

She dug her fingers into my hair as I took over her mouth, drinking deeply from her, ready for more of her, my appetite whetted by that new bit of skin she'd shown.

"There's some rocks a little farther down," she said. "Just keep walking."

We were pretty out in the open, but that didn't stop me from working my hand as far up her thigh as I could while still holding her.

She shifted position. I stopped to see what she was doing, and she swung around, straddling my waist and locking her ankles at the back. Now I could put my hands on her sweet little behind, round and tight beneath the stretchy dress.

We were face to face, and she bounced a little as we walked along. Her breasts swung just enough to tease me. She caught me staring and looked around us, up and down the beach. "Seems pretty empty tonight," she said, and let one arm come away from around my neck.

Before I could figure out what she was up to, she'd pulled her arm up and out of the sleeve of her dress. It clung to her, just barely, as she wrapped the freed arm back around me and did the same to the other side.

When both arms were back around me, I couldn't tear my gaze from that loosened top. It was tight enough to stay roughly in place, but each step we took sent it slipping a little farther down. The suspense was torture as I took bigger strides, encouraging it to fall.

Jenny threw back her head and laughed, knowing she was making me crazy. Her hair draped down her spine and tickled the backs of my hands where I held on to her.

She slipped a little, and I pushed her back up on my waist, shifting the bottom of her dress. And that's when I felt the warm smooth contact of her skin down there.

She wasn't wearing panties.

I lost it, my raging need of her too intense for another moment of this torture. I stopped right there on the shore and brought one hand around, pulling that infernal dress down to expose her beautiful sweet breasts.

My mouth closed over a nipple and she gasped, clinging to my head. I pressed that breast up and into my mouth, kneading it, reveling in its full round softness.

She squirmed against my waist, and knowing she was exposed against me made me a little crazy. I shifted her body up against my jeans and slid her down, imagining that pretty unprotected part of her getting the full treatment of the rough denim.

She groaned and pushed harder, her breathing rapid. I was beginning to really regret the beach idea. I lifted my head from that luscious nipple, about to suggest we get back in the limo.

That's when I noticed the rocks she'd been talking about, just a bit farther down the shore. It was an outcropping, and I could see why she mentioned it. It gave a little protection, something less exposed than standing in the middle of the unbroken sand.

I headed straight for it. Jenny leaned her head down, resting it on my shoulder. Her dress was pushed together at her waist now. I wanted to set her down, look at her, touch and taste everything.

The rocks were surrounded by upshoots of weeds. There was no place to lie down, but that didn't matter. Once we were inside the shelter of their towering sides, I set her in the sand and jerked the dress down from her body. Now, I only had to plan my nonstop worship of her skin, starting at her ankles.

# 11

## JENNY

Holy shit-sparkles. This guy was intense and I was naked on the beach.

Hidden among the rocks, I felt less exposed, not that I wasn't an exhibitionist. Enough people had seen me naked to populate a small town. But getting arrested wasn't on the agenda tonight.

Chance knelt down low, his hands massaging my ankles, his mouth kissing the inside of my knee.

I leaned back against the wall of rock, rough and gritty. He was heading north, and seemed intent on making a rest stop at —

Yes. There.

I clutched at his head as his tongue slid in all the right places. This was crazy, even for me. The beach. A stranger. I inhaled sharply as he sucked at me, his hand lifting one of my thighs to rest on his shoulder.

His other hand worked his magic. Just as I thought. Strong, deft fingers.

The world was already starting to splinter. It had been a while, and my body sang to his strumming like a Stradivarius. I didn't care if I was mixing musical metaphors. I just wanted more, to shatter, to get what I'd been missing all those months.

He moved up, his hands still working on me, until his mouth reached a breast. One tweak there and that was it, I was over the top, shuddering against his palm, hanging on to his hair for dear life, crying out, long and slow. Random words. Then his name. Chance.

My knees started to give out, and he clasped my waist. My skin sizzled despite the chill.

"You okay, darlin'?" he asked, pressing me in.

I nodded against his chest. I fingered the bottom of his shirt, ready to see this boy who'd just turned me inside out. I pulled it overhead and let it fall. It hit the sand with a whisper.

Our little spot was dark, hardly any moonlight straining in, but I could see the contours of his chest. I ran my hands over those hard shoulders and down the bulge of his arms. I reached those talented fingers and squeezed.

He unfastened his belt with a jingle of metal. I couldn't see much in the shadows, but his boxers were light colored, visible as he pushed his jeans down.

The pale fabric bisected him in the dark. He was erect and pushing against the elastic band. He kicked off his shoes and the jeans.

The waves crashed in the distance as I reached for him, feeling hot again already. I pushed the boxers down and out of my way.

The length of him was plenty enough and my fingers encircling him tingled with the knowledge of his girth. I worked him a little and he braced his hands on the rock on either side of my head. Without my killer heels, I stood well below him, my face right at the center of his chest. I leaned in to lick that hollow between his pecs. He was salty and warm, smooth and hard.

His breath hitched. "I have a condom," he said.

Good idea. I was on the pill, but I didn't know this boy, where he'd been, how often he did things like this.

"Wallet?" I asked.

"Yeah." His voice was low and hoarse. He was working hard to keep control as I kept one hand on him, easing up and down his length.

I liked that he was having a hard time.

I bent down for his discarded jeans. He reached to cup my bottom, not a squeeze or anything rough, but reverently, like I was fragile. I managed to lift the heavy denim one handed, but I couldn't free his wallet without letting go of him. So I released him and turned away to get the condom.

He closed the gap between us, grazing me from behind with that extended erection. He groaned as I fumbled to find the little package.

His fingers started working me again, and sparks burst through my head. I gave up on the condom for a moment and braced my hands in the sand, glad for the flexibility earned through years of modern dance class. I felt both his hand and the rest of him sliding along between my thighs, hot friction laced with the tight circles around my swollen nub.

God, I was going to go again.

I pushed against him, suddenly desperate to have him inside. The condom. I needed it now. I opened his wallet and found it.

Desperate, I tore at the corner, releasing the lubricated disc.

Chance pressed against me, dangerously close to being inside already. I opened for him, reveling in that feeling. Then he hit just the right spot and I lurched forward, crying out.

And dropped the condom.

"Shit!" I cried.

He pulled away immediately. "Did I hurt you?"

"No!" I said. "I dropped it."

"The condom?"

"Yes."

"That's all right. It's safe in the package."

"But it wasn't. I took it out." I felt around in the sand until I found it. It was coated with sand, sticky and gritty.

Chance exhaled in a long rush. "That's all right. We can drop by somewhere and pick up some more."

I wanted to weep. He was right there, right where I wanted him. "Just tell me you don't have anything catching."

"I don't."

"I'm on the pill."

His fingers continued their fervent press against me. I leaned back, wanting him back where he was, to keep going.

He bent over my back and lifted my hair from my neck with his free hand. "You sure?"

I pushed harder, feeling him at the entrance again, and that pulsing need that seemed to draw him in.

"Yes," I managed to say. "Please."

He pressed forward, the delicious tip slipping inside. I groaned as I expanded for him. It had been too damn long.

He rested his hands on my hips and slid the rest of the way

until his body was flush against mine.

I cried out, overcome with sensation.

Chance started an easy rhythm, holding me in place. I turned to the stone wall to brace my hands, rocking into him, urging him on.

He matched my pace. My body shifted along with his, my hair tickling my naked back, the breeze from the ocean caressing my tender nipples. I felt so crazy alive there, on a public beach, sheltered by nature, taken by a total stranger who could probably make me orgasm with his voice alone.

I learned the sounds of him, his throaty exclamations. And his grip, fingers tight on my hips. The flat muscled planes of his abs bumped against me with every shift we made into each other.

He picked up speed, and I could hear myself groaning along with him. As he rushed into his climax, he reached around for me again, teasing my tender flesh, touching me with the knowledge he'd gained just moments ago.

I didn't think I could go again, but I did, and when I began to shudder around him, my voice hitting that higher pitch, he released into me, jerking me hard against him, squeezing everything he touched, elongating the moment, wringing it for every ounce of pleasure.

My palms were raw against the rock, my toes deep in the sand. The wind had whipped my hair into chaos. But I was so high, so crazy elated. I wasn't sure if I should cry or laugh or be embarrassed by the insanity of what we'd just done.

He lifted me up against him, his arms crisscrossing my belly, palms protectively cupping my breasts. His mouth kissed my hair, my head, my ears. I realized tears were streaming down my cheeks. Above us, the wind rushed over the rocks, and the stars were easy to see on the edge of the vast ocean. We stayed like that a little while, just holding on, like two refugees stranded together with only each other for comfort.

# 12

## CHANCE

Something had just happened, and I couldn't explain it. It was emotional, like a tender blues song coming to life.

Jenny laid her head back against my shoulder. I was holding on to her, doing my job keeping her warm, like she asked, although her body was still hot and worked over.

She shuddered a little and I felt the unmistakable drop of a tear on the back of my hand.

"Hey," I said softly, close to her ear. "You okay?"

She nodded. "I'm fine," she said. "That was...unexpected."

I knew what she meant. "Yeah. Weird, huh?"

Jenny laughed a little. "For lack of a better word."

"I'm not known for my pretty talk."

"Just your pretty singing?"

"People say I'm not half-bad."

She turned around in my arms to face me. "So sing me something soft and romantic." Her face was upturned, but I couldn't make out much more than her eyes.

"Any requests?"

"The first thing that pops into your head."

I started singing, and only after a few words did I realize it was the opening line to "Fools Rush In."

Damn. That's over the top. Falling in love. Not being able to help it. My gut tightened at saying anything like that to anybody. I wasn't up for entanglements. I'd only just managed to sever everything that had been dragging me down when I left Tennessee.

But now I was committed to the line, or I might upset her. So, to lighten the mood, I pressed my hand to my heart and shifted to falsetto. "I…can't…HELP…"

She smacked my chest with a giggle. "Okay, okay, stop."

"What?" I asked. "You're not impressed with my crooning anymore?" I put my hands on her slender waist and lifted her up. "Rather I use my mouth for something else?" I blew a loud phbbbttttt on her belly.

She shrieked and wiggled against me, trying to push off. "Aaaaah, stop! It tickles!" She laughed and fought against me, but I kept my grip and did it again.

This time she managed to work loose and took off across the sand. "No zerberts!"

I chased after her in the dark, the ocean roaring and powerful in front of us.

She made it to the first waves and shrieked again at the cold. She ran with high steps and now that we were out in the moonlight, I could see the bouncing of her breasts as she ran.

I glanced up and down the beach to confirm we were still alone and chased after her.

She dashed farther out, gasping. When I reached the water, I sucked in a breath. Damn, it was *freezing*.

"You're crazy!" I told her.

She laughed. "You're just now figuring that out?" She splashed me with water, and it hit my skin like ice.

I blasted a wave back at her, and she jumped away. She was still only thigh deep in the waves, and I could see every delicious inch of her skin.

I lunged for her, dragging her against me. "I'm supposed to be keeping you warm." She was covered in goose bumps.

"So do your job." She jerked her chin high and her hair fell down her back.

I wrapped a handful of dreads around my palm and tugged. "God, this hair makes me so hot."

She laughed again. "I think I might be noticing that." She backed away and looked down at how I was standing at attention again despite the cold. "So much for shriveling!"

She ducked her head to get me to let go of her hair. I released her, and she spun away to run through the waves. I followed her, thinking just how insane we were, like little kids running naked after a bath.

The moonlight kissed her skin as she dashed back to the shore. It was an image I didn't think I'd forget for a long, long time.

"Clothes!" she shouted and sprinted back for the rocks. "I'm so damn cold!"

I hurried behind her and caught up just as she bent to pick up her dress. "*Now* we have sand everywhere," I said.

"We're going to be a jacked-up mess going back to that party," Jenny said, pulling the dress over her head. "I'll stay in the limo."

"You look beautiful," I told her.

She pushed at me. "I look tragic. I can't have any photographers catching me now."

I shook sand from my boxers. "You worried about the shot somebody took in the garden?" I remembered that guy draping an arm over her. She might be avoiding the party on purpose.

She smoothed her dress down over her legs. "Nah, that one was okay." Something in her voice had changed.

"You sure?"

She bent down and scooped up my shirt and smacked it against the rocks to remove the sand. "I'm sure."

The easy camaraderie we'd felt in the ocean seemed to evaporate. We were back to near strangers having a one-night stand.

But it was just as well. I really couldn't give her any more than that.

As if she knew the directions of my thoughts, she asked, "So are you in LA to stay, or just passing through?"

I frowned as I felt sand trickle down from my jeans to hit my feet. "Sand really does get everywhere." I smacked at the legs. "I like being on the road. I haven't stayed anywhere more than a week."

She picked up my shoes and turned them upside down. I couldn't see the sand dump out of them in the dark, but I was sure there was plenty. "Where all have you been?" she asked.

"I zigzagged pretty good," I said. "Nashville, Chicago, Minneapolis, Kansas City, Dallas, Austin, Phoenix, Vegas."

"You started in Tennessee, then?" she asked.

I jerked on my socks, trying to ignore the grit. "Yeah, I'm from Chattanooga."

"People are actually *from* Chattanooga?"

"A fair number of people call it home," I said. "Tennessee River runs right through it. There's a big ol' park smack in the center."

"LA must seem like a dirty maze in comparison."

"Not from what I've seen," I told her as I shoved on my shoes. "But we came in early evening and went straight to those swanky mansions."

"Not all of LA is like that, of course," she said, bending down to feel along the ground.

"I know. There's some poor parts." I watched her fumble around. "Did you drop an earring or something?"

She stood up. "No, just don't really want to leave anything behind."

I realized she meant the condom and smiled in the dark. "I can stick it in my pocket."

"There's a trash can out there. Gotta be responsible, you know, since I'm such a law-abiding citizen." She took my hand, and just like that, the awkwardness was gone again and it was like we'd known each other a long time.

We tramped through the sand to one of the cans. The temperature had dropped again, so I pulled her close. The limo waited in the parking lot.

"You like the beach?" she asked casually, and the question was so simple, almost silly, that I stopped and swept her up again against my chest.

She smacked my shoulder. "You're always carrying me."

"You're easy to lug around."

Jenny laid her head on my shoulder. "I don't normally seduce strangers on public beaches," she said.

I kissed the top of her head. "It was definitely one hell of an introduction to the West Coast."

"I guess we have to get back to reality," she said.

I started walking toward the limo. "Yeah, I can't lose my gear. I carry my life on my back."

The driver appeared and opened the door to the limo. "Sorry about the sand," Jenny said.

"Not a problem," he said to her.

We ducked inside, and he closed the door.

"Uggh, we're bringing half the beach in with us," she said.

The black carpet was strewn with sand. Every movement sent another cascade down.

We settled back on the seat. I let my thoughts drift back to the rocks, and Jenny, her responses to me. I'd had a lot of solitary encounters, but they were usually unremarkable. Just bodies and actions. No real connection. Not like this.

I drew her close. I actually felt some regret that we'd met this way, gone this direction. I would have liked to have gotten to know her. But I had a feeling her life was complicated. There was this limo that wasn't hers. And the party where she didn't belong. And that man putting his arm around her.

"You going home after this?" I asked her.

"Yeah, it's about a two-hour drive. I'll probably sleep," she said. "You going to play with that band more?"

"You mean tonight?"

"I mean other gigs."

"Beats me." And I didn't know. Even if they asked me to, I'd be reluctant. "I'm not really one for getting tied down."

She stiffened, and I realized what that sounded like. But I didn't correct it. It was true either way. I needed to roam.

*But LA was the final destination*, my conscience reminded me.

Still, I had no plans to stay anywhere, as long as I could keep supporting myself with song. I didn't know if LA would suit me.

Although, if it meant I could see Jenny again…

Maybe.

# 13

## JENNY

So this Chance guy wasn't into relationships. Check.

He was hot as hell. Check.

He was seriously gifted in bed. (Okay, on the beach.) Check.

And as a bonus, a singer.

Perfect. Bloody. Fit.

I hated that I wanted him. I mean, just thinking it meant I wanted a relationship. Which I never did. The only time I'd ever committed to a man for more than five minutes was with Frankie, and that was under contract. For money. And perks. And no sex.

I couldn't believe my brain was working this way.

Time to apply the brakes.

"Well, I live in San Diego," I said. "I'm not even going to be in LA while you're here."

His thumb, which had been rubbing my bare arm, went still. "It was a fun night anyway," he said.

"Since we're never going to see each other again," I said, "and

I don't even know your last name, tell me something." I was feeling sort of bold now, and pulled away to face him.

"What's that?" His face looked wary in the dim light of the limo.

"Why did you leave home? What chased you away from the great metropolis of Chattanooga, Tennessee, with its river running through town and the park smack in the middle?"

I knew I sounded a little bitchy. It helped give him a reason to pull away. No rejection then. I controlled it.

He released me. "No reason in particular." His voice had gone cold.

"Really? A guy takes off from home with nothing but what he's carrying on his back, and it's for no reason?"

"Just wanted to see the country."

"That is so 1960," I shot back. "Give me something real."

His eyes were hard, glittering as he glared at me. "There wasn't anything worth staying for in that town," he said.

"No family? No girl? No job? Nothing?"

"Nothing," he said again, and now his voice was bitter enough for me to know not to push it.

Which, of course, made me push harder.

"You piss off somebody's husband? You croon for the wrong bimbo?"

"It's in the past," he said harshly. "Drop it."

I sat back against the seat, not touching him now. This was good. If I couldn't have him, I might as well not be all morose about it. Not liking him as we went our separate ways made it a whole lot easier.

The limo slowed as we turned into the gates of the party. Cars were still parked all over the lawn. It seemed as though nothing had changed. Maybe time stood still while we were out on that beach.

The thought made my cold resolve melt a little.

"It was fun," I said. "I'm glad we did it."

Chance let out a long slow exhale and relaxed a bit. "Yeah. Good luck with whoever that dude was at the party."

"What?" I shot out. Then I remembered. Frankie. Hell, this guy thought I'd stepped out on a boyfriend. "Oh. Yeah. He's more like my boss. This is his limo."

"Oh." He sounded unsure. "I hope you don't get in trouble."

"No, no," I said. "It's not like that. It's — complicated."

The limo slowed to a stop by the front steps.

"I bet."

My throat felt a little tight now that we were actually at good-bye. There was no way I was stepping out of this limo, sand in my hair, salt water dried all over me. Besides, I'd had enough for one night. My glory days were at an end, and I needed to just ride off into the sunset.

"Good luck with your gigs," I said to Chance. "I hope you find what you're looking for."

This made him pause. "Thanks," he said. He hesitated, then leaned in and placed one last lingering kiss on my lips. "I'm sure I'll be thinking of you for as long as there is still sand in my jeans pockets."

I laughed. "Get on out of here, Chance the Crooner. Go seduce more girls with your love songs."

He pulled away and moved toward the door. Brandon's impeccable sense of timing kicked in and he opened it at just the right moment.

I watched Chance hop out of the limo and make his way around the side of the house. I felt a lump grow in my throat. Now that was a boy worth knowing, right there.

At least I'd had a little piece of him.

"You going back to the party, Miss Jenny?" Brandon asked.

"No," I told him. "Let's head back to San Diego."

He closed the door.

I sat by the window as the limo moved forward in the drive. I couldn't see into the darkness at the side of the house, so I wasn't given any more glimpses of Chance. For a moment, my heart rebelled, and I wanted to go back, to chase after him.

But instead I lay down on the long seat and put my feet up. Sleep, Jenny, I told myself. Tomorrow is the first day of the rest of your life.

No more Frankie. No more fancy parties. Just finish college, get a job, and be part of the boring old world of grown-ups.

# 14

## CHANCE

The band was packing up the van when I made it around to the side of the house.

"Lover boy returns!" Paul said, setting the amplifier inside the back door.

"Let me help grab your gear," I said, and followed the bass guitarist back to the stage.

The party was thinner now, most of the crowd sitting at the tables. I wondered if the gig had gone better after I left, or if everyone had drifted away from the stage again. The Sonic Kings should probably update their set list, pacing out the shows, but I wasn't the one to tell them that. They had some talent. They were just disorganized and a little apathetic. It showed.

I picked up a drum box, already feeling stupidly nostalgic about the party. I paused, looking down where Jenny had stood at my feet and I hadn't noticed for an entire song, still scanning the crowd for her pink dreadlocks.

I hopped to the ground, staring at the path we had taken to the gardens. She'd kissed me there so unexpectedly, just in time for that photographer to catch us. I hadn't even noticed any cameras at the party until then.

Strange.

I headed back to the van. There wasn't a lot left to gather up. The caterers were pulling their equipment too, loading a sleek white delivery truck next to the boys' ratty van. I wasn't sure what I'd do next. Take off walking or ride somewhere with the band. I figured I would just go along with whatever opportunities arose.

What I didn't expect was a hand on my arm as I was about to round the corner of the house. I paused and turned to a gorgeous redhead who seemed vaguely familiar.

"I heard you sing," she said. "Your voice is divine."

Jazz, the drummer, came up behind us with a snicker. "You're something else," he said as he passed.

I ignored him. "Thanks," I said to the woman.

"I'm staying here at the house. You want to come up for a drink?" She kept her poise, her body held in place like she was in a photo shoot, hip cocked, arm angled away from her fitted black dress.

That's when I placed her. She was on a TV show my mother used to watch. I could see her in a cop uniform. Her hair was longer then.

Paul came up and took the snare drum from my hands without a word.

"Seems you have some time to spare." Her smile was perfect, something you'd see on a billboard.

But about as fake.

"I'm just the help," I said. "I need to get everyone packed."

She let go of my arm, her smile unchanging, like it was painted on. Then she frowned, rubbing her fingers together like something was stuck to them.

"Sand," I said with a laugh. "Sorry."

That was when I realized, yeah, no way was I going near this woman. She was like a cardboard cutout compared to the warm, spontaneous ease of Jenny.

"Oh," she said with confusion, as if trying to solve the puzzle of how I had gotten sand on me at the party.

"Thanks for the offer," I said, and strode away toward the van.

When Paul jumped out of the back door and saw me, he pretended to pull his hair out. "What are you doing here, man? That was Vanessa Price! You could totally be doing her right now!"

The keyboardist stepped around the bumper, smoking a cigarette. "He's already had action tonight, man," he said. "That pink girl."

I said nothing, just hopped in the back to locate my guitar and backpack. I wasn't sure I was going to hang with them after all. I needed a shower and a change of clothes, though, for sure. I felt like I was carrying half the beach in my boxers.

Jazz lay between drums on the floor of the van. "I'm wiped."

Paul closed the back doors, reappearing in the driver's seat. "I think we got it all," he said. He turned around. "You going to chill with us since you chickened out with that actress?"

I couldn't really afford a hotel. Their place was a roof over my head at least. "Yeah, sure," I said.

Jazz picked up a water bottle from the floor and chucked it at me. "You could've been shacking up with that redhead."

I deftly caught the bottle and set it down. "I just got here. I don't need woman trouble straight off."

"You check to make sure that other girl wasn't hitched before you jizzed her?" Jazz asked. "Because we really don't want to have to shovel your ass off the concrete."

"She was alone," I said.

Jazz sighed. "And now so is that redhead."

Paul fired up the engine. It sputtered a moment, then caught. "I'll stop by QuickieCash and split the check," he said as we circled to the front of the house.

"Nah, man, they'll take too much," Jazz said. "I can cash it at the bank Monday morning."

"I was gonna give Tennessee here a cut, with him making the crowd actually notice we were there and all," Paul said.

I sat with my back against the wall of the van. "Not necessary," I said. "I'll settle for a sofa to crash on."

"Right on," Jazz said. "You can hang with me. My roommate is outta town."

We passed through the iron gates. "Still a lot of cars here," Paul remarked. "They should have extended the gig."

"Nobody was paying any attention once the crooner here took off," Jazz said. "'Sides, the food was leaving. The people weren't going to hang much longer."

"That reminds me," Paul said. "They gave us a box of leftovers. It's by the amp."

"Righteous," Jazz said, but didn't make any move to open it.

I scooted closer to the front of the van and found the plain white box. Inside was a pile of perfect triangular sandwiches and a stack of cookies. I pulled a couple of each and passed the box up to the front to the keyboardist in the passenger seat. I hadn't eaten since breakfast in Vegas.

"Thanks," Paul said. "So where'd you go with that pink girl?"

"Some beach," I said.

"Dude, never have sex on a beach!" the keyboardist said. "Sand is not your friend."

"Total chafing," Jazz said.

"It went all right," I said. I didn't want to admit to them I'd never been to a beach.

"So you gonna see her again?" the keyboardist asked, his mouth full of sandwich. "Is that why you blew off the actress?"

"I don't even know who she is," I said.

"No number exchange? Nothing?" Jazz asked.

"Nope," I said.

"Slam, bam, thank you, ma'am," Jazz said. "Just the way I like it."

The bass guitarist spoke up from where he was wedged between boxes near the back door. "Like that shit ever happens to you."

"Yeah, yeah," Jazz said. "I don't see you getting any either."

"Face it, friends," Paul said. "Tennessee here is the sum total of our action. We have to live vicariously through him."

"We'll write songs about your pussy quest," Jazz said. "Like the knights of old."

The keyboardist reached back and thumped Jazz on the head. "We haven't written an original song since you insisted they all sucked," he said.

Jazz nudged my leg. "You write your own shit?" he asked. "If so, you can tell your own damn tales."

I brushed crumbs off my hands. "I've done a few."

Jazz let out a whoop. "He's got a huge talent!" he laughed. "No wonder he gets all the ladies."

We pulled up to a red light, and Paul swung his head around. "So let's hear something, Tennessee. Show us what you've got."

I wasn't in much of a mood for it, but the boys were eager, and they'd given me a killer night. So I reached over for my guitar case and flipped it open.

"You've got a lot of shit in there," Jazz said, peering through the gloom.

"Carrying my life around," I said, pulling out the pale cherry Seagull, surrounded by tightly packed clothes. This guitar was new, but still from Tennessee, one of the few things I had from my life before this journey. I'd bought it when I knew I was going to walk away from everything and everybody I'd ever known.

"You got a song that tells your story?" Jazz asked. "Because a dude like you on the road has got to have a story."

"Nah," I said. "My life isn't worthy of a song."

"Awww," Jazz said. "Well, give us something good."

I strummed a few chords and adjusted the tuning. "I don't know that this one is about anything in particular, but it tends to turn a few heads when I sing it."

I picked out a tricky little introduction that I'd put together over a couple weeks shortly after I graduated high school, some six years ago now. I still felt pretty good about the world back then. Sometimes when I played it, a little bit of that happiness and optimism would stick. It never lasted long, but it was all right to feel it for a while.

I came back around to the C chord, and sang the opening lines.

*I've been staring out this window all night long*
*Hoping maybe I will see the light*
*This world's no place for an honest man*
*Simple but uncouth*
*Some people will never understand*

As always, I forgot where I was once I got started, the crowded van and the rumbling floor beneath me disappearing as I went into song-space.

*Just strangers to the truth*
*And she done left me*
*She done left me*
*Right on the center line*

Then it went back around to the tricky progression and a couple more verses.

When I strummed the last chord, Jazz let out a whoop. "I knew you were country! That was seriously country."

I flattened my hand on the strings to kill the sound. "Well, I guess I'm from the country."

"But you sure could sing the blues too," the keyboardist said.

I looked out the front window at the unfamiliar city whizzing by. I thought of Jenny then, and how she must be getting close to home by now, in a whole other place. I'd never even know where.

Yeah, I could definitely sing the blues.

# 15

## JENNY

I woke up in my rainbow explosion feeling like I'd been on a bender.

My head was heavy from the dreadlocks. Maybe I'd cut them all off. What had I been thinking adding all these extensions?

My green dress lay draped over the back of a chair, sand scattered beneath it.

Last night I'd dragged myself into the shower even though I wanted to feel nostalgic about the night with Chance. But I was just too gritty. So I washed it all away, down the drain.

I would never even know who he was. I had nothing but his first name.

I stretched, knocking a plush pink unicorn off the bed to the floor. A third grader could probably live happily in this room.

Uggh. My hair. My room. My life.

Shut up, I told myself. The world is full of haters, don't start hating on yourself.

I kicked off the comforter and stumbled out to the hallway. No way was I up for making my own coffee. I did that all day at work.

Not that I'd been going in that much. I might be fired for all I knew. God. I had relied too much on Frankie. He'd taken over everything, paying my rent, buying me gas and clothes and grocery delivery.

This was the worst day of the rest of my life.

I decided I was too poor for Starbucks, then remembered the Keurig Frankie had bought me early on. I'd never used it. I opened a cabinet and pulled out the box. After several minutes of fumbling with packaging, I had it plugged in and the first cute container of breakfast blend percolating. Or whatever it was a Keurig did. Magic, maybe.

I plopped onto a fuzzy yellow chair and pulled my phone off the wall charger. I had sixteen text messages. What the hell? When had I gotten so popular?

A sense of unease spread through me as I read through the first page, all from Tina and Corabelle with varying versions of "Call us right away!"

Then one from Frankie, saying, "You got 'er done, all right. Call me if you feel panic. I can put some people on it."

God. What were they talking about?

I couldn't squint at the phone any longer, so I switched to my pink-jeweled laptop. I felt irritated at the bling and wanted to scrape it all off. This was what I got for drawing attention in every way possible.

I knew the news of my kiss and betrayal was bound to be on the gossip sites, or in the tabloids, or both. They had some pictures. How they put it all together was the real question.

I opened the laptop and waited for it to power up. Then for the wireless to kick in. Then to examine my nail polish for chips. Then to situate myself more comfortably in my fuzzy chair, which Tina affectionately called "The Baby Chick Hole."

Procrastination. Did I really want to see what I had done?

I ran my hand along the yellow fur stretched over the papasan base. This wasn't a Frankie gift, but something my mother had picked out for my bedroom long ago. I thought about her for a minute, remembering my squeals when I opened my bedroom door at home and saw it. She understood me. A good thing in a mother, maybe.

Sigh. I supposed I did have to look eventually. Face the music.

I didn't have to go far. Yahoo was my home screen and there I was, mugging out with Chance, right there on one of the slider photos on the celebrity news. Below us, the caption read "Movie director's heart in shambles after tawdry display at premiere."

"*After* the premiere," I corrected. This was about what I'd expected to happen. I guess my friends didn't think they'd run a picture of an actual kiss.

Feeling a heck of a lot calmer, I got up to fetch my coffee. This was nothing. I could handle it. Frankie was the one who had to deal with people thinking he'd been a fool.

I blew on the coffee and settled back in my chair. The steam opened my pores. I relaxed. This was okay. Weird about Frankie, though. He normally didn't spook easily. He should have anticipated what would happen, and yet he'd written me offering some help as if we'd done something unexpected.

I clicked over to my favorite gossip site, one that had actually put up a few solo pictures of me now and then when I wore something particularly fabulous. I had a bit of a fetish for five-inch platforms and short skirts. At one point, they'd done a little spread on Frankie's pink-haired plaything, showing my skirts shrinking and my boot height growing. I had printed it out and put it in my scrapbook.

I didn't see anything obvious on the home page, although there was a "stars get wild" montage that was new. I shouldn't have made that, since I wasn't an actress myself. But I clicked anyway, to see what I was up against for click bait.

I felt startled when I realized the first image was of Chance, but not with me. He was talking to Vanessa Price, and she had her claws on him. They were still at the party. The caption said, *"Copper Field* star paws pretty boy at Hollywood soirée."

Was it taken before or after Chance had been with me on the beach? I peered in closely. He was holding a drum. So they were packing to leave. No way Vanessa would have been there when they set up.

My stomach fell. He hooked up with yet another woman after me?

I felt seriously sick. I'd picked a real winner. No condom either. Crap. I'd have to get a VD screen.

Stupid.

I clicked to the next picture and realized this whole "gone wild" montage was from the party. The couple who had cozied up in the sunroom when I arrived apparently got a lot more daring out in the gardens. The actress hopeful was naked and holding on to a tree, black bars covering the strategic areas, and the man was behind her.

So I was definitely not going to be the hottest click from that photo shoot, if I was in it at all.

The next one was Avery Klaus, an actress who had gone for Chance when he came offstage. Her dress could scarcely be called clothing, with its outrageous cutouts. It barely covered her nipples. The angle of the shot accentuated this as she lifted her arms to the stage.

The next shot had her to one side, Chance in the middle, and me in the corner. Well, my pink dreadlocks anyway. You couldn't see my face.

The timing of the shot made it seem as though Chance was choosing between us. Another black bar appeared to cover Avery's nipple slip, although it was probably slapped on whether it happened or not. They did this all the time to make images appear dirty even when they weren't.

I didn't think there would be any more of me, since I wasn't really the subject of the montage, but when the next image was Frankie looking perturbed, probably just a random shot taken who knows when, I had a feeling I knew what was coming.

I clicked. Yes, the kiss picture. And this one had one of those infernal unnecessary blackout bars that made it appear my skirt was hiked up and Chance's hand was up it.

Why had I ever liked this site? Grrr. Below the image was a link that said, "See the sordid history of this cotton candy tart."

What they hell could they possibly have on me? I was nobody until I met Frankie, and I had strictly upheld my contractual code of conduct since.

I clicked through with a sinking feeling.

Jesus. Pictures they'd used before, this time with strategic black bars, made it look like I was getting felt up, flashing girl parts, or otherwise behaving badly. They must have put a whole team on finding images where the bars could create the illusion of something raunchy going on. One of them was a random passerby on a red carpet, looking over my shoulder at no telling what, but the bar over the neckline of my strapless dress made me look topless.

Right. People went topless to premieres.

God.

I hoped my parents didn't go to these sites. Or any of my mother's snoopy friends, who might send links to her.

I got up from the chair and paced the room a moment. I wasn't a public figure. Could I sue?

Did I care?

I tapped out a quick note to Frankie. "What are my options?"

He wrote back immediately. "I would ask the boy before you involve him in any court filing. It will fan the flames initially."

Why would I have to talk to Chance? He wasn't even in any of the worst photos, just the kiss.

Unless there were more.

My throat tightened. "I was talking about the black bars in the *Falling Star Gazette*," I typed.

"Didn't see those," Frankie responded. "Is it worse than the video segment?"

What?

Oh, God. Surely I hadn't made the television gossip. If so, I'd be everywhere by the end of the day.

I flipped on the flat screen to watch the entertainment news, but after ten or so minutes of commercials and the intro to a show, I realized it would be faster to go to their online videos.

I tapped in the link with trepidation, feeling even worse than when I'd first started looking. If it went that high, they felt they had something really good.

The doorbell rang. Crap. Who could that be? I felt paranoid that some reporter or photographer had tracked me down. I peered through the peephole, flooding with relief when I saw Tina and Corabelle.

I opened the door.

Corabelle had a stack of tabloids. "We bought them all!" she said. "I mean, it's just the one daily that got you in this fast, but we bought all the copies."

She dumped them on the coffee table. I hadn't been the lead story, but a small photo in the corner hinted at a scandal inside.

"Have you seen the video segment?" I asked them. A summary from them before I saw it might calm my rising panic.

Tina plopped down on the sofa, pushing a sequined pillow out of her way. "I haven't seen any television stuff, but I see you're waiting for it." She pointed at the entertainment channel. "You going to record it?"

"I was just about to go to their website to see what it was about," I said. I pointed at the stack of tabloids. "How is that article?"

"Not too bad," Corabelle said, flipping to it. "A lot of destroyed love stuff, like you'd planned. They also hinted at a love triangle, but not with you and Frankie and this boy." She turned the page to me. "Some actress named Avery?"

They had the picture with Chance between us. "Great," I said. "That's probably what's feeding the frenzy." I hadn't considered the possibility that an A-list actress would be in any of the pictures and boost their popularity.

"Lover boy is a singer?" Tina asked. "You picked a pretty one."

My heart hurt a little to see the picture in front of my friends. The loss stabbed me acutely now that we could talk about him. "Yeah, he was."

"So what happened?" Corabelle asked. "Did you like him? Is he local?"

I gave them the rundown on the evening, the band, the song, the interested actresses, and the beach.

"And that's it? You haven't heard from him?" Corabelle asked. She pulled her feet up to sit cross-legged on the sofa and tweaked her black ponytail.

"I don't know his name, and he didn't ask mine," I said.

"Well, he knows it now if he's paying attention," Tina said, pointing to the article. "They have you listed right here, Jenny Gillespie, a UCSD acting major who has been seen on the arm of movie director Frankie Sharp for the past four months."

"Acting major, whatever," I said. "They sure did their homework."

"Acting, liberal arts," Tina said. "All the same to them."

I grunted. "Did they figure out who Chance was?"

"No," Corabelle said. "He's just listed as a new member of the Sonic Kings, the band playing at the party."

"He isn't a member," I said. "They picked him up hitchhiking earlier that day."

"Oh, wow," Corabelle said. "Then he really isn't someone you can easily track down."

"Yeah." I dropped back into my yellow chair. "I guess we better see what this video is all about. Frankie already wrote me about it, asking if I wanted to put his people on it. He acted like I might want to take legal action."

"Whoa," Tina said. "That's hardcore."

I pulled up the website, but before I spotted the video, Corabelle pointed at the television. "I think this is it," she said.

Just looking at the opening image, I thought I might faint.

# 16

## CHANCE

I woke with a start at Jazz's apartment, the rough cushion of the ratty sofa imprinted on my cheek.

The front door was swung wide, drenching the cave-like living room with light.

"Rise and shine, country boy," Paul said. "You're famous." He sauntered into the room with some guy I hadn't met before.

I sat up and fumbled on the floor for my bag, pulling out a clean T-shirt. Yesterday's jeans were still drying in Jazz's bathroom. I'd washed them in his sink, definitely leaving the porcelain cleaner than I found it.

I jerked the shirt over my head and yawned. I normally didn't sleep late, but something about the dark room must have kept me out.

Paul tossed a tabloid news magazine on my lap. "I was grabbing some cigarettes for breakfast and saw this."

A giant headline pronounced that some big actor had left his bride at the altar. I wondered why the hell Paul was shoving this in my face.

Then I saw it.

In the corner, a picture from the party. Me and Jenny in the gardens, kissing.

I shoved it aside. "I knew they took that picture. No big deal."

"I thought you said she was single," Paul said. "Says here she's some big movie director's chick."

I frowned. Jenny told me the guy was her boss.

But it didn't matter. I was sure her little angry rant in the limo at the end had to do with making sure I didn't follow her around. Probably due to that guy.

"I don't exactly plan on proposing to her," I said. "It's in the past." I tossed the newspaper beside me on the sofa.

Paul plopped down in a brown recliner with the stuffing falling out. His friend headed toward the kitchen. That guy had *presence*, and I wondered if he was a musician too.

"You getting back on the road?" Paul asked. "Because we've got another gig tonight. The way you rocked it, you could definitely sweeten our take. We get tips on this one, and you can get a cut of that action, since you draw the *ladies*."

"Maybe," I said. I hadn't really thought about what I'd do next. Probably walk around a bit. Spot any smallish coffee shops that would let me play. But if the Sonic Kings gig was decent, I might make more there, maybe enough to cushion a day or two without having to worry about my next meal.

I glanced down at the picture. I tried to act all casual as I reached beside me and flipped to the page number listed by the cover photo.

"Awww, yeah, Tennessee wants to see what they're saying about him," Paul crowed.

Jazz stumbled into the room, blocking the light with his hand. "Shut that door, man," he said. "You're going to let rats in, or something."

"Let 'em out, is more like it," Paul said, kicking at an abandoned pizza box on the floor. "You were definitely raised in a barn. And that is an improvement over this place."

Their sniping at each other gave me the opportunity to scan the article inside. Paul was right, it did say Jenny was a movie director's girlfriend. And an image of his despondent face, obviously unrelated since it wasn't even what he was wearing last night, confirmed that he was the guy who draped his arm around her at the party.

I'd been played. Dragged into some stupid publicity stunt, maybe. God. No wonder she'd been so flirty across the room, sipping her wine then disappearing like a fairy girl. Stupid pink hair. Stupid dreadlocks. Stupid me, for being stupid.

Paul kicked my shin. "You got a hate face on. Bros don't let bros hate on themselves over dames."

The other guy came back in the room, and Paul said to him, "Yo, Dylan, let's get this boy some breakfast."

Now I recognized the guy who'd passed through. Dylan Wolf. He'd been a street busker like me before signing a big record deal with Morris Music.

Crazy luck. Last night I had movie actresses hanging on my arm. Today a rock star the size of Adam Levine had shown up to take me to breakfast.

LA was definitely where it was at.

"You'll get used to that bullshit," Dylan said, waving at the tabloid. "According to that, I've got six girls in every city." He gulped a bottle of water.

"Nearly cost you Jessie a time or two, as I recall," Paul said. "Bloody leeches, that's what they are." He stood up. "You coming, Tennessee? Might as well get to know somebody who actually makes money in this business."

Dylan shook his head. "The only difference between me and you is dumb luck," he said.

I dragged my second pair of jeans out of the bag, and jerked them on. I barely had my boots shoved on my feet before Dylan and Paul walked out the door. "You coming?" Paul asked Jazz through the doorway.

Jazz still had his hand over his eyes, as if he was allergic to the sun. "Nah, man. You go on. Hair of the dog over here," he said.

"Cool if I leave my stuff here?" I asked Jazz.

"It's cool," he said. "I'll be here until the gig tonight."

I followed Paul and Dylan outside to a sleek little blue Maserati. I could admire the ride without feeling any sort of need to own it myself. I'd already figured out that owning things just tied you down, and freedom had been my only valuable possession for a while now.

I ducked into the backseat. The engine started so quiet you could barely tell it was running.

I sat back, thinking over the crazy luck I'd had since arriving in LA. Running into the band, singing at the gig, Jenny, and now meeting Dylan.

But just saying her name in my head made my thoughts turn back to her. The beach, her hair flying as she ran naked in the dark, splashing in the surf. The images were seared into my head. A longing for her started to pulse in my chest.

I had to forget it. She belonged to someone else anyway. And she'd been so crazy, doing all that with me despite her boyfriend or whatever. She'd do it again. One thing I knew, cheaters never changed. It wasn't the first time I'd found out a girl had something on the side.

My thoughts only glanced against that dark muddy night in Chattanooga before I forced them away. Hell, I was acting like I was interested in a relationship or something. I didn't even have a place to sleep.

Dylan and Paul were talking nonstop about somebody they knew, a guy in another band. I tuned it out and stared out the window. We weren't among posh mansions anymore, but gray streets and sketchy-looking businesses up close to the curb.

People walked along the sidewalks, headed for bus stops or just strolling along, oblivious to the world. I took it all in, already feeling inspired by this city to write a song about seeing it for the first time.

Words came to me, and a line of a melody. These were the best days, when the muse was sittin' on my shoulder.

*You might be right*
*We might both live to regret it*
*We might just lose everything*
*We worked so long and hard to build*
*But what I felt last night*
*Well, I never will forget it*

"So what's your name?" Dylan asked.

I met his eyes in the mirror. "Chance McKenzie," I said.

"From Tennessee, I take it," Dylan said.

"Used to be," I said. "I reckon I'll figure out a place to settle down eventually."

"LA's not a bad base." He pulled up to a light. "Nashville seems like it would have been a good fit for you."

I shrugged. "I tried it. Not my scene."

"You write your own stuff?" The light turned green and we took off through the intersection.

"I do," I said.

"He sang one last night," Paul said. "It was all right. The boy's got talent."

Dylan turned into the parking lot of a diner. "It's a tough business," he said as he pulled into a spot. "Everybody's got to make their own way. We can talk about your plans if you want to."

I didn't know how much I wanted to bandy about my plans, since I didn't have any, but I could definitely put away some breakfast.

As for my past, I kept those cards pretty close to my chest. But it wouldn't hurt listening to what this guy'd been through to get where he was. Not that his way was the path for me. I didn't need any glitz or glory. But probably he had experiences I could learn from.

I'd forget the girl. Focus on today and nothing but today. I'd been doing it for a long time. No use changing it now.

# 17

## JENNY

I could barely stand to look at my own television. Corabelle let out a squeal.

"Holy shit," Tina said.

The minute I saw the grainy black footage of Dockweiler Beach, all the blood rushed from my face. It didn't even occur to me that anyone might follow us in the limo. I was nobody. Chance was a random stranger. There didn't seem any point in wasting a photographer's time on us when there were A-list stars back at the party.

But somebody had.

"Please tell me they aren't going to get you—" Tina cut off when the shaky video showed me running naked from the rock shelter, censor bars covering strategic parts.

"Oh, they did," she said with a sigh. "Did you have to go skinny-dipping on a public beach?"

I couldn't answer, petrified that there would be something of us actually getting down to business. My own live sex tape. God, God, God.

Chance came running after me, just a shadow in the moonlight. I was pale and more reflective, apparently. I wasn't sure I could watch any more of it.

The announcer came back on, flashing a lurid grin. "The girlfriend of director Frankie Sharp had a little fling with a singer after the premiere party for the new blockbuster film *Brontosaurus Rampage*."

They displayed an image of me and Frankie from a month or so back. Frankie gazed at me adoringly. I felt a pang for how bad this looked for him.

"Her mystery crooner didn't stop there, though. He was spotted with the *Copper Field* actress Vanessa Price as well as Avery Klaus, the star of *The Neighbor Connection*."

Images flashed onscreen to support his words, Avery in her scanty dress, then Vanessa sidling up to Chance after the party.

The show went back to the anchor with an image of me running naked, my dreadlocks flying, displayed on a side screen. This one was from the back, and they didn't bother to black out my butt.

"But he chose this little hottie to romp with on the beach," the guy said.

The shot widened to show a woman anchor next to him. "I think they have a drink named for that," she said.

"No telling where the sand got lodged," the man responded with a laugh.

I kept my fists clenched tight, but the show moved on to another segment. I let out a long gust of air as I realized there wouldn't be any sex footage. At least not on the show. Someone could still have it. The online sites could pop up with something any minute. Getting rid of it would be like trying to catch a thousand cockroaches.

"Well, that was something," Tina said.

I curled up in a tight ball on my yellow-chick papasan chair.

"You okay?" Corabelle asked.

"Somebody do some online searches," I said. "If that photographer was there with equipment, he could have anything."

"I'll do the honors," Tina said, heading for my table and the laptop. "You think they have your name? It wasn't on the show."

"They have my everything," I said.

Corabelle looked at the door. "Will they come here?"

"I can't imagine. I'm just not worth it. They might stalk Frankie, though."

"What about the boy?" Tina asked from the dining area. "You think they'll figure out his name?"

"Probably," I said. But after seeing that segment, I wasn't sure I cared. He probably woke up with Vanessa. Or Avery.

Or both.

Corabelle scooted down the sofa closer to my chair. "You need us to do anything?"

I covered my eyes with my hands. "Not sure what there is to do. I guess I'll hole up for a while."

"You think it will blow over by Monday?" Corabelle asked. "Will you go to class?"

I had no idea. I leaned my head back against the fur and closed my eyes. "I can't believe I didn't think that they would follow us."

"You were on a public beach," Tina said. "Anything could

have happened. Cops. Kids with cell phones."

I knew she was right. But we had checked. There hadn't appeared to be anyone around.

"Don't beat yourself up," Corabelle said. "It was a perfect storm. You trying to get some publicity, the actresses being there."

"He must have been one hot potato to get you naked on a chilly beach," Tina said.

I didn't answer. He had been. I'd been oblivious to everything. Perfect storm was right. The dry spell. The song. The way he'd sung it just for me.

*When a man loves a woman.*

I wanted to throw something. When a man *plugs* a woman was more like it. Chance had moved on in a heartbeat. I didn't know why he'd even bothered to spend a moment with me when he had these other starlets eating out of his hand.

Anger felt good. It was a hell of a lot better than moping. I hoped Chance realized that I knew. Hell, he probably didn't care. He was just another entertainer trying to crawl his way to the top. Maybe he even knew I had been with Frankie. Or saw me talking to the other big shots and thought I was an easy in.

I unfurled from my tight ball and forced myself out of the chair.

"I think that TV show got exclusive rights or something," Tina said from the table. "Because I'm not finding the beach stuff on any of the gossip sites. It's starting to appear on YouTube, though, illegal recordings of the segment."

"That's good, though, right?" Corabelle asked. "If they got an exclusive but didn't use any other footage, nobody else can use it either."

I headed over to Tina and the laptop. "Maybe. Those photographers are pretty smart. He would hold on to anything the show wasn't willing to air and see if he could get a higher bid for the rest."

"So he won't just stick it on the Internet for free, then," Tina said. "Still good."

She was right. I could have Frankie track down the photographer. He was probably submitting his stuff all over. He wouldn't be hard to find. Maybe Frankie would buy the footage from him.

"Aren't you a private person, not a public figure?" Corabelle asked. "Can't you sue?"

"Not if she's on a public beach," Tina said. "Technically, she was committing a crime."

Corabelle's eyes got wide. "Will you get arrested?"

"Not likely," I said. "They'd have to want to make a point with me, and generally it's not worth it."

I turned back to my kitchen and dug out more K-cups for coffee. I had a feeling I was going to need a lot more of it as this got sorted out.

"You going to tell your mom before she sees it herself?" Corabelle asked. "You know how much she loves the entertainment shows."

I fired up the Keurig for another round. "I probably should. Although they don't say my name on the show, and she hasn't seen my dreadlocks."

"Moms know their kids," Tina said, still clicking around on the laptop. "And there's that super-clear shot of you and Frankie."

Right. Crap. "Okay, I'll call her." I braced my hands on the edge of the counter. "This is like the worst day ever."

Corabelle came up behind me and lifted the heavy dreadlocks. "It'll pass." But her voice was tight. And I knew she was thinking of her worst day ever. This was nothing compared to that.

Corabelle and Tina both had been through a lot. They knew each other because both of them had given birth to babies that had only lived a short time.

They didn't know as much about me as they thought. To them, I was this colorful, pink-haired friend who partied too hard and never took anything seriously.

I didn't talk about my past, or the things that haunted me at night. I was barely able to keep them aside enough to keep going at times. I certainly didn't want to have to live like that girl, the sad one.

I went back to the laptop and took control of the trackpad. Tina pulled her hands away. I navigated back to the spread with the screaming headline that read "Cotton candy tart."

"Print that one," I told Tina. "That defines me just about as well as anything."

Tina shook her head but sent the wireless command through to the printer on the desk in the next room.

Being that silly attention whore who nobody takes seriously was a whole lot easier than anything else. Probably if Chance saw the ruckus I caused, he wouldn't have given me the light of day this morning anyway.

At least if I never saw him again, I didn't have to deal with his disappointment or disgust.

# 18

## CHANCE

It turned out Dylan was totally laid back. Despite his megabucks and the hot wife and a baby on the way, he was chill about random fans who spotted him and started screaming. And it happened. Even at our breakfast in a dumpy diner.

The group of three girls who approached us seemed easygoing at first. One shyly came up and asked if he was the real Dylan Wolf. He smiled and nodded at her.

She rummaged through her purse looking for something to get him to sign. When she produced a little notepad, he dutifully scribbled out a message and his name.

I thought they were done, when one of the girls in the group whirled around and shouted, "I can't stop myself!" and nosedived into his lap in the booth.

He very carefully extricated himself and lifted her off the seat. Her friends dashed forward and dragged her away. She started wailing that she loved him, and by then the manager was holding open the door for them to leave.

When they were gone, Dylan shook his head. "By tomorrow she'll be telling *Star* magazine that I'm her baby daddy."

"How do you deal with all that?" I asked. My tiny taste of fame was more than I wanted already.

"You pay people to manage your publicity," Dylan said. "And you hope your family will be understanding. My wife, Jessie, really had a hard time at first. But once you realize the people typing up the lies are just trying to pay their bills, you realize it isn't personal. If it wasn't me, it'd be some other target."

"I've got none of these problems," Paul said, talking around a toothpick. "You pretty boys deserve every piece of shit you go through."

Dylan punched him on the arm, and Paul pretended to fall back. "Police, police," he called out weakly. "I'm gonna sue!"

Dylan huffed out a rueful laugh. "I think half my money goes to lawyers."

"But you can still eat at normal places like this?" I asked. I was sort of surprised that only those girls had noticed him. One of his songs was in the Top 40 right now.

"Sure," he said. "It's funny how many people really don't pay attention, or don't believe it's me. Generally I'm golden until somebody gets crazy. Then everybody else figures they've got to get in on it."

I thought about Jenny and that kiss she'd given me. Obviously it was staged. I didn't know why she went through with the rest of it, the beach and all. Hell, maybe I was in a porn movie now and didn't even know it.

But that was the anger talking. Jenny wasn't that sort of girl. I could tell that. And we'd had an honest-to-God connection out there. Maybe she regretted the pictures. Who knows? It wasn't like I'd ever see her again.

"He's mooning over the pink dreads girl again," Paul said.

My head snapped up. Dylan and Paul were watching me, amused.

"He's a goner," Dylan said. "I know that look."

"Ain't nobody gonna tie down this hunk of man-meat," Paul said. He lifted his rail-thin arms and pretended to flex his muscles.

"There's girls who are into guys like you," Dylan said.

"Pass them over," Paul said. "Cuz all I know is that when Tennessee got up onstage, I was a stinking pile of dog shit."

"But you guys got the gig in the first place," I said. "I've never played for more than twenty people at a time before."

"Dylan here got the gig," Paul said. "He's nice to the little people."

"We're all little people," Dylan said, picking up his coffee. "Just some people don't know it."

My phone buzzed in my jeans, startling me. It had been months since I had used it. After I refused to answer or respond to anybody back home the first few weeks, interest in what had happened to me tapered off. My mom tried every now and again, but eventually I blocked her. Pretty much the only person I'd even pay attention to was Charlie, and her only because she worked at the care center where my sister was.

I tugged the phone out and glanced down to make sure the message wasn't anything about her. The number was unfamiliar. Probably random. I was about to tuck it away again when a text came through. The first few words showed in the preview pane, and when I saw "naked," I clicked through in a hurry.

*What were you doing naked on that California beach?*

"Shit," I mumbled.

"What's gettin' you, Tennessee?" Paul asked.

"Why does anybody know I was naked on a beach last night?"

"You were *what?*" Paul exclaimed.

Dylan leaned forward. "Did a photographer follow you from that party?"

"I don't know," I said. Surely Jenny hadn't sold the story somewhere.

Or maybe I *was* starring in a porn movie.

"Wait," Paul said. He shook his hands next to his head. "Let me get this straight. You took off with pink dreadlocks and went streaking on the beach?"

"Among other things," I mumbled, wondering now what all was out there.

"Who was this girl exactly?" Dylan asked.

I set down the phone, trying to cool my jets. My head felt about ready to pop off from anger. "I just met her at the party. She said the movie director guy was her boss. She felt out of place."

"And you nailed her on the beach?" Paul's face was full of shock.

"Did she act strange in any way?" Dylan asked.

"She kissed me unexpectedly at the party," I said. "Some photographer took a picture."

"Then she took you to the beach?" Dylan's face was etched with concern.

"Yeah. But that was my idea. Not hers." I pictured her again, curled up against me between the rocks.

Dylan slid his phone closer to his plate and began tapping. I stared out the window at the broken asphalt of the parking lot. People walked by, going about their day. I wanted to be one of them now, not having unknown numbers telling me my own private business.

"Well, you've hit the big time," Dylan said. "I searched the news for 'naked beach musician' and I'm getting a lot of uploads of a segment from an entertainment news show. There's footage of you and a girl skinny-dipping."

"No shit," Paul said, grabbing the phone. "My country boy here is in a real live LA scandal on his first day?"

He angled the phone so we could all see it. I didn't really want to look. But seeing Jenny's bare backside made me lean in to the phone.

"A whole segment," Paul said. "Who'da thunk it?"

"They don't know who you are," Dylan said. "She's getting the worst of it."

My phone buzzed again. Then again. All people I used to know, ones I hadn't bothered blocking because they hadn't even wondered where I'd gone off to. The messages were all the same.

*Saw you with that chick! Hot damn!*
*Who was that naked girl on the beach? Where can I get one?*
*You know how to get out of town all right! Saw your pictures!*

Then another from the unknown number. This one made clear who it was.

*Chance Arthur McKenzie! What in God's name were you doing cavorting with some California hussy in front of cameras? You better call me right now. I'm on Aunt Gertie's cell phone. I can't even leave a voice mail for you when I use mine.*

My mother. Just about the last person I wanted to ever see again. And Aunt Gertie was right up there. I was not going to give them the time of day.

I blocked the new number and shut off the phone.

I'd had just about enough of LA.

"Gentlemen," I said. "If you wouldn't mind giving me a lift back to the apartment, I need to gather my stuff and head on out of here."

"What?" Paul said. "You can't leave us now. Things just started getting interesting!"

I didn't want to tell him the whole reason I'd gone away was to blend in and become invisible. LA had just blown my cover.

"Let the boy adjust," Dylan said. He slid out of the booth and dragged Paul along with him. "It isn't every day you become a viral video."

Thankfully the boys were quiet as we headed out to the car and drove back to Jazz's place. I was still in a pisser about the messages.

My mother. Of all people to chastise me about anything. She was the one making everyone suffer.

I knew it was my fault. But it was her fault too. And my pissant friends. All of them.

The image of my sister in that facility, her chest rising and falling with the ventilator, flashed through my vision long enough to remind me why I'd left the whole lot of them behind. The only one I cared about would never walk again, never talk again, never do anything but waste away until she died. If our mother ever let her go in peace.

I didn't have a word to say to a single one of them ever again. And now this stupid video was making them all track me down.

I would toss the damn phone if it wasn't for Charlie. But maybe even that wasn't good enough. I could write down her number and then chuck this stupid thing. I should have done it months ago.

I would this time. And as soon as I did, I wouldn't be able to get out of this godforsaken city fast enough.

# 19

## JENNY

Tina and Corabelle spent most of the day with me, probably thinking they were on suicide watch or something. But I was fine.

I practiced what I would say to my mother if she spotted the video or the tabloids. I didn't think she went to any of the gossip sites, but who knew?

I was grateful that, at the very least, the gossip rags weren't digging into my past. I didn't need sob stories about my poor, poor tragic family. They didn't know anything, and if they wanted to put some sort of pathetic spin on my life choices, I'd torch every last one of their offices.

Yeah, maybe Tina and Corabelle were actually on arson watch.

I wondered if Chance had seen any of this yet and how he was taking it. Frankie had called an hour ago asking if I was okay. I told him it didn't matter. So what if I was the naked tart? I didn't ask if it meant none of his friends would hire me now.

Although who knows, after the naked pictures were plastered

everywhere, I might have too many offers. The wrong kind.

I flung myself on my sofa after they left, sort of glad to be alone. I propped the laptop on my belly and clicked back through all the images, saving the good ones showing Chance.

Nothing had popped up showing us between the rocks, so either the photographer didn't have anything or he was still working a deal. Judging by the limitations of his equipment in the moonlight photos and how dark it was in our hidden spot, I was guessing nothing had really turned out well, if he had it at all.

I could see the image in my mind, though. Chance, kneeling in the sand, his mouth working up my thigh. My body did a little involuntary clench just thinking about it. I could feel it today. A few aches here and there. Delicious. Just enough to be a reminder. Not enough to hurt.

I wasn't under any contractual obligations now. I could sow my girl oats all I wanted, and I knew exactly what would fix a post-boy melancholy. Hair of the dog.

Although, I should probably get checked out first. Make sure there were no lasting remnants of Chance's prodigious parts. Condom in the sand. God. How stupid was that?

I idly flipped through the images, studying Chance. I tried to put together everything I knew about him.

He was a singer.

He had hitchhiked from Chattanooga, Tennessee.

Hmm. That was about it.

Well, that and length and girth. My body hitched again, and I closed the laptop. I was tired. It had been a late night and a stressful as hell day. For once, I was actually ready to go back to class.

Now *that* was tragic.

# 20

## CHANCE

I didn't intend to go back to the beach Jenny took us to, but somehow, I'd ended up there.

The waves crashed along the shore. Everything looked different in the light of day. A few stragglers in jackets walked along the sand. No one got in the spray. Far out from shore, I could see a sailboat, its white triangles disappearing into the blown-out sky.

I held my guitar case in one hand, my backpack slung over my shoulder. I was supposed to be heading north to catch a ride to Portland, maybe, or Washington State. But my feet had led me here.

I'd sold my cell to a guy on a street corner paying cash for old phones. My past couldn't catch me now. Those old ghosts were as invisible as air.

The sand crunched beneath my boots. I didn't know what had led me here, really. I was acting like a fool boy with a crush. After everything I'd seen of Jenny, I should be done with the whole mess. She'd singled me out and used me to get some publicity.

But she'd been so genuine, her highs and lows, passion and intensity, laughing and then letting tears flow down my hand.

I kicked at a rock peeking out from the ground. I was approaching the outcropping where we'd hidden.

*We'd hidden.*

If she'd wanted to get caught on camera, seems like she would have stayed out in the open. And the beach had been my idea, not hers. And she pointed out the rock.

I didn't get it. None of it. I approached the rock. Other people had been here since us. The place was scattered with footprints and two half-buried soda cans.

I stepped into the sheltered space. I set my guitar case in the sand, and just for a moment, pressed my hands against the rough surface of the rock. In that instant, my past aligning with my present, I could see her, the shadow of her, looking up at me.

I closed my eyes and when the smells and sounds kicked in, I felt like I was back there. The sharpness of the sea air. The roar of the waves pounding the shore. The gritty feeling underneath my feet as the sand shifted.

I thought of heading to San Diego instead. Of finding her.

Then I pulled myself together.

Hell, no.

I pushed away from the rock, breaking the spell. She was probably out with her movie director guy, all glitzed up, practicing her come-hither look for some other unsuspecting sap they could laugh about over cocktails.

I snatched up my guitar and headed back to the street. One thing had been sure about LA: no matter how promising everything had seemed at first — the band, the party, the celebrities — it wasn't my friend.

I had a long walk ahead. Nobody would pick me up until I was out of the city proper. But I was used to it. I would hightail it away from the crowded streets and back into the open. Then my next set of possibilities would split wide, and I'd forget everything. The mansions. The stars. The beach. The actresses.

As I took off down the road, heading roughly north, I did admit one thing to myself, though. It was going to take a lot to forget about her.

# 21

## JENNY

I went to class on Monday, big fat sunglasses on my face like I was a movie star trying to be incognito. But when that felt stupid, I yanked them off.

Then two guys started staring at me outside the library, and I just knew it was because they recognized my hair from the video, so I put them on again and tucked my dreadlocks into a bandana.

Maybe I should cut the extensions off. I went to World Lit with a chip on my shoulder, sure that everyone was looking at me and picturing me without my black bars. I hunkered down in my seat, feeling exposed. I didn't hear a single word of the lecture. I might as well have stayed home.

After class I met Corabelle at the quad and we sat in our usual spot on the diamonds of grass, but I felt edgy and vulnerable.

"Can we go somewhere less public?" I finally asked.

"Sure," she said. "You want to go sit in the chairs by the food court?"

"That's pretty public," I said.

"By the statue?" she suggested.

"Still public!"

Corabelle took my elbow and dragged me to my feet. I wished I had a less beautiful friend, as the two of us together tended to attract attention. "Do you have any sunglasses you could put on?" I asked her.

"Whoa, you are way over the top," she said. "Let's go find a quiet corner somewhere."

I followed her through the forest of trees in the center of campus, glad she was straying off the path. We wound up at the base of the library, off to one side where nobody ever ventured. I sat down on a rock.

"What's going on?" she asked me. "You always liked the spotlight before."

"I wasn't naked before!" I said. "People keep looking at me!"

She dropped her backpack to the ground and plopped down next to me. "People always look at you," she said. "You stop traffic. I don't think anybody's really figured it out."

"Lumberjack did," I said. My ex-boyfriend, boy toy, whatever he was, a TA from astronomy last fall, had been calling me nonstop since the photos hit social media over the weekend. I'd ignored him. He didn't seem to care about how I felt about the pictures, but kept asking if we could go to the beach sometime.

Jerk.

The station must have successfully squelched a lot of the illegally recorded segments of the show, as they weren't getting out nearly as much as my naked butt picture on the beach. I had quit logging into anything so I wouldn't have to keep looking at myself.

Fortunately, the dreadlocks were so new that my family hadn't put it all together. My name had been in the segment and in the tabloids, but wasn't attached to any of the viral images.

I was possibly getting off luckier than I could have.

"You heard from the hunky singer?" Corabelle asked.

"I don't expect to." I picked at a leaf near my plum Uggs boot. The color cheered me up a bit. "It wasn't like we exchanged numbers or anything."

"Just bodily fluids, I know. You keep saying that. Still, he has your name if he noticed."

"Chance didn't strike me as the type to follow celebrity gossip," I said. "Besides, he was on the road. Hitchhikers don't exactly get cable."

"You think he's gone already?" Corabelle asked.

I looked up through the spindly trees at the pale sky. "Probably. If I were him, I'd be done with LA."

We sat for a bit in companionable silence. Corabelle was good at that. Just being outside and away from people and devices and news magazines made me calmer.

I squirmed a bit on my rock, feeling a little strange in the girl parts. "That's what I meant to do," I said aloud, then wished I hadn't.

Corabelle looked up from her notebook. "What's that?"

"Never mind," I said.

She put her pad down with a look I recognized from my mother. It was new to her. She'd taken to being a stepmom to Gavin's adorable four-year-old like a kid to a cookie. She had the mom voice and the mom stare and the mom hug. She was born to it. I hoped they'd get to have a baby of their own eventually, although I knew they had a long way to go to get there.

Just not now.

I needed her more.

"Spit it out," she said.

"I think I need to go to the clinic," I said.

"Oh," Corabelle said. "Right. You didn't end up with a condom, did you?"

I shook my head. "And I feel a little weird."

"Let's go over there right now," she said. "You can make an appointment. The doctor there is super nice. I went for the exact same reason as you last fall." She tucked her notebook in her backpack.

"Really?" I asked. "A VD screen?"

"Yeah, and a pregnancy test. Not a fun combination. You feel like a two-bit tramp with no common sense."

I got up from the rock and brushed the dirt off my wool miniskirt. "I feel like that most of the time."

"You don't have to keep trading them out, you know," she said as we cut back through the trees. "You can find a good one and hold on to him."

"That's the trouble," I said. "There aren't any good ones."

She didn't point out that Gavin was her husband, or that even Tina, who had always sworn off second dates, was also engaged now. Corabelle was good at letting the I-told-you-so go unsaid. That's probably why we were friends. Otherwise there would be nothing else to say. I screwed up at the speed of ejaculation.

I balked as we approached the small door of the health clinic. "I can't be seen going in there," I said. "I'll just call them later."

"I don't think anyone is watching you," Corabelle said.

I looked around. Students walked in every direction, talking on cell phones, listening to earbuds, or chatting with friends. They all looked legit, but then, I hadn't known I was being watched on the beach.

"Can't do it," I said. "I promise I'll call."

"Don't put it off," Corabelle said. "Waiting will make you crazy, and you need to focus on your grades or you won't graduate."

"I don't know. Another term at good ol' UCSD probably wouldn't kill me," I said. "Not like I have anything else to do."

We passed by the health building without going in.

"I have to get to class," Corabelle said. "Maybe it will get quieter in a little while and you can sneak in."

"Maybe," I said. I really did want to get that over with.

She reached over for a quick hug. "I'm glad you came to campus today. You can't let this derail your life."

I nodded, but I felt doubtful. My life was already derailed. My old best friend had gone and gotten married and was mired in family and change.

Then my new best friend had fallen in love with someone else. I was still feeling the loss of Frankie. And not just his money. I didn't realize how much he kept me feeling good about myself. Appearing to be in a fun, stable relationship had made it seem real.

And as much as I didn't want to admit it, I liked it.

I sat on a bench a couple buildings away from the campus clinic. I didn't have another class for an hour. I watched people walking by, and just like Corabelle said, it cleared out not too long after. Everyone was either in class or heading home.

I adjusted my sunglasses and checked my bandana. I couldn't

hide the entire bushel of dreadlocks, but it was pretty good. I should have worn a hoodie. The day had a bit of a chill, which was why I'd pulled out the Uggs and the skirt. Navy and purple were my thing, a perfect foil for my pink hair. Pretty soon it would be summer and my amazing wardrobe would be the wrong season.

Back to old Jenny clothes.

Back to old Jenny.

Just to be sure no one was following me, I walked quickly between a couple buildings and circled back.

Nobody was around.

Okay. I could do this.

I rushed up to the small glass door of the clinic and hurried inside.

A woman sat behind a desk, friendly and easygoing with short gray hair in a girlish bob. Two girls waited in chairs. They glanced up at me, then returned to their cell phones.

"Can I help you?" the woman asked.

"I wondered if I could make an appointment," I said.

"What did you want to be seen for?" she asked.

I squeezed my hands in fists. I really didn't want to say this out loud. I leaned forward. "A VD screening," I whispered.

"Are you showing symptoms?" she asked.

"I don't know," I said. "Maybe?"

"Let's see when I can fit you in." She tapped on her screen. "Can you come back Wednesday?"

"I'm in class until 2."

"That's fine, just come after," she said.

I'd have to return to the building, but I guessed I was committed now.

"What's your name?" she asked.

I was grateful for Frankie one more time as I pulled out my custom business cards, designed by his assistant and paid for by him. Now I didn't have to say it out loud.

The woman tapped in my information and passed back the card. "Pretty," she said.

"Thanks." I held it in my palm like a relic from better days. It was soft pink, almost white, and had an intricate swirl in one corner. It read "Jenny Gillespie. Assistant and Social Media Management for Public Figures."

I shoved it in my backpack as I left. I couldn't manage my own social media at the moment. I had no business acting like I could help somebody else with theirs.

One life problem at a time. Now I had to go to class and act like I wasn't yet again having to deal with my impulsive stupidity.

# 22

## CHANCE

The vegan cafe in downtown Portland was quiet and small. The tables were full, though, and the little stage in the corner was just right for a single musician.

I kept everything light and soft, easygoing music for the dinner crowd. The owner of the place, a tall spindly woman with frizzy gray hair tied a wide scarf, stood by the swinging doors to the kitchen and watched. She seemed pleased with my choices. I figured if I did all right, she'd let me come back again tomorrow night. One less thing to worry about as I settled in the new city.

The people here were older, looked to be well off, and had an appreciation for things money couldn't buy. They were polite and tipped well. This was my second set, and my first one had gotten a bigger take than my past three gigs combined, for just two hours.

I was feeling fine.

A woman in a long blue dress that kissed the floor came up and dropped money in the silver bucket the owner had provided me. Then she leaned in close. "It's my anniversary," she said, pointing to a friendly-looking guy at a table by the wall. "Do you know 'When a Man Loves a Woman'?"

I tensed up at the words, but I nodded. She beamed at me, so excited that I would sing her request.

I played back through the chorus on the song I was finishing up. The conversations were hushed, and fabric on the walls kept the noise levels low. I diddled through a bridge to shift me from one key to the next. Then I strummed the opening chords of her request.

I almost couldn't do it. When I got to the opening line, the world burst wide, the cafe disappeared and instead, the crowd at the base of the stage from the movie party filled my vision. Jenny looked up at me, her pink dreadlocks on her bare shoulders.

This time, I didn't see just the green dress, but the way it peeled off her against the rock. The madness of that one night washed over me. I had trouble focusing on the song.

I shook my head and forced myself to make eye contact with the woman who'd asked for it. She and her man were cuddled close together, watching me. I had to make this good for them. I tried to picture their wedding day, probably a couple decades ago, judging by their age. This got me through.

When the song finally ended, the crowd really clapped. Quite a lot of people got up to put money in the bucket. A couple more requests came in. The night became a lovefest of romantic songs.

As the evening wound down, the owner came over. "You were a real hit," she said. "I've been over there thinking, would you like to do this regularly? We could call it 'Romance Night' and they could make requests. I'm happy to pay you a regular wage on top of tips." She glanced into the bucket. "Though it looks like you did all right. What do you think? Once a week?"

I packed my guitar in the case. I knew damn well I couldn't sit there and sing love songs to happy couples all the time. And even the promise of regular money felt like a trap.

"I'm mighty flattered," I told the woman. "But I'm only in Portland a couple more days. I won't be around for anything regular. But it's a mighty fine idea."

She nodded, her lips pursed together. The fringed end of her scarf brushed against her shoulder. "You look like a boy who's running from something."

Did everybody have me pegged?

"No, ma'am," I said. "I just figured it was best to hit the road before life tied me down."

She settled back on her heels, arms crossed in front of her crinkly cotton dress. "Come over here," she said, and sat at an empty table.

I latched my case and followed, sitting opposite her in a hard-backed chair.

"Give me your hand," she said.

"You a fortune-teller?" I asked.

"Just give it to me," she insisted.

I stretched my arm across the table. She flipped my hand over, opening my fingers.

"You aren't just a guitar player," she said. "You used to do manual labor."

"Poured concrete," I said. "Had to set a lot of forms."

She nodded. "But you don't have a lot of highfalutin aspirations."

"I prefer to just get by."

She stared a while, then let go of my hand. I wasn't sure if she was a palm reader after all, or if she didn't want to relay what she saw there. "You've been on the road a while," she said. "And it's about time for you to go home."

I sat back in my chair. I guessed I was about to get a lecture. "Don't reckon I really have one of those."

I was ready to get out of there now. I'd found a $25 a night hotel earlier that day and was looking forward to sleeping in an actual bed. Today's take was good enough that I didn't have to feel guilty about it.

"Oh, but you do. You just don't want to admit it," she said. "Let me pack you a meal before you go. Collect your money. And the offer's good if you want to come back. You were real popular with my customers. Several of them stopped me just to comment on it."

"Thank you," I said, and pushed away from the table.

She headed to the back and I returned to the little stage. I sorted through the night's take, stacking the bills. I'd done all right by a long shot. Maybe I'd buy a bus ticket, go all the way across the country and start on the other side.

The more I thought about it, the more that sounded like a good idea. New York. The East Coast. Virginia. All places I'd never been.

I was a fool to think the journey was supposed to end in LA. Nothing had changed back home. I had made it this long. Maybe this was the life I was supposed to lead.

I picked up my case and my backpack, feeling real good about the decision. The owner came out with a box of food. I took it from her and thanked her one more time.

I headed out into the cool night air, ready to hoof it to the Greyhound station. There was no reason to change a thing. My luck was holding out, and a life on the road was turning out to be just about perfect.

No commitments. No obligations. No expectations.

All fine by me.

# 23

## JENNY

Wednesday and the doctor visit came around a little too fast for my taste.

But Corabelle had been right. Things were blowing over. I was just the flavor of the weekend, and thankfully, another actress had a meltdown and shaved not her head, but her boyfriend's, in his sleep. And HE was a very prominent actor scheduled to host an award show this weekend.

Way more interesting stuff.

I had a love-hate relationship with celebrity gossip. I found it fascinating and endlessly entertaining as long as it was about somebody else.

I decided to look sweet and innocent for my appointment, hopefully to offset the fact that I was coming in for a VD screening. After class, I planned to head to Cool Beans, a coffee shop where I allegedly had a job with Corabelle, and see if our boss had canned me completely or if he could be swayed into giving me hours.

I'd only been to work one day in the past month, and not much more in the previous ones. Frankie had needed me as he geared up for his premiere. I couldn't be expected to stay out half the night and then get up and grind beans at some ungodly hour.

It had made sense at the time. If I was fired, I'd have to find something. My dad paid my tuition and my mom paid my rent. But anything else I needed in life, I had to pay for myself.

I knew I had it lucky. And I'd do the right thing. The whole Hollywood experience had definitely gone to my head. But it was over. I hadn't heard from anybody about a job, and the more days that passed, the less likely it was that I would. LA had a short attention span. Graduation was just a couple months away.

I straightened my navy blue beret. It gave my dreadlocks a bohemian effect rather than alternative-edgy. I pulled on a simple hunter green sweater and a soft blue and green plaid skirt. I looked positively schoolgirlish as I finished the look with suede flats.

The hair was still a little wild, so I tamed the dreads into a loose low ponytail that fell over one shoulder. Perfect. That small change aged me up to a model from a college Benetton ad rather than prep school.

I was probably overthinking this.

I drove over to campus. I headed to World Lit in a fog and probably didn't pay any more attention to the lecture today than I had on Monday. Corabelle would help me when it came time for finals. She was ace at this stuff. As long as I had the reading list, I would be fine.

When the class finally ended, I was the last to leave my seat. I felt sure the doc was going to tell me I had sixteen diseases, half of them incurable.

The walk along the paths felt long. It seemed happy couples were everywhere, all twitterpated or whatever with spring. The thought of the movie *Bambi* and the love-struck animals made me miss my mom. I hadn't called her or told her anything. It seemed weird to involve her in my grown-up problems. But maybe I needed a mom right now.

Just not to talk about the VD screening.

I slowed down as I approached the glass door of the health center. Even if nobody cared anymore, and surely no one was stalking me by now, I looked around to see who might be watching.

I considered limping or coughing so that my visit would clearly have some other cause. Then I realized I was being ridiculous and just walked in.

The waiting room was busy, almost every seat full. Great, I would probably have to sit there forever. I checked in and plopped into a seat that was uncomfortably close to a boyishly cute basketball player holding a ball in his lap.

Normally I would have come to attention and tried to chat him up, but my heart wasn't in it anymore. Besides, I'd probably no more strike up a conversation than they'd open the door and ask Jenny Gillespie to come back for her VD test.

He must have given off some manly testosterone vibe, though, because sitting by him made me think of Chance again. Probably the only reason I was so hung up on him, well, other than his outrageous hot factor and the way he sang "When a Man Loves a Woman," was because he hadn't been hung up on me.

He ditched me like I was nothing. I could still see Vanessa Price's greedy paws on his arm.

But if I thought about what I'd do if Brad Pitt propositioned me, I got it. How often does stuff like that happen to us plebes?

Still, it smarted. And now I was here, checking for God-knows-what on my privates.

I pulled out my phone, catching up on everything I'd avoided while my butt was viral. Instagram. Snapchat. Two new sites nobody seemed to really be using. I was tempted to check the gossip rags online, but decided not to get my heart rate up before they checked my blood pressure. Still, I typed in Frankie's name to see if he had gone public with his new boy.

Most of the hits were still about his broken heart, but one made me click. A small sidebar mention showed Frankie laughing with another man. The text said he was "sealing a new deal" with a screenwriter, but I knew better. His face was radiant. This was the guy.

Frankie had never looked at me like that. In fact, I wasn't sure anybody ever had.

I sank a little lower in the chair. Where had my moxie gone? I was usually impervious to self-doubt. The one-two punch of ending things with Frankie and this singer knocking me off-center was having its effect.

Basketball Boy got up when his name was called. I stared at his butt as he walked away, but I wasn't feeling it. Instead, I pictured Chance, running after me in the waves, thinking I was so crazy for dashing out into the freezing water naked.

"Jenny?"

My head popped up with cold fear when I heard my name, certain some reporter had discovered me getting VD screened at the health center.

But it was just the nurse, kind and broad-faced, braids

encircling her head. "You ready?" she asked.

I followed her pink scrubs through the maze of hallways. I began to wonder if I shouldn't have gone to my regular ob-gyn for this, but then my mother would have gotten the insurance statement. At least here, all the documentation came straight to me.

The nurse led me into an exam room. "So you want a screening?" she asked.

I stepped up on the ledge to the exam table and sat on the paper runner. "Yeah. I guess whatever the standard workup is."

"What symptoms are you having?" she asked, pen poised over her clipboard. She said this like it was perfectly natural to have this horrible conversation. I guess on a college campus, she saw this a lot.

"Mainly, paranoia," I said.

She laughed. "No itching or burning or pain with urination or intercourse?"

"No. I just had an encounter with a man whore and the condom got lost in the sand."

"Ouch," she said. She came forward and wrapped a blood pressure cuff around my arm. "How long ago?"

"Friday," I said.

She nodded as she pumped air into the cuff. "We'll swab you, but we might not detect anything that new. If you have any problems in the next couple of weeks, you might want to return for a repeat."

Great, I'd have to do this again. I hadn't even thought there might be an incubation period.

"Okay," I said, but she wasn't listening, intent on the blood pressure dial.

She released the air. "All looks good here. I'll send Dr. Alpern in. Undress waist down and cover with the sheet."

I nodded.

I kicked off my shoes and piled my clothes on a chair in the corner. Then I waited, deciding to skip looking at my phone. Just be.

But as soon as my mind had nothing to occupy it, Chance came right back. Singing. Looking at me from the stage. Hopping down next to me despite all those hot actresses swarming around him.

He'd chosen me. My body warmed over. Why had he done that, only to switch to the A-list after? Maybe he had mistaken me for somebody else.

Or hadn't gotten what he really wanted. I had to bite my cheek to banish that depressing thought.

Two swift knocks on the door startled me. "Everyone indecent?" a voice asked.

"All good," I said.

The doctor entered, older, gray-haired, in a traditional lab coat, something I didn't see much anymore. He extended a hand. "I'm Dr. Alpern," he said.

"I'm Jenny."

"Well, Jenny, let's take a look." He flipped through a chart. "We're going to do a quick panel. It also looks like you need a new script for your birth control. So we should do the full annual so I can sign off on that."

I remembered seeing at least one full pack plus a partial when I took my pill that morning. "I don't think so. I can do that next month when I run out."

He frowned. "You should be out now. In fact, what are you using for birth control?"

My head spun. "The pill," I said.

He nodded and smiled. "Okay. Maybe you overlapped last time and had some extra. You come back when it's time." He sat on a stool. "Go ahead and lie back and scoot to the edge."

I fell back on the paper pillow, but my head was spinning. I didn't remember having extra, but that had been a year ago. I knew I had gotten a little sloppy here and there with taking the pill, but I was with Frankie and it didn't matter.

We had a lot of late parties, and unexpected overnights in LA with my pills in San Diego. The blood drained out of me as I thought about just how often it had happened, and if that might have meant I missed too many.

"How many can you miss and still be safe?" I asked.

Dr. Alpern looked up over the paper tented on my knees. "Generally a missed pill here and there isn't disastrous," he said, "although it does put you at risk."

My heart started thumping. "What if you were sort of sketchy about taking it over a long period?"

He paused, concentrating on the task of sticking random things in me for a minute. Then he withdrew and rolled back. "I'd say it's time for a different form of birth control."

I sat up. "Okay, I'm listening."

"There's IUDs, patches, and the ring," he said.

"I'll look them up," I said. "I'll decide before I do the annual exam."

"Sounds like a good plan," he said. "Do you think you could be pregnant?"

"No, no way," I said. But I felt a niggle of doubt. "At least, I don't think so."

"When was your last period?"

"A couple weeks ago, but it's not late or anything. I haven't—" I swallowed over the lump of fear in my throat. "I mean, I've only had the one time in like four months."

He patted my shoulder. "I'm sure you're fine, then. Just watch for that period since things are a little uncertain."

I refused to even be concerned. I'm sure I was better than I thought I was with the pill. And I had taken it that morning of the party, I was sure of it. And every day since. Except maybe the morning of the viral video.

Shit.

"When will I hear about the test?" I asked.

"Two days," he said. "We'll give you a call."

"Thank you," I said.

Dr. Alpern left and I bunched the paper sheet up in a ball. At least this part was over. Hopefully I would be all clear and could forget about Chance and this whole crazy weekend.

# 24

## JENNY

The break between the winter and spring quarters approached and I tried to decide how to spend it. My dad in Florida hoped I would fly out, but I really felt it was too late to get a plane ticket. It would be stupidly expensive and probably take off at some hideous hour when a party should end, not when you have to get up. Six a.m. or whatever.

For some stupid reason, once my pictures dropped out of social media, I missed the shock and awe of popping on and seeing myself all over my feed. There was probably a diagnosis for this sort of behavior, but I didn't care. The thing about being the center of your own world was that you could decide if you had gone too over the top.

I had, and now it was over.

I met Corabelle in the quad on the last day of class before the break. I was feeling fine since my screenings had been all clear. I'd dodged a bullet. It had been two weeks since my collision with

Chance, and I was totally over it.

So I kept telling myself.

I lay back on the grass diamonds, my head on my backpack. The weather was superfine, and I had switched to cute little bare-shouldered shortie rompers and four-inch wedge sandals.

I was ready for another man. Maybe, just maybe, I'd actually date this one a little.

Maybe.

Corabelle had her head stuck in a book. She had one last final to go. I'd taken it easy this quarter, and other than World Lit, I had nothing to study for. With only one last term to go, I should sail into graduation in June without too much trouble.

"What are you and Gavin doing during the break?" I asked.

Corabelle looked up. "I think we're going to stay in Mexico for part of it."

"With the baby mama?" Corabelle's husband had a baby with a woman from Tijuana. The little boy was four now.

"No, just hanging out. We try to remember Manuel is from there, and to be comfortable with the culture."

"You are doing so much better than I would," I said.

Corabelle shrugged and flipped a page. "You deal with what life hands you sometimes."

"At least he's cute," I said.

A pair of seriously hot undergrads with their shirts slung over their shoulders caught my attention.

"Having trouble choosing?" Corabelle asked.

"No need to have just one," I said. "There's time to spare these days." I peered over my sunglasses at the boys, but they were engrossed in conversation and didn't even notice me. Drat.

And it was true. With Frankie out of my life, I had too little to do. My classes were easy. I was working barely ten hours a week as the manager started rotating me back into the schedule at Cool Beans.

"You going to see your dad?" Corabelle asked.

"I don't think so," I said. "It's so awkward going there, and he'll be up for graduation in a couple months anyway."

She nodded. "You should probably pick up some shifts at Cool Beans anyway, if you really want to keep the job. People will be grateful."

I shielded my eyes from the sun with an arm over my face. "Uggh, don't remind me about our grunt job."

Corabelle pushed at me with her foot. "You should have planned ahead for when Frankie ended the contract."

"I know," I said. "It was just so sudden."

"You didn't have any idea he was dating someone?"

"I don't know, I guess," I said. He had seemed happier there at the end. Didn't matter. That life was past. Frankie's movie premiere was in two weeks, and I didn't even have tickets in the cheap seats.

Now I was really depressed.

Corabelle stood. "I have to get to this final. Let me know when you're around next week. I'll only be gone a couple of days."

I lifted my arm. "Will do." The sun was starting to get to me. I sat up as Corabelle shoved her arms through the straps of her backpack.

Immediately I felt hot and sick, a blast of nausea rising through me like a tidal wave.

I rolled to one side, panting a little, trying to manage the sudden shock to my system.

Corabelle knelt beside me. "You okay, Jenny?"

I couldn't answer. I pressed my hand to my mouth. I would not throw up in the quad. No way, no how.

I breathed in and out, wondering when I got so sensitive to the sun. I felt overheated, like I'd been frying myself with baby oil on the beach.

"You look really pale," Corabelle said. "Did you eat something bad?"

Maybe that was it. The cheese sandwich. The more I thought about it, the hot cheese curdling in my belly as I sat out in the glaring light of high noon, the more certain I felt that this was it.

I calmed down, and this brought the misery down a notch. I managed to sit up. "I think it was the cheese," I said.

Corabelle nodded. "I don't have a lot of time, but I could help you to your car."

I waved her off. "I'll be fine." To prove it, I got to my feet. "I'm done anyway. I was just hanging with you."

"Text me when you get home," she said, concern creasing her brow.

"I will."

She walked with me until she had to peel off toward her class. I continued on, feeling a little better with each step, until I got to my car. I opened the door and let the stuffy air out before I got in. Then I blasted air-conditioning on my face.

That was better. I had no idea what had just happened, but it seemed to be over.

Time to start my vacation.

# 25

## CHANCE

I was staring up at one of the wonders of the modern world, and I just wasn't feeling it.

Times Square buzzed with people. Giant screens flickered with color and light, advertising soft drinks and Broadway shows and trendy clothes.

Ahead, the red steps were covered with tourists taking a rest. It was spring break for a lot of people, and New York was crazy since the weather was apparently good for this time of year.

I'd been busking for days in the city, sometimes on street corners, other times in the subway. I had a bit of a cushion from Portland, which was good, since the outdoor gigs weren't nearly as lucrative and everything in this town cost a fortune. I'd been living on vendor hot dogs.

Maybe I looked wrong for the part. So many of the street musicians here were edgy. They had a certain style that got attention.

I probably looked like a country boy farmhand who'd just left his mama.

As much as I didn't want to admit it, I felt lost. I was world-weary. When I'd first arrived in the city, I'd loved it. Lights all the time. I could just wander, get caught up in the movement and sound. But now I wanted to sit a spell, talk to somebody. Everyone here had a place to go.

I turned off the square and walked for blocks until the city quieted down. Here, cars lined the curbs bumper to bumper. Delivery trucks blocked the road, taking boxes down into basements via little caged lifts. If there was anything green or leafed out, it was in a pot or a planter.

I headed toward Central Park, which always helped. I could sit on a bench by the pond, or watch kids run along the walks, and feel better. Of course, I had to fight the realization that what made it better wasn't the trees and grass and water. It was the families. In the park, people didn't hustle in high-end clothes or tourist garb. They talked and laughed and meandered a bit.

The sun was out, so I unzipped my jacket and sat on a bench by the famous arch, picturing all the movie scenes I'd seen set there. I pulled out the crappy pay-by-the-minute phone I'd picked up after I sold my real one and dialed Charlie. She should just be getting off.

"Hey, Chance," she said, her voice as abrupt as always. She didn't really like me, but she had sympathy, and that would have to be good enough.

"Hello, Charlie," I said. "Everything still okay over there?"

"Sure. Hannah's the same as always. Your mother is still visiting every day after work. Your aunt Gertie was here and seemed in a huff over something."

"Aunt Gertie is always in a huff over something."

Charlie laughed. "Nobody could take that woman in hand once your Gram died."

"Nope," I said, relaxing with the talk of people and things that I knew, even if I'd left them behind for good reason. "And no man ever caught her either."

"Imagine if she'd had kids," Charlie said.

"Oh, let's not," I said.

"You doing okay now that all the talk has died down about that girl in LA?" Charlie asked.

"Yeah. I'm anonymous here. Nobody knows that even happened." A beetle headed toward my boot and I watched its slow progress across the sidewalk.

"It'll be a while before they stop talking about it here," Charlie said. "You ever call that girl?"

"No reason to call her," I said. "Over and done."

"I'd like to give her a piece of my mind," Charlie said.

I smiled, amused. Charlie might profess to hate me, but she had my back. It was hard to pinpoint exactly what she was to me now. Growing up, she was the older girl who disapproved of everything I stood for. After the accident, when my sister ended up in her care, I realized she was the only person I really trusted.

"You going to come home eventually?" Charlie asked. "You got to face all of this one of these days."

"Nothing to face," I said. "You know I can't go there without seeing Hannah. And you know I can't see Hannah without wanting to…" I trailed off. We were rehashing old stuff we couldn't do anything about.

"I know," she said. "But Hannah will turn eighteen in a couple months. Is that when you're planning to head back?"

I sighed. The beetle was caught on a rock. "Won't do any good. Mother will get power of attorney and they'd take her wishes over mine anyway."

"You can fight her if you want, Chance. You should start now if you're going to." Charlie's voice had a strident tone.

I couldn't summon the urgency to argue or the passion to agree. Distance had taken its toll. All I had left was the dull ache of regret. "Maybe Mom's right about just letting it be."

The phone went silent for a moment. The beetle got over its rock, only to turn around and get caught on it again. Foolish creature.

"Something changed you in LA, didn't it?" Charlie asked. "Was it that girl? I thought she was just a fling."

"She was," I insisted. But I could still close my eyes and smell the sea. The sand crunched under my feet. I cleared my throat. "It's no big thing."

"Well, all right," she said. "I'll let you know if I see anything on our side, legally. If your mom starts paperwork."

"Thanks, Charlie."

"Sure," she said.

The line clicked. I held the phone against my ear another moment, then shut it off.

The beetle started heading for me again. I watched its progress, wondering what I'd do if it started crawling up my leg. But when it got close, it turned and went another direction, as if I had some sort of force field around me, deflecting it.

Maybe I did.

I stood up. This country boy was all wrong for New York. I

was glad to have seen it, but it was time to move on. I had a feeling I'd get a better reception in Virginia. So I'd head there next.

Still a lot of country to see, and a lot of forgetting to do.

# 26

## JENNY

I was so screwed.

I lined up the pair of pregnancy tests on the counter. I hadn't summoned the courage to unwrap them yet. But after three days of nausea that came and went, and a couple trips to the toilet that had actually been productive in that department, I had a bad, bad feeling.

My boobs hurt to touch. I knew these symptoms. All I needed to complete the stereotype was a craving for pickles and ice cream.

Except I hated pickles.

I sat on the toilet lid, staring at the tests. All I had to do was pee on them to know for sure. But maybe I was wrong. Maybe I had some little bug. My period was due. That was probably what the boob thing was about.

But deep down, I knew. I had known since Dr. Alpern said I should have been out of pills. My carelessness was going to cost me.

I should have gotten my act together before striking out on a boy quest.

The white wrappers shined under the bathroom lights. I was torn between getting it over with and never taking one at all. Maybe I wasn't up for facing facts.

But I should know. I should stop taking the pill, if it was true. Figure out what I was supposed to do. Take vitamins or something.

I'd been holed up since the first time I threw up. It was the second day of break, and Corabelle was in Mexico and Tina was working. I had to go in to Cool Beans in about an hour to work a shift. That was going to be awesome.

I twirled the stick in a circle, like it was the center of spin the bottle. Stop here, baby. Stop there, no baby.

If only.

"Fine," I said to the sticks. I tore the wrapper off one and pulled off the cap. Now what?

I dug the instructions out of the box.

*Hold the end into the stream of urine for fifteen seconds.*

Fifteen? Did I even pee that long?

I could also stick it in a cup of pee, but that seemed gross. I shoved my shortie pajama bottoms to the floor and tugged on my green flowered underwear.

Panty dropping. I had a feeling this was NOT what they meant.

I stuck the stick between my legs, but this made me not have to go. I sat there, swearing at my parts, insisting they cooperate. Still nothing.

I reached over for the faucet, turning on the tap. "Sorry," I said to the flow, and all of drought-ridden California, and the Water Board.

Finally, a stream of pee came out of me. I held the stick, counting slowly, but the dang thing was saturated. I yanked it out and stuck the cap back on.

Shoot. I should have read the rest of the directions.

*Lay the test on a flat surface and wait fifteen seconds.*

Another fifteen. Had they done experiments to find the ideal time frame or was it just a random number? I pictured the marketing guys talking about it. "Hey, Joe, make sure they leave it long enough. Put in some crazy time frame so they won't stop too early."

I braced myself on my elbows, watching the little window. The moisture began cutting across, setting off a red line. Was that it? A positive already? My chest tightened and I snatched at the instructions.

No, it was just the control line. Two lines meant pregnant.

I stared at the empty spot, willing it to stay blank. But it appeared, just a faint hint at first, like a mirage, then gaining color. Before it could fully develop, I picked up the stick and flung it across the room.

This could not be happening.

I pushed away from the counter and began pacing the entire apartment. Hall, bedroom, living, dining, kitchen, dining, living, hall, bedroom. Back and forth, again and again, as if maybe when I found another unexpected room, I could pass through a door into a life where this wasn't happening.

A baby. A BABY!

I could barely take care of myself!

I paced, again and again, front and back. The hour to leave for Cool Beans came and went. I got a phone call, but I ignored it. A coffee shop job wasn't going to support a baby anyway.

A baby!

Even though I knew the tabloids no longer cared about me, I could see the headlines anyway.

Movie tart pregnant with singer's love child!

Director devastated, destroys film negatives.

Ha, whatever. It was all digital.

Writing headlines always cheered me up. I sat on the sofa, picturing the spread. Me, with a Photoshopped belly. Frankie pictured in an oval, the words "SHOCKED AND ANGRY" angled over his head.

Then something of the actresses. "Vanessa determined to win back the hunky crooner." They'd have some old image of her looking pissed off.

I kicked my feet up on the coffee table. This made me look at my belly, flat beneath the stretchy top of my pajamas.

The kid was in there. I stared at the pale green stripes as if I could see through them. I had no idea what it looked like. A miniature infant? A fish, swimming around?

My laptop was on the floor, so I bent down and picked it up. I opened up a browser and typed in, "What do you do if you're pregnant?"

That was a mistake. I got a million religious sites about adoption and God loving your baby.

I typed in a new search. "What happens when you're pregnant?"

This time I got a bunch of medical and pregnancy sites. The image results filled with drawings and photographs of floating babies and strange little pink shrimp-like things.

How did they have photographs of unborn babies? Did they stick something up in you? Was that safe?

I shuddered. But still, I clicked on one.

The baby floated inside a clear bubble. Was it really clear? That seemed risky. I didn't want to move, in case I popped it. How did pregnant people walk around without feeling totally paranoid?

I angled my head, looking at the kid. It was sucking its thumb, all oblivious. The umbilical cord came out of its belly button, snaking and twisting around. That scared me too. If I turned in a circle, would I get it all tangled? I remembered making toy tornadoes in peanut butter jars as a kid. You twirled the jar and water swirled, tossing around the light bright pegs inside as if they were colorful telephone poles.

I could see the tornado in my belly. I'd have to quit dance class.

But people danced when they were pregnant.

God, I was so ignorant.

I was about to close the laptop and pretend this had never happened when I spotted an ad in the corner. "How far along are you? Use our tool!"

I clicked on it. It was some sort of pregnancy calendar. It asked for either the day of my last period or the day I conceived. Well, that was easy.

I typed in 3-6.

It took me to a new page that read "Congratulations, you are four weeks pregnant."

What? That couldn't be right. I went back to the previous screen and typed the date in again. The result was the same.

This time, I read the text. "You conceived two weeks ago. You are just finding out you are pregnant! Congratulations. Pregnancy is counted by the first day of your last period, so you may be adding two weeks to how long it's been since the baby was conceived."

Oh, okay. Got it.

There was a drawing of something out of a science book, a bunch of pink bubbles stuck together. Underneath, it said, "Your baby is the size of a grain of sand."

I looked down at my belly again. Sand? Seriously?

It really had gotten everywhere.

~*´`*~

I typed up multiple texts to both Tina and Corabelle to tell them about the baby, then deleted each one.

I thought I could talk to them about anything. Secret fake boyfriends. VD tests. Boy hopping, sometimes without a whole lotta time in between. Boinking my astronomy TA.

But I couldn't talk to them about this.

Corabelle's baby had died of a heart condition when he was only a week old. Her now-husband Gavin had gotten a vasectomy afterward. They weren't sure they'd ever have a child together.

Tina had given birth at seventeen, but her baby was born too premature to survive.

I couldn't tell them I'd gotten knocked up by a total stranger. It was too close to home for them. I would say something wrong, destroy our friendship.

Terror started to set in. What was I going to do? I still had one more quarter term before graduation. But I didn't have a job. And who would hire me if I was pregnant?

I flipped on my belly on the sofa, ready to kick my arms and legs like an angry toddler. What the hell had I done?

My face smashed into the cushion. I was stuck. I had no idea where Chance was. Or even who he was. No way to contact him. If the tabloids hadn't tracked him down, I surely wasn't going to have any luck.

But had they tried?

I snatched my phone from the coffee table. I typed in "Chance Tennessee musician."

I found one guy born in 1925. And a whole lot of want ads for musicians to play in gigs, a "chance" to do something or another.

Why did he have to have a name that was a common word?

I dropped the phone to the floor.

If I couldn't talk to Tina and Corabelle, then who? Frankie? I couldn't imagine that conversation. Besides, he was outed with the new boy now. The last thing he needed was speculation that my swelling belly was HIS love child.

Tears threatened then. I was so not a crier, but I could feel them coming. Probably the hormones. A whole host of new horrible things were about to happen, if Buzzfeed videos were anything to judge by. Was I really going to get hemorrhoids and leaky boobs?

I had five-inch spike platforms! Designer dresses! Pink godforsaken dreadlocks!

I clutched a handful and resisted the urge to yank. Stupid hair. I couldn't even afford to keep it up, and now I would have a baby?

I collapsed back on the sofa. I never wanted to leave the house again. But I had to pull myself together. I had a vague notion that I was supposed to eat certain things, but not others. And there was something about diet drinks. And hot tubs.

How did people know all this stuff?

I got up and paced the room, feeling like a lion in a cage. I needed help. Big-time help.

Then I paused by a framed photograph. It was taken when I was nine, before all the bad things happened. When my family was still a family, and not a bunch of cinders scattered everywhere. My mom, my dad, and —

My mind froze on his name. Bry Guy. My little brother. He was seven in the picture, a mess as usual, hair everywhere and his collar crooked. He was a tornado, tearing through our lives with laughter and energy.

He'd died when I was ten. Nothing was ever the same after.

I switched my gaze to Dad. He lived in Florida now. I hadn't gone to see him like he wanted. Probably a good thing, given what had happened.

And Mom. She lived here in San Diego. Despite the way our family blew apart after Bryan died, she was a good, solid person. She didn't understand me and my crazy ways. But she would listen. She'd try to dress me in normal clothes and would shake her head at my hair.

But she'd be there.

I raced to my bedroom to put on my most normal outfit. I knew what I needed now.

I needed my mama.

# 27

## CHANCE

Now this was better. I could see the song lyrics in my head, how I would write out the scene.

The rolling hills were green and dotted with trees. The battlegrounds rose and fell in gentle slopes. Along a line, blue cannons on big spindle wheels stood sentry, clean and perfect like soldiers on the march.

The whole thing felt too pristine, too tidy for the bloodshed that went on here. A Civil War with spectators, northerners who came to the battlefield to witness the quick defeat of the backwater Confederates. Instead of witnessing a decisive victory, however, these voyeurs ended up running in smoky chaos when the battle raged like war does, with death and gunfire and devastation.

Only a few tourists walked the grounds at this early hour. The morning was cool, a light mist rising from the ground as if the ghosts of the old soldiers were getting up for a day's work.

An intricate wood fence was pieced together like a puzzle of timbers, angular and neat. I couldn't get past how idealized the battlegrounds had become. How long did it take before something so horrible became beautiful again? At least one hundred years, judging by this park.

I walked along the slope past the sturdy stone house with its blood orange-red door. My father had visited these places once, I knew. He told me stories about these fields when I was young, when he still lived with us.

I wondered if he had been back here since, if this was still a favorite place for him. After he left my mother, we got only a rare word back from him, although I know he sent her money. I saw the deposit slips once. But he did not try to see me, or Hannah, who was too young when he left to even remember him.

Water sluiced down a path, perhaps from a faulty irrigation line, or maybe just a hose left on. The deep, heavy footprint of a boot broke up the perfection of the path. I imagined it could be a relic from some soldier's tread, or maybe even the mark of my own father's passage here. I stared at it until an old man carrying a toolbox stopped to peer at me. His shoe matched the print.

"Can I help you?" he asked.

I shrugged off the strange disoriented feeling and shook my head. I turned away, knowing I needed to get back to a city, play for money, earn my next meal. I was burned out, done with this, but still in no mood to go home. I supposed I could look for work, pour cement again, someplace far from Tennessee.

I felt lost, unmoored, and no longer in a good way.

I set down my guitar case. I tried calling Charlie but the signal out here was no good with my cheap phone. I wanted to toss it, hurl it onto the battlefield.

But I needed it. I had to keep that one last line to home, to my sister, to my past. Maybe Charlie was right. I should go home and wage that battle with my mother. Hannah needed to be let go. But I didn't think I was the man who could do it. I had failed her in every way, been exactly the wrong sort of person, a bad brother, a terrible influence. And in the end, I was responsible for what had happened to her.

No, it was better that I was miserable, alone, and walking the world with nothing but a guitar and a change of clothes. At least I could do those things. Because of me, my sister could not.

# 28

## JENNY

To avoid getting dragged on any outings that might make me crazy, I didn't text my mom that I was coming until I was a couple miles away from her condo.

I took a deep breath before typing the words.

*Just got through shopping at H&M and thought I'd drop in.*

Both things would make her happy. Shopping at "normal" stores, "non-alternative" stores. And coming to see her.

I really had stopped by H&M and picked up a maxi dress, figuring I'd need a tent to cover up this belly eventually. Might as well start now. It was right up Mom's alley, navy and white striped with double straps. It made my eyes cross and had enough fabric for three normal outfits for me. Maybe six. It was long.

Her complex was simple, four two-story condos in each building, set off with yellow stucco and palm trees. When I parked in a visitor spot close to her door, she stepped out on the porch.

I could tell the moment when she saw my hair, because her hands clenched in that way they did when she was trying to control herself.

I plucked the shopping bag from the passenger seat. I wanted to throw up, and not in the way I'd felt the past few days. Pure nerves. I swallowed hard and headed across the parking spaces to her tiny yard lined with pink bougainvillea.

"My sweet Jenny!" she said, enveloping me in a hug. She looked every bit the urban mother in a smart twin set and slender slacks, her work clothes. Her hair was blond and short and styled into a feathery bob.

She tugged at one of my pink dreadlocks. "Isn't this an interesting style?"

I bit my lip. "It's new."

"It's definitely different. So to what do I owe this surprise?" she asked.

"It's spring break," I said. "My friends are all out of town."

She laughed and led me inside. "Glad I'm the company of last resort."

"How was work today?" I asked as I sat at a tall bar that separated her sunny kitchen from a breakfast nook.

"Same as usual. Lots of paper shuffling." She worked for an accounting firm, mainly in billing. I was pretty sure I'd rather die than ever do something like that.

"How was the winter term?" she asked.

"I did fine. Just one to go," I said.

"We should make plans for a graduation party," she said. "Maybe I can get your father to spring for the club."

I tried to picture how much bigger I'd be by then, belly

popping out of my graduation gown.

"Oh, no, something simple. Maybe here?" I looked around as though I admired the place. It was nice enough. Just too boring for my liking, decorated in beiges and browns.

"We can talk about it later," she said, her code for "I'll get my way in the end."

It didn't matter. All our plans were about to be shot.

"Show me your shopping," she said.

I reached down and pulled the dress out of the bag.

Mom lifted the fabric. "Just lovely," she said. "Glad to see you're getting a little more conservative." Her gaze raked over my tight pink T-shirt and rhinestone-studded jeans, which were, hilariously, the most *conservative* things in my closet. "Have you given any thought to what you're going to do after graduation?"

"I talked to some people two weeks ago," I said, tucking the dress back in the bag. "In the movie business. Social media management, stuff like that."

"Interesting," she said. "I guess there isn't a lot to do with a liberal arts degree unless you're going to grad school."

I plucked an apple from a bowl on the counter and turned it in my hands. "Something will pop up."

My belly button, for example.

"I could ask around the firm," she said. "See what's coming available."

God, accounting. I'd rather turn tricks. But I had to be gracious and grown-up for what was coming, so I said, "Sure, Mom. Sounds good." I thought about taking a bite of the apple, but then my stomach went queasy. I set it down.

She went to the refrigerator and filled a glass with water. "Can

I get you something to drink?"

Actually, my mouth was already dry with the unsaid news. "That would be great. Water's fine."

She filled a second glass. While she was still looking away, she said, "I can't help but wonder what's really going on, Jenny. You're being way too agreeable."

Mom was good like that, knowing how to segue into a tough conversation, leaving the door open for me to lay whatever I'd done lately right on her.

She turned and set the glasses on the counter. "You want to tell me what's really going on?"

I took a long sip, trying to steady myself. There was no way to do this but be straight.

"I'm pregnant."

Mom was so startled by my words that she knocked over her water, sending it cascading onto her pale blue cardigan.

"Oh!" she cried, snatching the glass before it crashed to the floor. She pulled a dish towel from a hook and began soaking up the spill.

"Sorry, Mom," I said, not sure what all I was apologizing for. The words. How I said them. The mess.

"It's okay," she said. "Just let me get a handle on this."

I waited in the tall chair as she soaked up the bulk of the water. I thought she might go back to her bedroom to change, but then she started giggling like a teen. "Wait. Have I gotten the dates wrong? Is it April first already? Is this your April fool?"

Oh, crap. I broke her. Mom never laughed like this and she certainly always knew the date.

"You all right, Mom?"

She bent forward, bracing her palms on her thighs. "You were always such a practical joker, Jenny." She glanced around. "Did one of your movie friends set up a hidden camera? Are you trying to make a viral video?"

I clutched the edge of the counter, trying to figure out who this woman was, standing in front of me, completely losing it.

"Mom, it's not a joke. You're scaring me. Please go back to being the straitlaced organized mother who sees the practical side of everything."

She held the dish towel to her face despite the fact that it was dripping wet.

"Mom?" I asked. Now I was getting worried. "Are you okay?"

She stepped forward and dropped the towel on the counter. "Just let me…adjust."

I wiggled on the chair, feeling like a little kid in trouble.

She continued to pass the wet towel over the counter for another minute. Then she stopped and looked up at me.

"You're serious, aren't you?" Her face was drawn tight with confusion. "Was it that movie director man? He's so much older than you, Jenny."

I shook my head.

"You're seeing someone new?" she asked.

I shook my head again.

She slid onto a stool on the opposite side of the bar. "Well," she said, "the baby has to have a father."

"He's not in the picture," I said, deciding not to mention that I didn't know his last name or if he was even inside the state lines anymore.

"All right." She pressed her hands against the counter, still streaked with water. "Have you considered your options?"

Now, that was unexpected. I didn't think she'd get all progressive on it.

"I haven't thought about anything yet," I said.

"How far along are you?"

"I looked at a website online, and it said four weeks."

"Did it give you a due date?"

I shook my head. "I can look." I pulled out my cell phone to find the site again.

Mom got up to pace the kitchen, walking to the fridge and back.

I focused on the little screen of my phone. I wasn't sure what I wanted from her. Condemnation. Anger. Disgust.

Maybe a hug.

"I never thought this would happen to you," she said. "I thought you were so independent. Cautious."

I figured I'd get a little stern talk, so I kept tapping. My stomach felt like lead, but overall, it hadn't been as bad as I had imagined.

I put in the conception date again and clicked past the part where it said the baby was sand. There was a link that said, "Reveal your due date."

Mom was back at the counter. "I don't think you are ready for a baby," she said.

My heart was thudding. Did she think that little of me? That I couldn't adjust?

But then the due date came up, and I dropped the phone.

"Jenny?" she said, her voice full of concern. "You're white as a sheet! Are you feeling sick?" She came around the counter to put her arms around me.

I couldn't stop staring at the screen. I rarely cried, but this did it to me, hot tears pouring from my eyes.

"What is it, baby?" Mom asked.

I pointed to the phone.

She stared at the date. "Oh my God," she said. "Oh my God."

It was a date we all dreaded, each of us, separately, on our own little islands of pain, a reminder of what we'd lost.

My baby brother's birthday.

# 29

## JENNY

Mom tucked me into bed in her guest room. I lay there in the gray light that filtered in through the curtains, a cool washcloth on my forehead.

I was a big believer in signs. Of all the days of the year, all 365 choices, my due date would fall on November 27.

Mom tiptoed back in the room. "Thought you might want this," she said. She sat on the edge of the bed and passed me Mr. Critter, a threadbare bunny I'd slept with when I was small.

I pulled Mr. Critter into my arms and held him close. "Thank you."

"It makes sense," Mom said. "I got pregnant with Bryan in the spring too. You were three. We didn't have the due date calculator sites, so I had to wait until we got to the doctor. Of course, the due date is just a guide. Bryan was a week late."

"So the baby might not come on Bryan's birthday?" I felt like I didn't know anything.

"Probably not," she said. "But it is still a powerful sign."

My head popped up. My mother was ever practical. She never talked about coincidences or karma or anything other than cold hard facts. It comforted me that she was bending a little.

"I don't know what I'm going to do," I said. "I don't even have a job."

"You can finish out your degree," she said, smoothing the covers. "Graduation is in June. One good thing about babies, they take a long time to arrive. You'll figure things out by December."

I laid my head back down, my thoughts swirling. A baby. Baby! The closest I'd gotten to one in the past ten years was Corabelle's stepson, Manuelito, and he was four. Potty trained and all.

"I don't know how to put on a diaper," I said in a panic.

"You'll figure it out," Mom said. She patted my shoulder. "And you'll be an expert within a day. They go through a lot."

"I guess I should see the doctor."

"Make an appointment. They won't see you for a few weeks yet."

I drew my knees up tighter to my belly, then brought them down again.

The baby was in there somewhere. I pictured a grain of sand floating around my gut. So much trouble over something so small.

"Do you..." Mom hesitated. "Not *know* who the father is?"

I buried my face in the pillow. The washcloth fell away. I didn't want to talk about this.

"Is he married?" Mom asked. She was clearly trying to come up with a logical explanation.

"His name is Chance," I said.

She exhaled in relief, glad, I guess, that I wasn't screwing half of San Diego.

"Are you going to tell him?" she asked.

I didn't answer. I would if I could. But I had no way to find him.

"Jenny? This is important. He should know there's a baby."

I turned my cheek to the pillow. "He's a traveling musician," I said. "I don't know where he is."

"Surely he has a schedule or a phone or something," she said.

"I don't think so," I said, and now tears threatened again. What was that about? So much emotion. Uggh.

"Do you not want to find him? Is he a bad person?"

I rolled onto my back. "Mom, I don't know him that well. It was just a — a one-night thing. We weren't planning on ever seeing each other again."

Admitting this to my mother was about the worst thing I'd had to tell her.

She sat a little straighter, as if this was a simple thing, something to be dealt with. "The problem," she said firmly, "is that it's not a one-night thing anymore. Did you like this boy?"

My voice caught as I tried to decide what to say. "He was nice. He was a really great singer. Amazing, really. He just didn't seem interested in, well, you know, ties. He likes to roam."

"Well, his roaming days are over. He's just as responsible for this as you are." She adjusted the washcloth back on my forehead. "I assume you protected yourself and it just failed."

I nodded under her hand. "I was on the pill."

She sighed. "This is where life's led you. I say we find this boy. Let him decide if he wants to be involved or not. At least you'll know. You can make him help financially, even if he isn't around."

Ha, Chance didn't even have a home. But one thing about moms, they were usually right. He ought to know about the baby. Maybe he would tell me to abort it, or whatever. Then I'd cut him off. But at least he'd know.

"He was singing with a local band when I met him," I said. "I could probably track them down and find out where he is."

"That's my girl," Mom said. "Problem solving." She stood up. "You get some rest. When you're feeling better we'll go shopping. You're going to need different clothes."

I had a feeling this was coming.

She looked around the room. "I could probably go part-time and watch the baby. We could make this a nursery."

She walked over to the window and touched the curtains. "A nice crisp yellow that would work for either a boy or a girl." She clasped her hands together as if she had a purpose finally. "I always wondered if I'd be a grandma."

Funny how fast she had adjusted to the idea. I watched as she walked the room, touching things, obviously making plans in her head.

Now I had to do the same.

My phone buzzed. It was across the room on a desk. Mom picked it up and brought it over. "Is it him?" she asked eagerly.

"He doesn't even have my number," I said. But the listing was unfamiliar. I sat up and cleared my throat before I hit the receive button. "Hello?"

"Jenny Gillespie?" It was a woman.

"That's me," I said.

"I'm calling on behalf of Tellmund Rogers."

That was Frankie's friend from the party. "Yes, hello," I said.

"He would like you to come in next week at your convenience to talk about some opportunities for you here at Red Bridge Pictures."

"Really? That's great."

"You will meet with our Director of Human Resources. How is next Thursday, April 2nd?"

"That should be fine." My head buzzed to remember my new class schedule for the spring quarter. "I am out of class at ten, I think."

"Why don't you call me at this number when you have a firm day and time?"

"Okay." My head was buzzing. "Who do I ask for?"

"My name is June. I answer the line."

"Great, thanks, June. I'll call when I'm sure about my classes."

"That will be just fine. Thank you, Jenny. Bye."

Holy crap. Did I have a job?

"What was that?" Mom asked.

"One of the contacts calling about a job." I was still freaking out a little.

"That's good news, right?" She sat on the bed next to me.

"Yeah." My head was spinning. So many things happening at once. I felt sick again and pressed my hands against my stomach.

"Are you worried they won't hire you if you're pregnant?" Mom asked. "It's illegal to do that."

It hadn't even occurred to me, actually.

"Just a lot of change really fast," I said.

She pushed a pile of dreadlocks away from my face. "It was always going to be, with graduation and all. You're just adding an extra facet."

A facet. Right. Like we were cutting diamonds. "I'm going to try and locate that band," I said, getting up from the bed.

"All right, Jenny," she said. "I'll be here. You're going to need some help. Let me know how it goes with Chance."

Oh, that was going to go super great. Especially if he was tying one on with Vanessa Price in a story line straight out of a daytime soap opera.

Tabloids, here we come.

# 30

## CHANCE

Chesapeake, Virginia, had a lot of the same feel as Chattanooga. Lots of water. Lots of green. The pace was mighty slower than New York, for sure. I was back in the south, and even though I was still a good ways from Tennessee, it felt like home. Without actually being home, which was a good thing.

I hadn't called Charlie in a couple days, still smarting over her insistence that I come home and fight for Hannah's rights. But the only thing worse than talking to a pissed-off Charlie was *not* talking to her. I didn't know anything that was going on, although if something big happened, no doubt she'd call.

My hand strummed an easy rhythm and I let the bridge go on for a while, bringing it back around over and over again rather than taking up the chorus.

I had scored a spot in a seafood joint on the east-side outskirts of town, playing for tips and all the fish I could eat. I mixed up the styles as the waves of people came and went. I just had a little corner of the restaurant, but it was pleasant enough. When I took breaks, people came over to chat me up.

I was packing up at the end of the second night when one of the waitresses plopped down on the floor next to me. She was young, barely twenty probably, and had a saucy attitude, like she knew how cute she was.

My trouble radar went off right away. I'd avoided entanglements since LA, and this one looked to be precisely the wrong way to get back in the game. I was betting she had a boyfriend named Buster who had a jealous streak that she liked to tickle. Having him go after any man who laid a hand on her was probably how she got her jollies.

She leaned on her arms, stretching out a long set of legs from her super-short skirt. She wore a flirty white top, off the shoulders, and her hair was every shade of blond and brown all mixed together, straight from a beauty parlor.

"So where ya from, cowboy?" she asked.

Cowboy. I had no idea where people kept getting the notion. Today's black T-shirt had a worn image of Jimi Hendrix flaking off. Still not exactly country.

I locked down the latches on my guitar case. "Tennessee," I said coolly.

"I figured, on account of the accent when you were singing," she said. "Been here long?"

"Just a couple days," I said, reaching for the tip jar.

The restaurant was shutting down. Wait staff circled the tables, filling napkin holders and checking ketchup bottles.

"I'm Angie," she said, leaning forward to extend a hand.

I hesitated, then reached down and shook it. Rather than sit around to count the money, I just shoved it all in my back pocket. I wanted out of there.

"You seem sort of antsy, cowboy," she said. "I don't think I caught your name when you were singing."

"It's Chance," I said, trying to bring down my anxiousness to leave.

It wasn't like I had anywhere to go. I'd been sleeping in the bus station since I got to Chesapeake. But since the weather was nice tonight, I might just hang out in a park. I didn't require a lot of downtime.

"I think you're just about the keenest thing I've seen walk into this seafood dive," she said.

My radar went off again. I glanced around the room, looking for anybody who might be watching. Buster was probably waiting for her out in the parking lot, getting more pissed off each passing minute that she dallied.

"Thank you kindly," I said. I set the empty jar back on the ground and picked up my case. "I'll just be heading out."

She jumped to her feet. "Now wait a minute! I was going to see if you wanted to get a drink or something."

I hesitated. I didn't want to offend the girl, but my tingly sense that I was going to get in over my head tonight wouldn't let go.

"I'm sure you've got some hometown boy who looks after you," I said. "Pretty thing like you."

"But I don't right now," she said. "I had one, but he left town. He's not around anymore."

I looked her over again. She was cute. That skirt sure was short. I didn't have to hurry.

"What did you have in mind?" I asked.

She squealed. "Finally! There's a place just a couple doors down. Beer's cheap and the music doesn't suck." She glanced down at the guitar. "Though I bet you'd be a lot better."

I shrugged. "I'm not much on drinking."

"Seriously?" She made a pouty face. "Well, I'm not legal anyway. We can just drink sodas. They have live music, though. Ain't much else open around here this time of night on a weekday. Thankfully they don't really card the girls." She fluffed her hair out from her slender neck. Her collarbone was smooth and created a little shadow, just right for burying your face in.

Seemed like maybe a place to do some forgetting.

Despite my better judgment, I said, "All right, then, let's go. You off?"

She untied her short apron that held a pen and an order pad. With a flick of her wrist, she tossed it on a table. "I am now," she said.

Yeah, this one was trouble. But I wasn't coming back to this place, seeing as they had a regular band the next few nights. So what the hell? I shouldered my backpack and followed her.

We passed through the tables and out into the near-perfect spring night.

I could see the place she was talking about, a big neon sign flashing the word "Woody's."

We crossed the parking lot and walked along the road, past a closed-up barbershop that used to be a regular house. It had a padded swing tucked in the corner of its long front porch, and I thought that might be a decent place to spend the night, depending on how it went with this girl.

Our feet crunched on the gravel as we got closer to the bar.

"So, Angie," I said. "You just waitress or you going to school?"

"I've been in and out of beauty school," she said. "I can't seem to get the hang of it, though. I got tired of sweeping up hair, so I started waiting tables to get by until I figure out what else to try."

"Your folks live here?" We arrived at the door and I opened it for her.

"Outside of town. My daddy's a plumber and my mom's just one of those busybody church ladies."

My jaw tensed at this. "I know the type," I said. "I've got one of those too."

"Ain't that the worst?" She beelined for a booth in the corner.

The bar was dark, but the stage was bright. A five-piece band of older guys played bluegrass. Just the quality of their sound perked my spirits. This was good stuff.

A waitress followed us to the seats. "Whatcha drinking?" she asked as I tucked my backpack and guitar under the table.

"Two sodas," Angie said, "and don't give me no grief about it, Kendra."

The girl whirled around and headed for the bar.

Angie shoved her chin in her palm, bracing her elbow on the table. "I went to high school with her. She's a piece of work."

I sat back against the vinyl seat and watched the lead guitarist pick out a tricky line. The urge to go up there and fill in another layer of sound was fierce.

I don't know how many minutes I stared at them so intently, but it must have been too long for Angie, because she bumped my shoulder. "Hey, you. You're mighty quiet."

"Sorry," I said. "You were right. These guys are really good."

"Ah, professional admiration," she said. "I guess you're always looking at other people playing guitar and comparing."

"Sometimes."

The waitress, Kendra, came over and plopped the two drinks down on the table. "Six dollars," she said.

"That is way too much for a dang soda and you know it," Angie said.

"It's all right," I said, before the girls glared holes into each other. I laid the money on her tray. "Thank you."

She looked me up and down a second, then whipped around to leave. She stomped away as if something more than a drink order had just happened.

"I take it you two did more than just go to high school together," I said.

Angie pulled her cup across the table. "Maybe she got mad I dated her ex. I don't know. It's high school. It's past."

I wondered if the ex had actually moved to ex status *before* the "dating" began.

"When did you graduate?" I asked. I was hoping it had been at least a couple years.

"Not last year, if that's what you're worried about," she said. "I've been out."

"All right." My eyes wandered back to the stage. It was worth being here just to listen to these guys, even if Angie wasn't exactly my type. I found myself comparing her to Jenny and made myself stop. Jenny was gone. A whole country away. We couldn't be much farther apart than we were at the moment.

Angie sipped on her drink a while, swinging her leg beneath the table to the time of the music, occasionally bumping up against mine.

Then she got antsy again and scooted closer. I knew I should be feeling it, the way she was pressing her body up against my arm. But I wasn't.

She leaned her head on my shoulder. "You wanna get on out of here?"

Normally I wasn't one to turn down an easy invitation. But we hadn't even said ten sentences to each other. "Let them finish their set," I said.

She sighed heavily, and I wondered what the deal was. Was she that set on a quick lay? A girl like her could pick up a guy whenever she wanted.

That tingly feeling came over me again. The waitress was leaning against the bar with a self-satisfied smirk on her face.

I felt Angie stiffen beside me and mutter a quiet "Oh, shit." She was looking at the door.

I no more turned my head to see what had gotten her attention when a fist slammed into my jaw.

# 31

## JENNY

I spent the night with my mother when all I could find for the Sonic Kings was a web page with an email address. I wrote them asking about Chance and then let Mom take me shopping.

We got what she considered an appropriate "interview suit" even though I knew I wouldn't wear that to the studio, ever. Only the bean counters came to work in stuff like that, but it made sense, since that was what my mother was used to.

I had a lot of other issues to deal with before I could worry about the job situation.

When I got up in the morning, feeling retched, sick, and tired, I checked my mail and saw some guy named Paul had written me back.

*Are you the girl from the beach? Saw the spread. Chance got kinda spooked by it and took off the next morning. No clue where he went.*

My heart sank. If they couldn't find him, I was really stuck.

*I need to find him. What do you know about him?*

He wrote back pretty fast.

*Not a lot. Why don't you come to our gig and the boys and all will figure out any intel he dropped. Tonight at Cain's. 9 p.m.*

I had no idea what Cain's was, but I'd look it up. I wrote him that I would come and thought about rustling up a date, then realized how ludicrous that was. Corabelle was in Mexico, but Tina might go, if I could extricate her from her hot doctor.

The band was in the middle of its set when Tina and I got there around ten. I hadn't told her I was pregnant. I couldn't find the words yet. And I certainly didn't want the band to know, so it was just as well the secret was only mine.

I explained to Tina that I wanted to track Chance down, and the band said they could help. She wasn't the sort of person to question motives. Dr. Darion had a late shift at the hospital, so she was fine with coming along.

The Sonic Kings were playing some dive bar in a suburb between LA and San Diego. It was an hour's drive, but it didn't matter. I wasn't going to be drinking anyway. That was one thing I already knew from drunkenly reading the surgeon general's warnings on the labels of thousands of bottles of beer.

The place was dark and half-empty. The band sounded about the same as they did at the party, decent but without any spark.

Tina and I sat down at a tall round table toward the back. I didn't really want to attract attention. Hopefully the shiny diamond on Tina's finger would keep random boys at bay.

And I didn't need to know what I was going to be missing out on for the next nine months. It seemed weird to do hookups with a bun in the oven. Although if Chance dissed me, then who knew? I guess I could do whatever.

A queasy feeling came over me, and I wasn't sure if it was the baby or the bar or the idea of Chance rejecting me. A cocktail waitress came up and asked what we were drinking. I told her water and she raised an eyebrow as if to say, "Then what are you doing in this dump?"

The order got Tina's attention too. "That's not like you, Jenny," she said. "You're going to need some liquid courage. Bring us both a margarita."

Great. Now I would have the temptation right at my chin.

Still, I said nothing.

The band launched into "Tell Me Something Good" and the nostalgia of hearing it at the party hit me in the gut. I could see Chance standing at the base of the stage, drumming his hands. A wave of melancholy passed over me. I had to get hold of these emotions. I was becoming somebody else already.

Somebody's mother.

Tina nodded her head in time with the song. "They don't suck," she said.

I watched the lead singer strum his guitar, his purple sunglasses flashing with the stage lights as he moved. I wondered if this was the Paul who wrote me, or if it was another member of the band. They'd introduced themselves onstage at the party, but I hadn't paid any attention to any names other than Chance. In addition to the singer, there was a bass guitarist, who never looked up from his instrument, a keyboardist in a ball cap, and a drummer.

When they ended this number, the scant crowd clapped for them, which was better than the response to the last one.

"Thank you, thank you," the lead singer said. "I'm Paul, and we're the Sonic Kings. We're going to take a little break and then we'll be back with more blues and funk for your listening pleasure."

So that *was* Paul. He stepped away from the mike.

"Should we go up to them now?" Tina asked.

The waitress set the drinks on the table and I picked mine up, almost taking a sip before I remembered not to. I faked it instead, and set the glass down. Tina paid for the round.

The guys from the band hung out at the end of the bar in a dark corner.

"Yeah, let's go talk," I said.

We picked up our drinks and headed for the boys. I casually lowered the glass and dumped part of it in an abandoned beer mug as we passed.

Their faces lit up that we were approaching them, then Paul nodded in understanding. "It's you."

"Yeah," I said.

The drummer turned around on his stool. "Man, Chance gave up a night with Vanessa freaking Price because of you."

I almost dropped my drink when he said that, so I set it on the bar. "What are you talking about?"

"She tried to get him to stay the night with her," Paul said.

"But he said, 'No dice.'"

My heart hammered. He hadn't been with Vanessa?

"Tell me everything that happened," I said quickly.

"What's your deal?" Paul said. "I don't want to give my boy over to a stalker chick."

The keyboard player smacked his arm. "She's not a stalker. She's just got the feels."

Paul stared at me. "Some girls are crazy."

Tina shoved Paul in the chest. "Well, this one's not. Just tell us what you know."

Paul took a step back. "No need for violence, ladies," he said. "We picked up Tennessee at a truck stop outside LA. We were on our way to the party that this here fine upstanding young lady attended."

The bass guitar player coughed into his hand to cover his laugh.

"Don't make me kick your ass," Tina said.

"Well, I was in the tabloids," I told her. "I get it."

"Did your sugar daddy movie director ditch you after he saw the pix of your sweet naked booty?" the drummer asked. He was obviously out to protect Chance. This made me wonder if he wasn't still around, and my heart sped up. He could even be here!

I took a deep breath. I couldn't blow the cover for Frankie, not even now. "We had already split up," I said. "I just went to the party with him so he would have a date."

Paul held up his palms. "Whatever. Doesn't matter to me. The fact of the matter is, we picked him up, he played with us." He pointed at the drummer. "He stayed with Jazz a night, and then he blew out of town like a Tasmanian devil."

"Why?" I asked.

"He saw the newspaper, baby," Paul said. "It said you were with that director. And cavorting with a crooner on the side. That was too much for a fresh-faced country boy."

Damn it. I knew it. "How can I find him? I need to find him. It's important." My words were a rush.

"Beats me," Paul said. "He got some messages that morning at breakfast and he got plumb spooked. Turned a little green around the gills."

Probably he got a lot of texts about the video segment, same as I did.

"He said he was from Chattanooga," I said. "And he'd been to a lot of cities. Did he tell you anything else?"

"He'd just come from Vegas," Paul said. "He'd been playin' some coffee shops. I got the impression he doesn't like bars."

"You think one of those shops would know who he was?" I asked. "Maybe they wrote him a check or got tax info."

Jazz shook his head. "Doubt it. They don't want paperwork. Most of these gigs are cash under the table. 'Sides, I'm pretty sure he only played for tips."

I held the edge of the bar with a death grip. "Are you sure there isn't anything else?" I asked. "I can't just go to Chattanooga and look for a Chance."

"Look for a chance," Jazz said with a laugh. "There's always a chance."

I wanted to belt him.

"Come on," Tina said. "These losers don't have anything." She pulled on my arm.

"Hey, wait," Paul said.

I turned back around. "What?"

"That guitar he had. It was a Seagull. And not any ordinary Seagull either, one of their rare wood ones. It looked pretty new. If I were playing detective, I'd call around Chattanooga guitar stores and see where he might have picked it up. There are few enough of them around that it might get you somewhere."

Now that was an honest-to-God clue. "Thank you," I said.

"I think he'll be happy to see you," Paul said. "He was pretty broken up about the director thing."

I nodded, feeling my heart soften. "Thank you," I repeated.

Tina and I walked out of the bar. "Let me drive," Tina said. "You have some thinking to do."

I handed her the keys. We'd both abandoned our drinks. I should tell her now about being pregnant, but I decided not to. Maybe the next person I would get to tell would be the baby's father.

# 32

## CHANCE

My whole body lurched back into the cushioned seat of the booth. Whoever had just waylaid me packed some punch.

Now, I might have been pussyfooting around the country like a peacemaker for five months while I played, but the twenty-four years leading up to it were full of more hellfire and fistfights than I had business surviving with my face intact.

So I didn't even bother to take a look at who was after me, or why. That was obvious. I just lifted the bottom of the table and sent it flying across the room so it was the hell out of my way.

Angie scurried out of range as the glasses and table crashed to the ground. The band stopped playing.

"You son of a bitch!" a voice raged.

I turned toward the sound. A hulking man about my age wiped soda off his face. I'd gotten a nice shot in without even trying.

He had me outweighed by at least forty pounds, but not all of it was muscle. I kept my arms loose at my sides, waiting for his next move. I really preferred to avoid injuring my hands on his ugly mug, but I wasn't sure I had any choice at this point.

"Reggie, stop it!" Angie cried out and flung herself in front of him. "Leave him alone."

He pushed her aside. "Who the hell are you?" he bellowed at me.

"His name's Chance," Angie said, flitting around him like a bee buzzing. "And he's twice the man you ever were."

Great. She had picked me to mess with him. Did women ever do anything but pit men against each other? Were we really so dumb as to fall for this?

I was disgusted, but there was nothing to be done about it. This guy had already clocked me once. There was going to be payback.

He took a step forward, and I saw my opportunity. I lunged forward and slammed my shoulder into his belly like a linebacker on the charge. He grunted, falling back, and I snatched a barstool as I tumbled onto him so I'd have a weapon when I got on my feet.

I jumped up, the stool out. The big oaf managed to roll over and stand. When he rushed for me, I smashed the stool into his thigh. He spun around, hopping on one leg. I had no intention of doing real harm, as a stool to his head could actually kill him, but I held it. I was done with this asshole.

He held out his hand. "This ain't worth it," he said, pointing at Angie. "You're not worth it, you filthy whore."

He straightened up and cracked his neck. He looked around the room as if to see who was going to witness his exit, and said, "You can have her."

Then he stormed back out.

I dropped the stool. This is why bars were bad. And women.

God, I was disgusted.

I didn't even look at Angie, but slung my backpack over my shoulder and picked up my guitar case. Since her asshole ex, or whoever he was, had gone out the front, I headed toward the back. Nobody said a word as I wound through the tables and headed through an exit behind the bar.

A couple bar-backs loading fresh kegs looked up. I passed through, aiming for the open door to the back lot. The night air felt good. I'd walk a bit, cool off.

My jaw didn't seem any worse for wear from the hit. I'd gotten free of the fight without hurting my hands. I was lucky.

And stupid.

I knew that girl was trouble and I went with her anyway. Damn fool.

I walked, and walked, and walked some more. The moon rose and held steady in the sky as I headed down a highway, not even thumbing it. I didn't want any company.

I realized when the air started to change and the breeze picked up that I was nearing the coast. I passed under a sign for Highway 58 that told me the beach was only six miles away.

Huh. One ocean to the other.

So I kept going. The night was calm and quiet. Virginia Beach, the signs said, straight ahead. The road went up and up, over a river. The tang in the air got sharper. The bridge came back down and the wide pedestrian walk ended, and I was on a city block. I knew where the water was by the high-rise hotels.

I kept going, no idea how many miles I'd gone. Hours had passed. But I pressed on, compelled to keep going, to get to the sand, to the ocean.

Finally I stood on the beach looking out on the black monster of the Atlantic. It was different from LA, no doubt, backed by hotels and businesses and bright lights rather than a campground and parking lot. But the sand still crunched beneath my boots, and the waves still roared up onto land.

Dawn was starting to break, so I sank down in the sand, weary and worn. I felt like I'd walked the world from end to end, seen all there was to see.

The water kept coming forward, flowing over the sand, then retreating, like something just out of reach. I dropped my head in my hands, trying to think. What should I do now? Go home? Settle somewhere?

But still, I couldn't shake the feeling I was where I belonged. It wasn't this sea air, and it wasn't this sand. But something just like it. So much the same, but as far away as it could be, a whole length of a country away.

And so I stood up, shouldered my bag, picked up my case, and started my travels back to the other ocean, the other side.

I was going back to LA.

# 33

## JENNY

I had five more days of spring break to find Chance. After that I'd be risking getting dropped from my classes if I didn't show.

Corabelle sat on my bed as I packed my suitcase. "I don't get why you have to go after him."

She was making it hard not to tell her about the baby.

"Sometimes you just know," I said.

She sighed. "Yeah, I get it. True love. I've never seen you like this. It has to be something."

"If I can't make it back for the first day, can you show up and get my attendance checked off?" UCSD was crazy about dropping you from a class if you bailed on day one.

"Of course," she said. "I only have one class that day, and it's not the same time as yours."

"Thank you," I said. "And don't worry about my job. Getting fired from Cool Beans is not high on my problem list."

"Okay." She passed me a stack of folded T-shirts. "What are

you going to do if you don't find him?"

I shoved a couple pairs of jeans in the suitcase. "That's not an option."

"Well, he's not going to be in Tennessee, probably," Corabelle said.

"But if a bunch of people were texting him about the photos, he has to have friends or family there. They'll know where he is or how to get in touch with him."

I snapped the suitcase shut. I only had ninety minutes until my flight. My mom had sprung for the ticket. I was grateful.

Corabelle threw her arms around me. "I think this is just about the most romantic thing I've ever seen," she said. "I hope you find him."

I held on to her a moment, feeling sad I hadn't told her my secret. "I will."

A taxi waited for me outside.

"Keep me updated," Corabelle said.

I got in the taxi and took off for the airport. My belly gurgled, and I rubbed it. Was it a sign I was doing the right thing? Or just some random result of breakfast?

I really needed some pregnancy books. I had no idea what I was doing.

I wound up sleeping almost the entire flight. I kept doing that, just crashing for no reason. Thankfully, I wasn't puking all the time. I'd always thought that being pregnant meant you hurled your guts 24/7. It was really more like a queasiness when I smelled something strong, or if I ate something weird. I could manage it.

I landed in Chattanooga just after lunch. My mind ran through the scenarios on how Chance would take the news. Denial? Rage?

Say it wasn't his?

As I walked through the airport toward the taxi stand, I fretted over how to actually say the words. If he wouldn't meet with me or tell me where he was, I would have to decide if I should do it in a phone call, or worse, a text.

I already had the names of four guitar stores in Chattanooga. I figured if I was trying to weasel contact information from a store employee, I'd better try it in person. This was something I was good at. I could eyeball somebody and instinctively know whether to flirt, be casual, or sneaky, or play hardball.

Still, my belly fluttered with nerves. This brought on a round of nausea.

It was all so connected. Each emotion affected every system. Staying cool and collected was harder than ever. This grain of sand was seriously impacting me in every way possible.

I figured Murphy's Law meant I would go to all four stores and it would be the last one that had the information I needed. So when I got in the taxi, I instructed the driver to take me to the one farthest away. Maybe I could cut to the chase, cheat ol' Murphy.

But when I arrived in front of the chain guitar store, it felt all wrong. Chance wouldn't go here. It was glitzy and aimed at amateurs and hobbyists. Not somebody who would play across the country.

I didn't even get out. I told the driver the next name on the list.

He turned around, his short cropped hair peppered with gray, like his mustache. "You sure?" he asked. "That's a pretty tough part of town, darlin'."

His accent was so much like Chance's that my heart pounded. "Well, I'm looking for a place that would sell a pretty rare but brand-new guitar. Some place that would cater to serious musicians."

"I know the one," he said. "Everybody who's anybody in this town buys their gear there."

"Have you?" I asked.

"Not me," he said. "But Chattanooga ain't a big city. There's only so many places, and I've lived here a long time."

I sat back on the seat, looking out. "It's a pretty place."

"There's two parts of Tennessee," he said. "The flat dull parts. And here, all green and mountains. This is what a lot of folks think of when they picture it. But the city they think of, Nashville, isn't like this at all."

"It's not green and pretty?"

"Not a lick."

"Can we see the river that runs through town?" I asked. It was one of the few things Chance had mentioned.

"Sure," he said. "We'll take Veterans Bridge right across the island and go up Riverfront. We'll pass all the tourist spots. The aquarium, museums. There's a cruise you can take up the river."

I doubted I'd have time to sightsee, but I was fascinated by the town Chance called home. I wondered if I could find his family. What they'd think of me. I had on the blue and white maxi dress. My suitcase was full of jeans. I had one killer outfit in the bag, to use only if necessary. And it would probably be necessary.

I had tucked my dreads into a big sun hat so they weren't too prominent. I'd whip it off at the guitar store if I thought the look would score me points in getting what I needed.

But I was probably not the girl you would normally bring home to Mother.

Particularly if I was knocked up.

My belly fluttered again, and nausea rolled in. I had to get control of this or I'd be too green in the gills to get what I needed from the stores.

We passed through the tourist district the driver had talked about. It looked like a lot of interesting things for typical visitors. Just not me. The only thing I wanted wore Grateful Dead T-shirts and jeans that hugged his butt just the right way.

I had no idea if I would find him, but I would sure as hell try.

# 34

## JENNY

I stood in front of the guitar shop, mentally preparing myself to go in. Maybe I should have gone to the other stores first, to practice what I would say.

Looking at the images of the local musicians whose event flyers plastered the front windows, I could see that taking off the hat was a wise idea. I wished I didn't have a suitcase to drag behind me, as it looked odd, but maybe I could incorporate it into my story. I had started to form one as I looked at the door. It would work. It had to.

I pulled off the hat and hooked it over the handle of the suitcase. Then I took a deep breath, and opened the door.

It jingled with my entry. A man with a long brown beard sat behind the counter, diddling on a guitar. The place was packed wall to wall with equipment. Amps. Cases. Shoulder straps. Two rotating racks were filled with picks. One wall was dedicated to strings.

A room to the left had its doors thrown wide, and inside I

could see guitars hanging floor to ceiling. I was drawn to it for a moment, so many colors and sizes, the warm wood of the acoustics and shiny gloss of electrics.

The man behind the counter finished whatever he was playing and asked, "Can I help you?"

I turned to him. "I hope so. I flew down to Tennessee to meet with a guitar player I discovered in LA. He's from here. He bought a beautiful rare wood Seagull from this shop and raved about it."

"We have a lot of 'em," he said.

I pressed on. "I apparently left my phone on a charger in the LAX airport and now I can't contact him. You are literally my only clue on how to meet up with him here."

"What was his name?"

This was the tricky bit. "Chance," I said. "He has the most delicious accent. He had picked up a gig with a band called the Sonic Kings at a Hollywood party I attended."

The man hit the mouse on his computer. "Did he buy the Seagull recently?"

"It looked pretty new, but he's been on the road for five months, so it would have been before then. It's such a rare guitar, I thought he might be easy to spot."

He scrolled through pages. "You play?" he asked.

"Oh, no, I have zero talent for any of it. But he was — wonderful. I have some friends who want to hire him. I work in the movie industry." Hopefully, I thought.

"Okay, I see him. He picked this up literally five months ago. I guess for this tour you're talking about."

I leaned on the counter. "Makes sense. I had his phone number. I hate that cell phones mean we don't write anything down!"

"He didn't give me that, but he lives just a few streets down from here." The man looked me over, head to toe.

"Great," I said. "Although I hate to pop in. Maybe I can just leave a little note with how to reach me. He's probably calling my missing phone, thinking I'm blowing him off." I put on my best distressed look.

"He's across from the middle school," he said, and gave me the address and rough directions. "Tell him I said hello."

I couldn't believe I did it.

I had an address.

I thanked him and dragged my suitcase out of the store. I really wanted to get rid of the suitcase as soon as possible, so as soon as I was certain I was out of view, I pulled out my phone to call the taxi service.

I hadn't been gone long, so the same driver picked up the fare. I was sort of glad to see his friendly face again.

"Did you find what you were looking for?" he asked as I got in.

"Yes. Are there any hotels near here?"

"Sure. We can drive by and you can take a look-see."

"Thank you," I said.

I stayed by the window to really take in all the places Chance once knew. I felt like I was getting to know him a little, seeing the shop where he got his guitar, and now going to where he lived. Or did. I wasn't sure if he'd pulled out completely when he left town. It might be a dead end. But if nothing else, I had a place I could send a letter and ask to be forwarded. It was something.

We drove by two nondescript chain hotels. "This one's fine," I said. "I really appreciate your help." I handed him the fare.

"Have a nice time here in Chattanooga," he said. "If you want me for anything, you can call and ask for Dan. They'll tell you if I'm on duty."

"Thank you," I said. It was nice to feel like I knew someone here, even if it was a taxi driver.

I checked into the hotel and called my mom to let her know I had an address for Chance, even if it was an old one. She told me to be careful and asked if I was feeling sick.

I told her as long as I stayed calm, I wasn't nauseated. After we hung up, I sat on the bed with the phone against my heart, glad at least somebody in the world knew everything. I appreciated her more in that moment than I think I ever had in my life.

I went in the bathroom to survey my appearance. I figured there were three possibilities for what I would find.

1. Chance himself.

2. Chance's family.

3. A new oblivious occupant.

The last seemed the most likely. But I had to brace myself for any of the others.

I took a second to Google the address to see if I could drum anything up. I found a rental listing from two years ago. Judging from the lack of lawn and family-friendliness, I assumed this had been where Chance had lived, not his parents.

It hadn't been listed since, so maybe he had roommates that were still there.

That might be the easiest scenario. His friends would tell me where he was. Surely.

Just in case it WAS his mother, though, I smoothed my dreads back into a ponytail and hid them under the hat again. Not to mention, it would be a dead giveaway to anyone who might have seen the video that I was the naked girl.

I felt prepared to face all the eventualities.

Maybe.

# 35

---

## JENNY

The house didn't look a whole lot different from the listing two years ago. Brown scraggly yard. Three trucks crammed into the driveway. So Chance had called this place home.

I gripped my purse strap tightly and headed up the walk. This was the worst part, hands down. But when I stepped on the porch, a buff cowboy in jeans, a plaid shirt, and a Stetson came out the front door.

"Oh, hey there," he said, his expression lighting up. "Who brought you here?"

My voice caught. Could this be a brother? Or just someone who knew Chance? I couldn't find any words.

His eyes were light blue and danced with amusement. "Quiet one, eh? You Redmond's new girl? You look kinda pretty for that scoundrel."

I took a deep breath. "Actually, I was wondering if Chance was back yet."

He took a step back. "You know Chance?"

"I met him" — I decided not to mention LA — "while he was traveling."

He squinted his eyes at me. "Are you that girl from the video?" He walked around me to look at the hair peeking out from the hat. "Bloody hell, it IS you!"

He opened the front door. "Redmond! Ace! You won't believe who is on our porch."

Shit. My heart hammered and my stomach turned over. Nausea flooded me. No, no, no, I could not throw up on their front stoop. I tried breathing slowly and carefully, wishing I had eaten some crackers.

Another guy came out, this one in workout clothes. "What are you talking about?" He stopped dead when he saw me. "Well, lookit that."

The third one pushed between them to take a gander at me. "It's dreadlock girl!" He was short and squat and watched me with suspicion. "Things not work out with your movie director?"

He had done his homework.

"Believe everything you read in a tabloid?" I shot at him. "Because I have an alien love child back home who wants somebody to probe."

The first guy slapped his leg, laughing with a deep boom. "This one's a corker. No wonder she flew all the way here chasing a ghost."

I frowned. "What do you mean?"

"Chance ain't been here in five months, and he hasn't written a-one of us back the whole time," the first guy said.

Short Boy said, "And he didn't respond when we pointed out

he'd made the news, either. He just doesn't care."

I held on tight to my purse. "Isn't there anyone he's willing to talk to back home? I really need to find him."

The boys looked at one another.

"Well," the first one said, "there's Charlie. She works at the facility where his sister is staying, so he'll talk to her. I don't think he's speaking to his mother, so Charlie would be your best bet."

"A facility?" I asked. "Who is his sister?"

The boys all looked at the floor of the porch. "Her name's Hannah," the first one said. "Hannah McKenzie. She's at the rehab place on Mercer Street. It's sort of an old folks' home, but they let Hannah go there."

Holy hell, I had his last name. Just hearing it made my heart sing a little. One more piece of information. McKenzie. Chance McKenzie.

"Is she okay?" I asked.

The boys looked at one another again. "We don't really know. We're not allowed to see her. Chance's mother is pretty tight-lipped and Charlie won't talk to us."

"What happened?" I asked.

"I'm not talking about this," the short one said. "I don't want anything to do with this at all." He went back inside.

"Don't mind Ace," the first guy said. "He was friends with Carl, and so much shit went down after the accident. He's just sick of it."

"Accident?"

"Our friend Carl hit Hannah's car while he was mud running," the guy who must be Redmond said. "It was a bad, bad night."

"Lots of bad feelings came out of it, and of course, Hannah

got hurt pretty bad," the first guy said.

"That was five months ago?" I asked.

Redmond tugged on his workout shirt. "More like six. Chance stuck around for a bit, until it was clear Hannah wasn't going to wake up. He and his mom had words over her care. She's real religious, and she wouldn't take her off life support. Chance didn't want to see her suffering on that ventilator, wasting away."

Wow. No wonder he was running.

"I've got his number," Redmond said. "But two weeks ago, it started giving us an 'out of service' message." He pulled out his phone. "I'm thinking he changed it after that little dustup with you on the beach."

"Oh," I said.

The first guy squinted at me. "So he didn't want to talk to you either?"

"We didn't exchange numbers at the time," I said carefully. "It was just going to be a one-night thing."

"So you changed your mind," Redmond said.

"I did."

"Good enough for me," Redmond said. "We can go see Charlie. You want me to drive you?"

"I can do it," the other one said.

"Back off, Pete," Redmond said. "I'm about the only one here Chance doesn't have a beef with."

"He's not exactly taking your calls," Pete shot back.

I took a step back. "I can call a cab."

"It's fine," Redmond said. "Let me get my keys."

Pete leaned against the column. "You sure came a long way to find him," he said. "Must be important."

I bit my lip. I couldn't let them figure out what was going on.

"True love," I said. "And maybe he has something of mine."

"Oh ho," Pete said. "How was he, when you saw him?"

I breathed a little easier knowing I had diverted his questioning. "All right. Seemed happy. He was playing with a band who'd picked him up hitchhiking."

"So you really don't have this other guy?"

"No," I said, knowing everything I said would be hashed over. "We were done. Chance was sort of a — rebound."

Pete nodded. "Well, I figure if anybody can find him, it'll be you. You're not his usual type, but I can see why he might get hooked."

Redmond came back out on the porch. He'd changed into jeans and a shirt and his black hair was damp. "Let's go before Charlie's off. I recall she only works days."

He passed me and headed toward one of the pickups in the drive.

I followed him and gave Pete a little wave. As anxious as I was, this was going better than I thought.

# 36

## JENNY

We pulled up to the facility, which had a few spots near a big circle drive under an overhang.

"Is this a nursing home?" I asked. It looked like one.

"Sort of," Redmond said. "They do some rehab things. I think they have a few other patients like Hannah, sort of in limbo."

"So what exactly happened?" I asked.

"It was a terrible car accident. A clusterfuck of shit that went down when everybody drank too much." Redmond stared out the windshield, his wrist over the steering wheel. "Changed everything."

"Is that why Chance took off?"

"He said he needed to see the country, live by the seat of his pants. He quit his job." Redmond pulled the keys from the ignition. "Running from demons, I guess. I don't blame him for blowing us all off. We deserved it."

"But his mom?"

"I hope he'll come around about her. She's a good lady, just a little preachy is all."

I touched my dreadlocks with trepidation. "She's not going to like me, is she?" I asked.

"If you can get her son back here, she'll love you." Redmond smiled and I could see why girls might fall for him. He had the same lazy grin that Chance had. It made me miss Chance all the more.

"Let's go find Charlie," Redmond said. "She's not going to speak to me, so you'll probably have to plead your case. She's kind of a tough one."

I nodded and opened the passenger door. I was getting good at these hard introductions.

We wandered into the visitors' area. A couple elderly women were seated by the window, their wheelchairs angled close. One of them lit up at seeing Redmond. "My boy is here!" she said.

Redmond walked right up and kissed her hand. "Hello, Mrs. Tate." He nodded to the other. "And Mrs. Johnson."

The old woman beamed. "I see you have a lady friend. Do you have some news for me? A wedding, maybe?"

"Not with this one," he said. "But I'll let you know."

"I want some grandbabies!" she said.

"I'll work on it. See you soon." He squeezed her hand and came back to me. We wandered toward a big round information desk.

"Is that your mom?" I asked.

"Oh, no," he said. "She thinks every young man who comes in is her son. I don't see any reason to correct her."

"Oh." I was starting to like Redmond.

We approached the friendly big-haired woman at the desk. "Is

Charlie around?" Redmond asked.

"Yeah, I think she's in the break room. She's leaving early today." She sat up a little straighter as Redmond leaned on the desk. He was definitely a charmer.

"Can we go back and catch her?" he asked.

Her lashes flitted down. "Sure. You know where it is?"

"Not a clue."

The woman smiled. "I'd show you myself, but I can't leave my post." She pointed down one of the corridors. "Go down the A hall, turn right first chance you get. It's a door marked 'Employees Only' on the left."

"Got it. Thanks." He turned to me. "Ready?"

I nodded.

We walked down the hall, passing numerous open doors of elderly people in beds or wheelchairs. Most of them were watching television. Everything smelled of antiseptic and medicine. I hadn't been in many places like this. My father's parents had died when I was very young, and my mother's parents were jet-setting all over the world in their retirement.

We found the break room. Redmond opened the door. Inside, a couple women in scrubs were chatting. One of them, a slender dark-haired woman in her early thirties, narrowed her eyes. "What are you doing here?" she asked.

The other woman scooted through the door. "Catch you later, Charlie," she said.

"Sure," Charlie answered, then returned her glare to Redmond. Finally she cast her angry gaze at me. "Who's this?"

"Chance's girlfriend."

I could see that caught her by surprise. "He hasn't said

anything about any girlfriend."

"So you *have* been talking to him." Redmond flashed her a wide smile. "Well, she met him playing a gig in LA. And she's trying to find him again."

Charlie looked back and forth between me and Redmond, unsmiling.

"If he wanted her, she'd know how to reach him," she said. "Sounds like you're getting involved in his business." She paused for effect. "Again."

Redmond held up his hands. "She tracked him down at the house. I had nothing to do with it."

"Charlie?" I said tentatively. "I think he might have lost his phone not long after I met him. Have you heard from him in the past two weeks?"

"Of course I have. He checks on his sister almost every day."

Redmond pulled out his phone. "Is it a new number?"

"I'm not giving it to you," she snapped. "Why do you think he changed it? You all ganged up on him over that pink-haired tart from the beach."

My face flamed red.

She looked at my hat, and then must have spotted the bits over my ears. She stepped up close and lifted the rim to look closer. "Unbelievable. It was you?"

I stepped back, but she was already pushing us toward the door. "This is a staff-only area. You are not authorized to be back here."

"Charlie, pry open that cold black heart of yours. The girl has got some reason to find him. You might want to ask her what it is."

"I don't care what it is. I saw the stories. She's got some big-shot boyfriend, and she doesn't need to be toying with Chance. He's got enough to worry about." She got us moved out into the hall. "Now, get out."

Redmond turned to face her again, but she slammed the door. I could hear a bolt falling on the other side.

"That went well," I said.

"Yeah, Charlie can be a little much." Redmond scratched the back of his neck. "Well, I'm not sure what else to tell you. She's about the only person who knows how to get to Chance at the moment."

I leaned against the wall. "Now what do I do?"

"I guess you let it go," Redmond said. "Pick up the shards of your broken heart." He sighed. "That idiot Chance. Can I take you somewhere? Are you hungry? Do you have a hotel?"

The urge to start bawling was fierce. I had come so far. I couldn't just give up.

"You think there's a chance that Charlie will tell him I came, and he'll want to see me?" I asked.

Redmond's face contorted. "Not sure, really. Maybe."

I pushed away from the wall. "I guess that's all I can do, then, hope Charlie will contact you, and you can contact me."

"I'll get your info from you. I'll let you know as soon as I hear, if I do." He looked concerned now. "Did something, you know, *happen?*"

He looked like he might be catching on.

The words stuck in my throat. I couldn't tell this total stranger the things that Chance should hear first.

"It's nothing," I said. "Don't worry about it. I'll figure something out."

"Are you in trouble? Did that director threaten you?" Now he looked angry.

"No, I just...I just regret how I left things," I said. That was true.

"Let me take you somewhere," Redmond insisted. "I can tell you all about growing up with Chance McKenzie."

Actually, that sounded kind of nice. If I wasn't able to track Chance down anytime soon, I could at least build a bunch of stories to tell the baby. Let him have something to go on.

Chance couldn't stay gone forever, right?

A rotund woman in a gray floral dress hurried toward us. "Redmond, is that you?"

He turned, and his expression changed again. "Oh, boy," he said.

"What are you doing here? Visiting Hannah?"

Redmond cleared his throat. "No, I came to see Charlie."

"Oh," she said. She noticed me then, and nodded politely. "How do you do?"

"Oh, Mrs. McKenzie, this is —" Redmond stopped when he realized I hadn't ever said my name.

I swallowed the shock that this was someone related to Chance, and said quickly, "Jenny. I'm from Los Angeles." I held out my hand.

She took it gingerly and shook it very slowly. "Chance was just in Los Angeles. I saw it in *Star* magazine."

No point beating around the bush. Chance's big exposé obviously had made the rounds. "He was with me, Mrs. McKenzie. We had a misunderstanding when he read the accounts of my relationship history. I'm here to find him, to set things straight."

"Oh!" she said. Then after a second, another "Oh!"

"Have you heard from him?" I asked. "I think he changed his number."

"He never writes me back," she said. "He's gone on quite the adventure, cutting himself off from everyone."

"'Cept Charlie," Redmond said. "She knew all about everything."

"Oh!" Mrs. McKenzie said again. "Maybe I should speak to her."

Redmond pointed at the door behind him. "She's holed up in there," he said. "But we can stand siege. Cut off all escape routes."

"Redmond, you were always such a card," Mrs. McKenzie said. She turned to the door and rapped loudly. "Charlie? It's Chance's mother. Let me in."

Nothing happened.

"Oh, for Pete's sake," she said. She knocked again. "Charlotta Jones, open this door this instant!"

Redmond stifled a laugh. Mrs. McKenzie turned to him sharply. "Hold your laughter, Redmond. I can speak to your mother as well."

"Won't be telling her anything she doesn't already know," he said, trying to keep a straight face.

The door opened. Charlie stood there, her face red, her long dark hair twisted in her hand. "I'm not going to give up his number to anybody," she said. "He's gone for a reason."

Mrs. McKenzie sniffed. "It's not right for a boy to turn his back on his family. Think of poor Hannah."

I thought Charlie's head was going to blow to bits, she got so red. "He thinks of her every day. You could stand to think of her a little too."

Now Mrs. McKenzie was the one with red cheeks. "She's my perfect little girl," she said. "She never should have gone out there after her brother. She was innocent in every way."

"Well, none of the rest of us are," Charlie said. "Including you."

Mrs. McKenzie closed her eyes like she was trying to maintain her patience.

Charlie sighed. "I have to get back to work. Go visit her. But don't skip the hand-washing and the masks today. We have two patients with pneumonia right now."

"Thank you for your advice, Charlotta," Mrs. McKenzie said.

Charlie took off down the hall, her black shoes squeaking on the shiny waxed floor.

"Well," Mrs. McKenzie said. "That girl needs a husband." She turned to me. "Would you like to meet Chance's sister?"

I felt lightheaded at the suggestion. Really? She was okay with me?

"Of course," I said. "I'd love to see her."

Mrs. McKenzie threaded her arm through mine. "I was once a wayward girl in love," she said. "I understand these things."

We continued down the corridor, the same direction as Charlie. Redmond followed behind.

"Chance was a wild young boy," she said. "In trouble all the time. When his father left, he just went crazy. I had my hands full with baby Hannah. I didn't look after him like I should have. The very devil got in his soul."

We paused outside a door decorated with a grapevine wreath in the shape of a heart. Hanging inside it was a hand-painted sign that read "Hannah." Mrs. McKenzie reached out and straightened it. Then she opened the door.

The room was dark and hushed. Monitors lit up both sides of the bed with a soft glow, emitting a quiet *beep beep*.

Mrs. McKenzie let go of my arm and headed to the sink. "There's antibacterial soap here," she said. She washed her hands and opened a drawer, removing two blue masks. "One for you."

I followed her lead, washing my hands and tucking the strings on the mask behind my ears.

Redmond stayed back in the doorway.

Mrs. McKenzie moved toward the window. "She needs some sunshine," she said.

As the curtains shifted, I could make out the girl on the bed. She had a tube taped to her mouth. Her chest rose and fell with the movements of a machine pushing air into her lungs.

Jesus.

Mrs. McKenzie took the girl's hand between both of her own. "Hello, sweet Hannah. I brought you someone special to meet. This is Jenny, Chance's girlfriend. She's from California!"

I glanced back at Redmond. His lips were pursed tight.

"Come on over, Jenny. Don't be shy," Mrs. McKenzie said.

I took a couple tentative steps forward.

Hannah looked to be in her teens, thin and frail with wispy mocha-colored hair. Her skin was pale and waxy. She was a pretty girl.

"I can see her resemblance to Chance," I said.

Mrs. McKenzie beamed. "They always did favor each other. Always sweet too. Chance was a protective big brother. There's an eight-year gap between them. I struggled to have another after my boy." Her eyes closed for a moment, her lips moving silently. I realized she was praying.

"Is she going to get better?" I asked, having a feeling I knew the answer based on the timeline and Charlie's accusations.

"Of course she is," Mrs. McKenzie said. "The Lord has his own timetable. We just have to be patient."

Redmond spoke up from the doorframe. "You ready for me to take you back to your hotel, Jenny?" he asked.

"Nonsense," Mrs. McKenzie said. "Jenny will come to the house. She can stay in Chance's room. She'll get a hoot out of his action-figure collection."

"I wouldn't want to put you out," I said.

"I'm so delighted to get to know you," she said. "You're such a sweet and pretty girl. I'm glad Chance finally found one worth holding on to." She reached out to tweak the edge of my sun hat. "Such a lovely dress and hat. A real old-fashioned girl."

I couldn't wait for her to spot my pink dreadlocks.

# 37

## CHANCE

I wanted a new path to California this time, so I headed deep south, toward Georgia. What I really needed was a damn airplane. The urgency to get back to LA was intense.

But that was a lot more money than I could get in tips on a typical night. Based on the gig in Portland at that vegan restaurant where I did so well, I knew I had to find the places catering to people with bucks.

Trouble was, the joints I kept landing weren't anything like that. The ritzy places weren't going to take me. The poor places netted me barely enough to keep going.

I sat on a bench in Atlanta near a mall I'd been to a thousand times with my mother. I was less than two hours from Chattanooga right now, and was seriously thinking of stopping by to sell my truck. Or drive it.

I could probably sell off some things, raise some cash to start over in Cali. I had stuff. Furniture still at Redmond's. A computer.

My old guitar.

The more I thought about it, the better this plan seemed. I'd done my stint hitchhiking. I'd played all over the country. Now I could just go straight to the place I liked best. I could look up the Sonic Kings. They'd bring me on a gig, I knew it. And if I had some cash, I could probably crash with one of them on the cheap, helping out with bills as I figured stuff out.

I stood up. This was a good plan. I just had to make this last stretch back to Chattanooga. An easy hitch. Or hell, I could even call somebody to fetch me. Any one of the old boys would do it, just to hear my tale.

Except…I didn't want them. I didn't want any of them.

My past came crashing down on my head, killing all my enthusiasm. If I went back there, I'd have to deal with my mother. And my so-called friends.

And Hannah.

I'd have to look at her again, wasting away. The worst thing she could have ever feared. Her biggest nightmare. She was living it.

Except she wasn't alive. She was being kept alive. She wouldn't want that. But I hadn't been able to change things. I hadn't done anything at all.

Except be part of what put her there.

I sank back down on the bench. I'd chosen this hard road on purpose. It was my punishment, my penance, what I deserved.

The night of the accident wanted to encroach on my thoughts, but I wouldn't let it. I'd done enough thinking these past five months to last a lifetime. I knew what I wanted now. Cali. The band. That girl.

Jenny.

Thinking about her pink dreadlocks made me smile. Remembering her spontaneous run down the beach soothed my tortured soul. She was just the ticket. Exactly what I needed.

I had to get there.

I got up, racking my brain for places I knew in Atlanta that might help with the cash situation. I needed a place that wasn't fancy, but catered to rich people.

I started walking toward downtown, but my phone buzzed. Charlie. I hadn't talked to her since New York. I should have called. If something had happened to Hannah…

I mashed the button. "Hello?"

"Chance McKenzie, I just met your pink-haired trollop and you probably better get back to Chattanooga."

For a minute, I just stood there, not sure what I'd just heard.

"Chance, are you listening to me?"

"Are you saying Jenny is in Chattanooga?" I asked.

"Redmond just brought her to the home. They thought they could weasel your phone number out of me."

I felt giddy and light. Jenny! She had found me!

"Charlie, this is great! Tell her my number! Hell, I'm in Atlanta! I can be there in two hours!" I wanted to laugh at the world, shout into the sky. Jenny was freaking *here*!

"You're in Atlanta? What the hell are you doing so close?" She sounded annoyed that I wasn't in Timbuktu or something.

"It's just where I wound up, making my way down from New York." I still couldn't get over it. Jenny! In Chattanooga.

"You want someone to come get you?" Her voice was full of uncertainty.

"I might have enough money for a bus ticket." I started

walking in the general direction of the station, even though it was miles away. "I don't want to sit here waiting for two hours."

"I can't believe you're racing here to meet up with that girl," Charlie said. "Have you already forgotten those articles? The video? She's trouble, Chance. Big trouble. Trouble you don't need."

I stopped walking. "Did you find something else out?" Maybe there was a problem over the news stories. Maybe something had happened with that director.

"Chance! It's obvious! She played you. I don't know how or why, but you can't trust this girl."

I let seconds tick by as I let this sink in. I had just gotten burned in Virginia. She might be right.

"Chance?" Charlie's voice was impatient. "What are you going to do?"

The sidewalk was a blur beneath my long rapid steps. It didn't seem to matter what my brain was thinking, any doubts Charlie was planting. My legs had their own agenda.

"I'm coming home," I said. "Don't let her get away."

# 38

## JENNY

As we left the nursing home, Redmond tried once more to convince me to go with him instead of Mrs. McKenzie.

He ducked his head in close. "You sure 'bout this, Jenny?"

Part of me would rather go with Redmond, the part who liked things easy. But if this woman was going to be my baby's grandmother, I was laying the groundwork for everything ahead.

"I'll be all right," I said. "She's a lovely woman."

"I hear every word you two are saying!" Mrs. McKenzie called out.

I gave Redmond a final nod and followed the stout woman to an old-model Honda, shiny and well kept despite its age.

"Have you had a chance to see much of Chattanooga yet?" Mrs. McKenzie asked as she manually unlocked the doors from the outside.

"I just got here a few hours ago," I said.

The car was stuffy and warm from sitting in the sun. I leaned forward to keep from smashing the back of my hat in a way that might reveal the pink hair. I needed to make a good impression on this woman before she figured out that little detail.

"Well, there's a lovely little bakery just up the road that I adore. Would you like to stop by for a refreshment?"

That sounded easy. "I'd be delighted, Mrs. McKenzie," I said.

"Call me Carol Ann," she said.

"All right, then, Carol Ann." I watched out the window as we headed along a quiet road with houses set well back from the street. "I've never been to Tennessee before."

"Oh, it's a wonderful place," she said. "So many lovely sights. And the music. This close to Nashville, you know. I think that's why my Chance took up singing like he did."

"He's very good," I said.

"How did you meet him?"

"I went to a movie premiere and he did a number with the band who played afterward." I did my best to avoid the word "party."

"What did he sing?" She turned down a side road with lots of cute cottages lined up, like a retirement village.

"The first one was 'Let the Good Times Roll,'" I said. "Then 'When a Man Loves a Woman.'"

She shot me a knowing look. "That Chance. He always was a charmer."

"It worked on me," I said, relieved to talk about him with someone who wouldn't mock how easily I fell for him.

We pulled up in front of a tiny bakery with only three parking spots. "Isn't it quaint?" she said. "You have to try their teacakes."

I wondered if this fuss had to do with my hat and maxi dress. I got out of the car, realizing I hadn't eaten in a while. As I stood up, lightheadedness caught me off balance and I had to catch myself on the doorframe before I stumbled.

Thankfully, Mrs. McKenzie was busy on the other side and didn't notice. I took a deep breath and steeled myself to get inside. We walked between two rows of rosebushes to enter the little shop.

"Hello, Lila!" Mrs. McKenzie called out as we approached a glass cabinet filled with pastries and cakes. My head swooned at the sight of them.

A tall thin lady with her copper hair tied up tight in a fat round bun smiled at us. "Carol Ann! So nice to see you."

Mrs. McKenzie turned to me. "This here is Chance's girlfriend visiting from California. She's in the movie business."

I extended a hand. "Just the back end. I don't act."

"Sounds fancy to me," Lila said. "Take a look at the goodies and let me know what you'd like."

*All of them,* I thought, but then simultaneously, a wave of nausea came over me. *Great, little grain of sand. Decide, already. Hungry or sick?*

Apparently the wayward speck had both things in mind. I pointed out an oversized blueberry scone, hoping to get a nice caloric bang for my buck while not inciting a puke-fest. Mrs. McKenzie ordered several teacakes and a pot of Earl Grey.

We settled on a horribly uncomfortable set of wicker chairs with a glass-topped table between us. "Tell me everything," Mrs. McKenzie said. "I haven't seen Chance in months. Is he well? Did he grow a beard? Has he gotten thin?"

I tried not to cram too much scone into my mouth despite the need for food firing through me like a cannon. When I swallowed, I said, "He is still clean shaven, although he gets pretty scruffy in the evening. He is definitely not thin." I paused to reflect on that hard chest and those corded shoulders. "He must be finding some way to work out on the road."

Mrs. McKenzie took a delicate bite of a teacake and sat back in her chair. "Lovely. So good to hear that he is well. Did he happen to tell you why he left?"

The bite of scone in my mouth suddenly went dry, and I coughed. I tried pouring the tea, but it was steaming and not even brewed yet in the pot.

Tears streamed from my eyes until my body settled down and I managed to get the bite down.

"Are you quite all right, Jenny dear?" Mrs. McKenzie asked. "You seem very excitable."

I decided to hell with it and sipped the bit of watery tea I'd put in my cup. My tongue burned instantly, but I felt better.

"He didn't talk much about home," I said finally. "Mostly he told me about his music, and places he'd been on the road."

"I heard a terrible rumor he was hitchhiking," she said, folding her napkin into a tight little square. "Is it true?"

I wasn't going to out anything Chance wouldn't want me to say. "I don't know. I only saw him in LA."

She frowned. "So what was all that nonsense in *Star* magazine? Those pictures were…" She unfurled the napkin to wave in front of her face as if she needed air.

"Faked," I said. "It's a sad but true part of the movie industry that bottom feeders use famous people as a way to sell papers and get television ratings."

She sat up. "I guess I knew that. But those pictures…"

Yeah, she was picturing them. My face burned.

"Photoshop," I said. "They have entire teams of people sticking one person's head on another person's body."

"Oh, my land," she said. "That's just awful." She reached across the table to squeeze my wrist. "I feel just terrible that I thought those terrible lies about you were true. I can see that you are really just a victim of a horrible scheme."

Yeah, right. A scheme I set in motion all on my own. I refused to feel bad about lying to Chance's mom. Everything I said was true, just not in my case. Not this time.

My stomach had settled and I attacked the scone with more energy. This was going well, really. And surely Charlie would report my appearance to Chance. And if he heard I was with his mother, well, maybe that would be what got him home.

"Do say you'll stay with me, dear. I'd love to hear every detail about my boy. I've missed him. I can take off work tomorrow and we can see the sights. I can show you all of Chance's favorite places."

As tough as it seemed, this was probably a good idea. The more I kept close to the people who knew Chance, the more likely I would be to find him.

But I'm pretty sure his mother didn't want *every* little detail.

# 39

## CHANCE

Bus tickets were a lot cheaper than I remembered and I had enough to easily cover the short trip back to Chattanooga. The bad part was the schedule wasn't very good and I had to wait an hour just to board. It might have been faster to hitch.

The ride back gave me time to think things through. Charlie said Redmond had brought Jenny around, so she must have figured out where I used to live. I pictured her on the porch with him and Ace and Pete and wanted to laugh. They'd think she was a wild thing with that crazy hair.

She sort of was.

I had this lightness inside I had forgotten I could feel. I'd lost it a long time ago, way before the accident, maybe as far back as when my dad left.

No, there were good times after that. Mom wasn't a crazy church lady right off. I think she believed Dad would come back.

She called his going away a midlife crisis, not that ten-year-old me knew what that meant. It sounded bad, though.

Maybe I lost it when Mom did figure it out. Hannah got sick with the croup and we had to go to the hospital. She had to sleep in a little tent thing. Mom tried harder than she ever had before to get hold of Dad. He'd been gone something like two years by then, so looking back, I wondered why she thought it might work. Maybe she believed he would come out of fear for Hannah.

He didn't. And I knew the score then. If he wasn't going to come back when one of his kids was in the hospital, he wasn't coming back at all.

About then she decide to let Jesus take the wheel. I had no opinion on the matter. We already went to church, and my Sunday school teacher was nice. We got cookies and coloring pages.

But Mom definitely took salvation seriously. As I got older, I couldn't stand how nothing was ever interesting to her unless it involved the right hand of God. I got wilder and wilder, because nothing got my rocks off faster than seeing her go ballistic in the name of the Lord. I'm sure He got a whole lotta earfuls about me.

Hannah handled Mom's deep end with a lot more grace. She was rebellious too, but in a quiet way. She buried herself in school activities, keeping to things that made Mom proud, like French club and orchestra. No cheerleading with short skirts or dance teams with their peppy gyrations, two things that made high school worthwhile back in my day.

I moved out at the first shot, but I could see by then my mother struggling to make ends meet. The only work she ever did was a few hours a week in the church gift store. Maybe Dad sent less money by then, with me grown.

So even though I couldn't much stand to be in her company, I did deposit half my paycheck into her accounts. When I left five months ago, I dumped pretty much every dime to my name into hers so she wouldn't be too hard up while I was gone.

Now I was going back.

I set aside how I might feel about seeing everybody and focused on Jenny. She was one pure good thing, no part of my past. I figured if she was here that meant she had told the truth about that man with his hand on her arm. He wasn't anybody to her but a boss, maybe a too-friendly boss, but still, not anybody she belonged to.

Outside the window, the familiar landscape of Tennessee soothed my soul. I'd seen a lot of the country now, end to end. I could appreciate my hometown in a way I hadn't before. It had a character all its own.

I wondered if Jenny liked it. Not that it mattered. LA suited me just fine, or San Diego, I guess, since she said she lived there.

Crazy, making any sort of plans on a girl I knew maybe three hours.

Another song started forming in my head. It'd been there a while, since the beach, but I'd ignored it, playing it off. I let it come along, though, now that I knew she was looking for me and maybe some song was playing in her head too.

*When you look a mess*
*How your eyes confess*
*How you see the best in me*
*Just a bead of sweat*
*Sliding down your neck*

*Things I don't know yet about you*
*It's a list that never ends*

At last the bus pulled into the Chattanooga station. Charlie must've looked at the schedule and figured out when I'd be arriving, because she was there, still in her work scrubs even though she must have been off a while. It was dinnertime.

She came up to me and didn't even bother with hellos, but said, "That girl has been all over town with your mother."

I shrugged. "So they'll get to know each other." A couple guys unloaded the bottom of the bus, and I watched for my guitar. I felt anxious to see Jenny, but maybe I wanted to get to the house and shower and things first. I'd given up my room to Pete, but I still had clothes and random things boxed up in the garage.

"Where do you want to go?" Charlie asked. "Redmond said she's staying at the Fairfield near the mall."

"Take me to the house first. I want to unpack some things."

We got in her car. "So you're staying, then?" she asked.

"For a spell," I said.

She started the car and pulled out of the bus station lot. Her jaw was set sort of hard, like she was angry.

"You pissed that I'm going to see this girl who flew all the way to Chattanooga just to see me?" I asked.

She concentrated on the road. Evening was setting in and some of the streetlights were coming on. I settled back, used to Charlie being mad. This was her natural state. Didn't bother me none.

"Doesn't it seem a little suspicious?" she asked, pulling up to a red light. "This girl finds you at a party, gets you caught up in some scandal, and then shows up at your door?"

She turned to me, her face all screwed up with anger. "Aren't you worried about who she is? What she's doing?"

I looked out my window at the businesses lined up along the road. Truth was, I wasn't worried in the least. For all I knew, we were both caught up in something that could have happened to anybody at that party. So many people were there looking for attention.

"We found each other at the same time at that party," I said. "And it was clear to me all along that she didn't really belong there. I don't know a lot about Hollywood and how it works on the inside, but these photographers and celebrity mags work whatever angles they can get."

"You were naked, Chance. And there were pictures of you with all these other actresses. It was like it was planned to be as salacious as possible." The light turned green, and Charlie jumped on the gas a little hard, sending us screeching into the intersection.

I wasn't sure what she meant by the other actresses. "What are you talking about? There was just the picture of me kissing her. And her boss looking annoyed, a shot from some other day since that wasn't what he was wearing that night."

Charlie slammed on the brakes and turned hard into the parking lot of a gas station. When we were stopped, she said, "Are you serious? Do you have no clue what all happened?"

My hackles started to rise. "What else is there?"

She jerked her phone out of the center console and tapped a while. Then she turned the screen to me.

I recognized the beach straight off. "Oh, shit," I said. Jenny was running naked, black bars on her. "She had to be mortified."

"Keep watching," Charlie said.

The news guy talked about the director, same as the article. It showed a picture of them together before Jenny got the dreadlocks. He certainly seemed like he was into her, but a picture could be like that. It didn't mean anything.

I sat up a little when they showed the pictures of me with those actresses. "Nothing happened with either of them," I said. Two people behind desks made some jokes about sand and then the video ended.

"You can't tell me this wasn't some publicity stunt," Charlie said. "It's too perfect. Is your girl an actress or a model or something? Is she trying to get press?"

"I'm pretty sure she wouldn't have wanted them following us to the beach," I said, sticking her phone back in the cup holder. "I just need to talk to her about it. Maybe there's been some fallout and she needs me to back up her story or something."

I didn't like that idea. I liked it a lot better when I thought she'd come for me. But now I knew to hold back my expectations. Truth be told, I had no idea what the next few hours were going to bring at all.

# 40

## JENNY

Wow, this woman was into Jesus.

My family wasn't religious at all, so when I stepped into Mrs. McKenzie's house, I got sort of wowed by all the crosses and statues and pillows with Bible verses.

"I like to surround myself with the Gospel," Mrs. McKenzie said as we settled into chairs in her living room. She leaned in conspiratorially. "I let the preacher handle the Old Testament at the pulpit."

She laughed like this was a great joke. I didn't quite know what she meant, but I smiled anyway. I could do this. She seemed like a sweet lady who would make it her personal mission to make sure every bereaved family would get a casserole.

"You must be tired of the hat," she said. "Lovely as it is. Want me to hang it somewhere?"

My hand flew to my head. "Oh, no, I couldn't. My hair is going to be a disaster after wearing it all day."

"Well, I can certainly understand that," she said.

"I'd love to see Chance's room, though," I said, hoping to shift attention. I realized I was at her mercy now, since I couldn't exactly get away without her driving or me calling a taxi. I should have thought this through.

No, this woman would be in my life for always. I needed to stay the course.

My phone buzzed with a text. Mrs. McKenzie dropped her gaze to my purse. "Do you think that could be Chance? Maybe he got a new phone and found your number?"

No way, I thought, but it was an excuse to take a peek. It was Redmond. I'd given him my contact info when we parted earlier. When I saw his message, I dropped my phone.

*Chance just got here. You want me to fetch you?*

"Are you all right, dear?" Mrs. McKenzie scooted forward in her chair.

What to tell her? If she knew Chance was in town, she'd insist on seeing him. And I really needed him first.

I chose my words carefully so nothing would be an out-and-out lie. "Redmond wants to come get me," I said. "I think he's gotten Charlie to help us get to Chance."

She sat up a little straighter. "Really? She seemed all fluffed up like an angry cat this afternoon."

I tapped out a quick YES and tucked the phone in my purse. I had no idea how far away Chance was. I was tired and travel-weary. If I had known he would come this fast, I would have gone to the hotel to get ready.

"I guess she came around," I said. "How about a quick tour of Chance's room before Redmond gets here?"

She popped up with more energy than I would have expected. I followed her down the dark carpeted hall, my nerves jangling. I was so close to the end of this search. But I didn't know what he'd think. Him coming was a great sign that he wanted to see me.

But I had news for him. Big news. I had to be prepared for his anger, his disgust. God, who knew how he would react?

My knees wobbled a little as I walked and nausea flooded me again. No, no, no, I could not get sick here. Somebody like Mrs. McKenzie would figure it out in a hurry. How many reasons could there be to track down a one-night stand? I felt like anybody could guess in two seconds if I didn't play every moment exactly right.

Mrs. McKenzie turned into a room on the left. When she flipped on the light, I actually took a step back. This didn't look like Chance at all.

First, the room was neat as a pin. Shelves held perfectly posed action figures from *X-Men*. On a small wood dresser were stacks and stacks of Pokémon cards.

It was all so…cute. It didn't suit Chance, who had this gritty edge. Maybe he'd been a normal kid. I looked at the brown and blue bedspread, the robot pillow, and thought — do I know this guy at all?

Then it hit me. There was nothing musical. This guy who'd left everything to sing across the country had absolutely nothing in his room to reflect that this had been a passion of his while he was growing up.

"When did Chance start playing guitar?" I asked.

Mrs. McKenzie held tight to the back of the desk chair. "Oh, I guess he did it pretty early, maybe ten or eleven? He took to it right away."

"I guess I expected to see some pictures of musicians or things that would show that side of him." I wandered the room, running my fingers along a perfectly tidy desk with a stack of Little Golden Books. Chance definitely wouldn't have had those around before moving out. Mrs. McKenzie had done some creative editing of his room.

His mother tapped the desk absently. "Oh, well, some of his posters and keepsakes regarding that were a little, how can I describe it? Dark."

I got it now. Chance had listened to bands that didn't fit Mrs. McKenzie's puritanical worldview. I suppressed another smile.

"I love it," I said. "Thank you so much for showing me." I fingered the Pokémon cards. "I collected these too."

"You seem a little younger than him," she said.

"Not much. I'm graduating the University of California in June."

This made her perk up dramatically. "Oh, how exciting."

"I didn't ever talk to Chance about schooling. Did he go to college?"

Her face darkened a little and she wandered the room, straightening figures that were already perfectly aligned. "Chance decided to learn a trade," she said. "He worked in home building up until he left town."

I wondered what his job actually entailed. I imagined him using those talented hands for hard labor. Maybe that had made them strong as much as the guitar playing.

I knew what Mrs. McKenzie wanted to hear. "Well, he's a lovely boy. Very well raised."

This brought her back around to me. "Let's make some tea

while we wait for Redmond," she said. "You promise me you'll come back tonight?"

I hesitated. "I'm not sure what he needs me for, but I'll do what I can to get back here."

This placated her and we headed back through the house. I let out a long-held breath. Compared to facing a potentially irate Chance, this might be the easiest part of my trip.

# 41

## CHANCE

Redmond was gone to fetch Jenny by the time I got out of the shower. I toweled my hair off and thought about that one night we'd been together. Just remembering her made me ache with need of her. I wasn't totally sure why she'd come, but I'd listen before making any judgments.

We were meeting at the hotel. I didn't want her here with all the guys around, and I certainly wasn't going to face my mother. I assumed Jenny would know better than to tell my mother about my return, but I could deal with that later if the cat was out of the bag.

Charlie had taken off in a huff after dropping me off. I was grateful for her help in all this. If she hadn't clued me in, I wouldn't have even known Jenny was here. When the dust settled, I'd make it up to her.

I pulled on my jeans and a shirt and walked out in the hall. Ace was sitting on the sofa, drinking a beer. "I jumped your truck," he said. "Battery was deader than a doornail. It's still running out there.

Pete is watching it."

"Thanks," I said, and sat down to pull on a pair of shoes I hadn't seen for half a year. It felt good to wear something other than the same boots day in and day out. Maybe I'd throw them out. I was definitely sick of them.

"You sure about this girl?" Ace asked. "Kinda crazy, coming all this way to find you."

"I'm curious to hear why," I said.

"I'm not gonna lie," Ace said. "I'm getting some weird vibes."

I stiffened but played it cool. Ace had never really been a friend of mine. "She's different. Grew up in Cali. Girls are different there."

He stared at his beer. "I reckon you know what you're doing."

I'd had enough of this conversation. "Thanks for the jump, man," I said. "Catch you later."

"Later," he said, still looking at his bottle.

I went outside. Pete sat on the bumper of my truck, a cherry red Dodge I'd bought after the accident, not wanting to ever drive the old one again.

"Damn fine truck," Pete said. "I shoulda stole it while I had the chance."

"If I'd known I was leaving, I never would have bought it," I said. "Just sat here gathering dust."

"'S'all right," Pete said. "Made this rathole look classy."

Money I could have given my mother, I thought. I had a lot of beef with her, but I didn't want to see her destitute.

The engine rumbled clean and easy. I opened the door and climbed in. "Wish me luck," I said.

"With a girl that hot, you'll need it," Pete said with a laugh.

"You don't deserve her."

"Probably not," I said.

He waved and turned for the porch.

I dropped the gearshift into reverse and headed out of my own driveway for the first time since last fall. Because the weather in November and March was so similar, it felt the same, like I'd never left.

Except now there was Jenny.

I didn't really have to drive over to the Fairfield. It was an easy walk. Redmond said Jenny had come on foot, so I'm guessing that's why she chose it.

But I wanted to have a way to get around town, just in case.

When I got there, I parked out front. I hadn't heard from anybody in a half hour. I wondered if they were stuck drinking tea with my mother, and had to grin at the thought of shit-kicking Redmond drinking from a rose-painted cup.

I sat up when I saw Redmond's truck pull in front of the entrance. The light popped on inside the cabin, but from my position, I could only see him. I guessed Jenny had opened the passenger door.

He asked her something, then nodded. Then I saw a girl in a hat appear on the other side and go in. She wore a long flowy dress that reached her ankles. Her hair was tucked up in the hat.

Was that Jenny?

Redmond didn't take off for a moment, and I wondered what was going on. The girl went inside the hotel.

Then my phone buzzed. It was Redmond, saying Jenny would meet me in the lobby when I was ready.

So that *was* her.

After Redmond took off, I got out of my truck and headed inside. The lobby was tiny, just a couple sofas on a rug on the opposite side of the room from the desk.

Nobody was there except the manager, who smiled at me but returned to her work when I showed no signs of approaching.

I sat on one of the sofas, tense, leaning forward with my hands clasped. She must've gone upstairs to her room first. I suddenly washed cold with doubt. What if she'd changed her hair, cut it all off? I might not even know who she was when she came down.

We'd been in dim places for almost the entire three hours we knew each other. I suddenly doubted my ability to recognize her.

The wait was interminable. I finally texted Redmond to say I was there and ask if I should get Jenny's direct number.

He said no, Jenny would give it to me. Just be patient.

So I sat a little longer.

The woman at the desk glanced at me occasionally. If our eyes met, I'd nod casually. After a while, that gesture seemed strained, so I made sure I never looked her way.

The elevator dinged, and I jumped to my feet. I straightened my collar. My heart was hammering ninety to nothing.

But when the doors opened, a little old lady in a walker inched forward. I sank back down to the cushion. I was actually starting to sweat it out a little. Was this one of those girl things? Making the guy wait?

Then I realized the lady was turning to thank someone behind her. I watched her move slowly out of the way, then an arm appeared, and a hip in jeans. Someone was holding the door.

When I saw the shoulder covered with pink dreadlocks, I stood up again. As soon as the older woman was clear, Jenny popped out of the elevator. She jumped aside to avoid the walker, then came to a dead stop when she saw me standing there.

She looked both different and the same. Her hair was as I remembered, long and pink and wild. I don't know why I even thought I could have forgotten that face. Seeing it again, I felt like I'd only looked at her just yesterday.

But instead of a fancy dress and killer heels, she wore soft jeans and a blue T-shirt with a giant daisy on the front. Her feet were encased in funny little hot pink high-tops.

She gave a little wave. I felt dumbstruck, seeing her again. This girl had come all the way from California, looking for me.

"Funny running into you again," she said.

I laughed. "It's a small country."

She smoothed her hair back from her face and sat on the other sofa. I lowered back down, returning to my leaning position.

"I can't believe you were so close," she said. "I thought it would take weeks to track you down."

"Just happened to be looping back across," I said.

"Did you hitch back here all the way from LA?"

"Nah. After I left, I went up to Portland for a few days, then I decided to just skip all the way across to New York. Took a bus."

"A bus." Her eyes flitted along my face, my button-down shirt, my jeans. "I don't think I've ever ridden a bus."

"Well, I'd never ridden in a limo," I said.

She huffed out a little laugh. "I never did up until Frankie." She frowned after she said his name. "I'm sorry about the gossip rags."

My fingers tightened. "So tell me about this director guy."

She bit her lip in such a cute way I wanted to nibble at it too. But we had this stuff to get through first. I waited for her to answer. She was clearly trying to put the right words together.

"We had an…agreement. I was sort of a publicity tool for him. Not a real girlfriend."

This made me sit up a little straighter. "Are you one of those high-end call girls?"

"No!" she said quickly, the sound echoing in the empty room. The woman at the front desk looked up.

Jenny noticed her and her face turned pink. "Maybe we should go somewhere else." She stood up and looked around. "I guess to my room."

She seemed hesitant, so I took the gentleman's route even though I didn't want to. "I have my truck. We can go somewhere. A restaurant, maybe."

Jenny glanced at the front door, then back at the elevator. "No, it's fine. We can go up." She shoved her hands in her front pockets and the innocent gesture had the opposite effect on me. The T-shirt pulled tight across her chest and all the images of her on the beach came roaring back. She and me, alone in a room. Sounded like a recipe for a crazy night, but I wouldn't make any assumptions.

Not yet.

"Then we'll go up," I said, and followed her to the elevator.

She seemed timid when we were closed up inside. She pressed the button for the third floor and stared at the panel. I could smell her bath soap, fruity and light. The urge to touch her pink hair was almost impossible to suppress.

"So how did you find me?" I asked. "Couldn't have been easy."

"I got lucky several times," she said. "The big tip was the guitar. It's rare enough that I was able to track down who sold it to you."

"Smart. Didn't realize you knew your guitars."

She shrugged. "I don't. Paul from the Sonic Kings told me. I found them to see if they knew where you were."

I was dying to ask why it was critical she found me, but I figured she'd tell me in her own time. No sense rushing things.

The doors opened to a standard hotel hall, patterned carpet and wall lights. She tugged her key card from her back pocket and slid it into a door a short ways down the corridor. When the handle clicked, she seemed to hesitate, but then soldiered on.

Curious. If she was so worried about being alone with me, why come at all?

It had to be connected to the newspaper articles.

I followed her into the room. She seemed unsure where to sit. The bed was still made, her suitcase open on the bedspread. "I should move this," she said, her voice at a slightly higher pitch. She shoved the dress she was wearing earlier into it and flipped the lid.

"Let me get that," I said. I lifted the suitcase and set it on the floor by the wall. The big hat hung over the corner of the television. I touched it. "You were hiding your hair?"

"Didn't know if color was a thing here in Tennessee," she said. "I was going out on a limb trying to weasel information out of people. I didn't want to look alternative."

"Redmond said you were with my mother."

Her head snapped up. "She's a lovely woman," she said quickly.

I walked up close to her. "She's a difficult woman." I gave in to my temptation to touch her hair, fingering the soft dreadlocks. "Did she see these?"

"I don't think so," she said, her voice catching. She was

achingly close. "But she apparently reads *Star* magazine."

"Yeah, I knew she'd seen the photos. Were they in color?"

"Yeah. Maybe she forgot."

Not likely. My mother had the memory of six elephants. "She was nice to you?" I asked.

"Very. Took me to tea. Showed me your bedroom." She shoved at my arm. "I saw your Pokémon cards."

"Yeah, that room is not the room I left," I said.

"I figured. Unless you left at age ten."

"She sanitized it. She thought my Grateful Dead posters were tools of the devil."

She laughed. "I asked her about that. Why there wasn't anything dealing with music."

"She had an answer for everything, I bet," I said. I didn't get mad anymore about how she'd destroyed my room. It was past. She needed her fantasy about the kid I once was.

I knew we were talking about that director guy when we came upstairs, but I didn't care about that part anymore. She was close, and I'd gone weeks without her, without anybody. I took another step in and pressed my hand gently at the small of her back.

She sucked in a breath, still looking at my chest rather than up at me, like she was trying to decide what she wanted. I was absolutely going to tip the scales in my direction.

"I think about the beach every day," I said to her, and it was true. "You are one crazy impulsive woman."

She looked up then, those silver eyes fixing on me. Her face was perfection, not a flaw on it. And she looked more natural today, not all glitzed up like at the party. Just simple. Easygoing.

I tweaked the hair near her forehead, using my hand on her

back to keep her close. She smelled even more divine. "I like you like this," I said. "Regular clothes. Like a real girl."

This made her smile.

She had told me she was with that other guy only for show, and I believed her. Who knew how those Hollywood types worked? But she was here with me now, and that counted for more than something.

I could feel the puff of air from her breath as I leaned down and brushed my lips against hers. She melted a little against me, and I knew this was where she wanted to go. Maybe the beach had haunted her too.

I pressed in harder, sliding my tongue across her mouth until she parted for me. She tasted minty, like she'd brushed her teeth just before coming back downstairs. Her hands stayed by her sides and it became a little challenge of mine to get her to hold on to me. I'd play it nice and slow until she was the one to urge me on.

My hand in her hair slipped into all the dreadlocks and cupped her head. I drew her even more deeply against me, plumbing the sweetness of her mouth, breathing her in. I massaged the small of her back, the soft T-shirt bunching up beneath my palm until I found her skin, hot and smooth.

At my touch on her naked back, she jolted beneath me, moving forward. Then it happened, her arms came up and hung on to me. I jerked her tight against me, letting her feel the raging of my need for her. We were back, not on a beach in LA, but in my hometown now.

She was mine.

# 42

## JENNY

I hadn't expected to get all up in Chance straight off, but here we were.

His hand was snaking up the back of my shirt, and I was pressed against that hard chest. His mouth was all over mine, and this boy, he had kissing *down*.

No way was I going to be able to resist this.

The lights were blazing, a nice change from all the dark of our first encounter. I wanted to see him, every muscle and plane. I wanted to get lost, let the world drop away, not think about the hard conversations ahead.

His lips made a trail down my jaw to my neck. He moved his hand from my hair to my waist, where it flirted with the hem of my shirt.

I squeezed my eyes shut, feeling his touch on me, the sensations spiraling up into a frenzy. I didn't want to push anything, just let things take their course. He owned me in the most intimate way, his grain of sand taking over my belly, and he didn't even know.

His hands moved up, finding the cups of my bra. "I see you went back to wearing underwear," he said against my collarbone.

"Didn't want to shock the southerners," I said.

His fingers moved to the band in the back and I felt it loosen as he unfastened the hook. His mouth found mine again, and my knees wobbled. What was so different about this boy that I really felt things? There was no awkwardness or disappointment or an urge to hurry it up or tell him what to do. I just fell in.

Something slid down one arm, then the other, and with a little gasp against his mouth, I realized he'd pulled my bra off from underneath the T-shirt. It hit the floor with a quiet thump.

"Talent," I whispered against his mouth.

"My fingers know what they like," he said back.

My nipples felt super sensitive against the shirt. He broke the kiss and leaned down, covering my breast with his mouth outside the fabric.

His breath was hot and I clutched at his head, feeling the urgency sizzling through me, more potent than ever before. I wondered if it had to do with the baby, because suddenly I was crazy with it. I could not wait. I needed him now.

I jerked his shirt from the waistband of his jeans. I wanted my hands on him. The hot band of muscle cording up his ribs fed my frenzy.

I reached his chest and reacquainted myself with the hard pecs. I pictured him working out to maintain this gold standard of man chest and my knees weakened a little more.

His breathing against my breast had gotten faster. His hands fumbled with the snap of my jeans, less agile now that the pace was moving from leisurely to breakneck.

I kicked at my high-tops, groaning when they were too stuck to come off easily. Chance noticed my problem and scooped me up to plant me on the bed. "I'll do the honors," he said, and untied my shoes.

He pulled off the sneakers and my socks, his palms wrapped around my ankles to smooth out where the pressure had left a mark.

I relaxed into the bed. The only thing really exposed on me was my belly where my jeans were unbuttoned. The air was cool and I pressed my hand there. I should tell him now, before this went any further.

Then his mouth was on my hand, nudging it out of the way. He kissed his way around my belly button. He paused only to say, "I'd forgotten you were an outie."

He peeled my jeans over my hips and slid them down my legs. My panties were pink, a match for my hair. Chance paused over me. "I like you like this," he said, his eyes raking my body. "T-shirt, no bra, lots of leg, and pretty little underwear."

He bent down and snagged the lace band in his teeth. He tugged on it for a second, then said, "I want to tear these off you."

I didn't say anything, just watched him look at me. He nibbled along my hip and waist, working his way up. He nudged the shirt aside and continued along my ribs. Then he exposed a breast and his lips in that tender spot sent me over a precipice and I cried out, so desperate for him now that nothing was going to distract me.

I heard his shoes hit the floor, but this was distant compared to the hot wetness sending spiraling waves of pleasure through my body. I lay flat on my back, eyes closed, just letting each sensation crash over me.

Chance took his time, bringing the pace back down. His hand slid up my thigh and I opened for him. He teased the satin aside and slid a finger against me. When he slipped inside, my body lifted to meet him with another cry.

"Mmm, keep making those sweet sounds," he said.

I couldn't stop if I wanted to. Every stroke of his hand was another intense push toward the peak I was headed for. I felt tears coming from my eyes, the emotion was so intense.

He moved back down, nipping with little bites as he made his way along my belly. The panties came down and he tossed them. He spread my thighs, and I didn't resist, letting him work me with both his fingers and his mouth.

I couldn't think anymore. I became nothing but the pleasure pulsing from below. I didn't move or touch him or do anything but let it build, tightening, spiraling into a coil only he could release.

His fingers moved deeply inside and when he sucked on the nub, everything let go at once. The orgasm crashed over me, hot and intense, sparkling and colored. I couldn't see or think or hear, but only feel, as though nothing existed but the places where he touched me.

I relaxed against the bed, coming down, and the tears flowed harder, hot and fast. He might notice if I drew attention to them, so I resisted the urge to wipe them away.

Instead, I reached up so I could unbutton this infernal shirt and get it away. When I pushed it off his shoulders, my breath caught just looking at him. I simply hadn't gotten my hands on many men this built before.

I sat up enough that I could press my cheek against his chest. I wanted him close now, skin to skin. I reached for his jeans and unfastened them. He rolled to the side and pushed them off, boxers and all.

I turned in to him. My shirt was still in the way, so I pulled back and whipped it over my head. Now we could lie flush against each other. I felt tears threatening again and groaned inside. *Enough, already*, I told my grain of sand. It helped, as I managed to keep them in check so I didn't get his shoulder all wet.

Chance lay on his back, and I began to memorize the lines and planes of his body. I ran my finger across his chest, down to his belly button, and bumped across his abs.

He was crazy erect and I followed the lines, gripping him tightly, base to end. He dropped his head back and closed his eyes.

This made it even easier to admire him, learning each part of him, bit by bit. How much of the baby would be like him, and how much like me?

I worked him, slowly and leisurely, feeling him pulse and throb beneath my fingers. His arm snaked around me, drawing me even closer, then gradually sliding me more on the bed. He shifted, rolling across me, until eventually he was over me and my knees were drawn up on either side of his thighs.

"A novel approach, for us," he said.

"No sand to get in bad places this time." I slid my palms up his body, belly to shoulders.

"You want me to get a condom this time?" he asked. "No sand to destroy it?"

I shook my head. "It's all right." For a second, I flashed with the women who could have been with him since me, during his travels. Then I just let it go. Such bigger issues to face.

He smoothed my hair back. "I haven't been with anyone since you."

I went still. "Really?"

His face was sober. "Really. Seems like nobody compares to a pink-haired girl cavorting naked on the beach."

I was going to cry again. I held my jaw tight, willing it to go away. Another moment had come to tell him, but I didn't trust my voice. It didn't matter, because he dropped his lips to mine in a soft probing kiss. Gradually his body moved over mine, nudging against me, opening me for him.

I sucked in a breath as he entered, pleasure blasting through me. Everything was so intense, so emotional, amplified by all I knew was still to come. He slid down and then back, starting a slow, easy rhythm.

My hands gripped his shoulders. Once again, I just let go, relaxed into the sensation, the joy. I wished I loved this man, that we were skipping ahead a year, when we were happy and knew each other well and had long-term plans. Then telling him something so dramatic would be a source of great wonder.

He buried his face in my neck, his pace increasing. I held on, feeling his energy and need, tense and coiled above me. I wrapped my legs around him and locked my ankles, holding us together. His breathing sped up, hot on my skin. His primal need broke through and he worked harder, faster, lifting away from me and plunging in.

I cried out as pleasure burst in me, a brutal desire for him that expanded to meet his. He moved his hands beneath me and pulled me up to him, controlling the thrusts, rolling them tight at the end, then pulling back, a tight hard movement that sent my body shrieking into another frenzy.

He didn't slow down and now I was matching him stroke for stroke, our bodies working in tandem, furious and hard. He began to groan and this response to me was the final straw. My body clenched down on his and the rumble of his voice reverberated through my skin as I blasted into another wave of orgasm.

I called out his name, loving the sound of it as it filled the room. He gripped me tight, and I felt the hot spurt flowing inside. I wanted to laugh, imagining the futility of the swimmers discovering their mission had already been accomplished.

I relaxed back on the bed. Chance held himself over me, his mouth soft against my cheek. The sounds of the hotel slowly filtered in. The hum of the lights. A thump from the floor above. The ding of the elevator.

We breathed together in quiet contentment for a while. I knew I had to start talking soon. I couldn't let this go on.

But we were so happy in that moment that I let it be. Maybe we could just have this night, let the words come in the light of tomorrow.

Chance pulled away and lay on his back, curling me up against him. "You all right?"

I realized my cheeks were wet again. But Chance didn't know I was not the least bit a crier normally. "I'm fine," I said.

He stroked my hair. "I'm glad you made it here," he said.

"You think you'll stay here or are you going to get back on the road?" I asked, not sure if I really wanted to hear the answer.

"I guess that depends on you," he said.

My heart hammered. "How is that?"

"You worked pretty hard to find me. I guess you'll eventually let me know why."

I buried my face in his neck. "Maybe just so you could do all this some more."

He laughed, the sound deep in his throat. "I could do this all day."

"Good," I said.

I felt his muscles suddenly go tense. I looked up at him. "What is it?"

"I think we need a little cleanup." He swiped his fingers at a splotch of red on his belly.

My vision blacked out for a minute, then roared back in a full-fledged panic. "Oh my God oh my God oh my God." I leaped from the bed and ran to the bathroom.

"It's okay, darlin'. I'm not afraid of a little girl business," he called out.

I slammed my hand against the light switch and lunged for the toilet paper.

Pink. It came back pink. I dropped it into the toilet and got some more. This, being less mixed with Chance's fluids, was darker. I tossed it too and tried again, pressing hard against me.

This one was bright red.

Tears flowed down my face, hot and furious. The baby. The baby. God.

I didn't know what to do. I didn't know anything. Should I go to a hospital?

I stumbled from the bathroom and scrambled for my purse, yanking my phone out.

Chance sat up on the bed. "You okay, Jenny?"

I didn't answer, frantically tapping a message to Corabelle.

She'd know more than anybody.

*I'm pregnant and bleeding. What do I do?*

The time waiting for a reply was ten years. I thought I might call my mother, but I didn't want to talk on the phone in front of Chance.

Thankfully, Corabelle was close to her phone.

*How long have you known?*

*Four days. I'm four weeks, four days.*

*How did the bleeding start?*

I hesitated, then typed.

*I just had sex.*

Corabelle's reply was a shout.

*WHO WITH?????*

I typed as fast as I could, grateful for autocorrect for once.

*With the baby's father.*

*The singer?*

*Yes.*

Seconds ticked by. I wrote again.

*Corabelle! What do I do?*

Chance knelt by me. "You okay? What's going on? Did I hurt you?"

I shook my head. I couldn't find any words.

Corabelle sent another message.

*Lie down. See if it stops. It might turn brown. I bled several times with Finn, especially after sex. There's a lot of blood going to that part of the body. If it stops, you're okay.*

I bent over the phone, relief flooding through me. So it could be okay. It could be okay.

I lay down right where I was, on the rough carpet of the hotel room floor.

Chance stroked my back. "Baby, talk to me. What's happening?"

I clutched the phone to my chest. I had to say it now. I had to find my voice.

"I'm pregnant," I said.

His hand stilled. "You're what?"

"Pregnant," I said. "I got pregnant that night with you. I found out four days ago. You're the only person I've been with for five months."

He pulled away. I curled up tightly, a shiver coming over me. I needed a blanket, or to move to the bed, but I was afraid to do anything, afraid of more blood, that it wouldn't stop like Corabelle said, but keep coming, a tidal wave, taking my grain of sand out to sea.

I started crying so hard that I shook with it.

"Hey, hey," he said. "Let's figure this out."

I could barely breathe. He wasn't mad or accusing or walking away. He sounded more worried than anything.

"You're cold," he said. "Let's get on the bed."

Just like on the beach and in the limo, he picked me up. I rolled into him, letting him move me to the bed. He tucked the sheets around me and pulled my head against him. "Tell me what's going on."

"I'm not supposed to bleed," I whispered. "I asked my friend Corabelle what was happening. She's had a baby."

"What did she say?"

"That if it stops, I'm okay."

I could feel the next question on his lips. What if it doesn't? But he held it in. We both knew the answer to that.

I didn't know if that would be a relief to him. I didn't want to know.

I just pressed my cheek into him and breathed in the scent of his skin. But my thoughts kept turning. Was I bleeding more? Had it stopped? Should I have stayed home? Did I cause this? I started crying again, hot fat tears that soaked the pillow.

Chance hung on to me. When I kept going, finding some endless well of tears that simply wouldn't stop, he hummed a melody that seemed kind of familiar, then slid into the song that he once told me was his favorite.

*Hush little baby, don't say a word, Papa's gonna buy you a mockingbird.*

At first I cried even harder, for no reason I could figure out, but as the song went on and on, one verse sliding right into the next, eventually my tears slowed down and my breathing evened out.

Then sleep took over and gave me peace.

# 43

## CHANCE

Jenny was asleep.

Her whole pillow was wet and her cheek stuck to my shoulder from the tears. I shifted carefully, taking care not to disturb her, and settled her a little easier alongside me.

My mind tried to wrap around what she'd told me. Pregnant. She'd gotten pregnant from that one night.

Pregnant.

I said it over and over in my head until it sounded foreign, like a made-up word.

Jenny hadn't seemed like the sort of girl who would get caught up in all that, but obviously she planned to keep the baby if she went looking for me. She was so upset at the idea it was in trouble that she clearly must want to have it.

The hotel room was quiet and cold. I should probably have gotten up and shut off the lights, maybe turned down the air-conditioning. But I didn't want to wake up Jenny. If she started bleeding again, she'd really panic.

I didn't know anything about babies. My friends could barely hold on to a girl for any length of time, much less start families.

A kid. Damn. I'd have to get back into concrete work, get something steady, something with benefits.

My traveling days were over.

Jenny's phone buzzed several times, probably her friend asking how she was. I let it be. The world had completely changed for me, but outside this room, nothing was any different than it had been an hour ago.

I looked down at her, the pink dreadlocks draping across her shoulder and the white pillow. I didn't know hardly anything about her. But we were bound together now.

I was used to not sleeping much, but this was the first real bed I'd been in for a while, and I must have dozed off. When I opened my eyes, Jenny was looking at me. We stared at each other a moment, not moving.

Then she said, "How long has it been?"

I glanced behind her at the clock. "About three hours."

She rolled onto her back, slowly and carefully, as if her body was made of glass. "I should check."

I could tell she didn't want to. "You want me to come in there with you?"

She didn't answer. These were intimate things, body and blood, sex and babies, life and death. But here we were, two strangers, sharing them before our time.

Then she nodded. I sat up, holding out my hand to her. She took it and slid evenly over the bed, jarring her body as little as possible. It made me wonder if she could keep that up for nine whole months. Seemed like the little critter needed to be able to handle a bit of motion. But I didn't know anything.

Jenny shifted on the bed so she could drop her feet over the edge. She stood with pained deliberation, as if every movement could bring about a terrible end. With small, gentle steps, she headed for the bathroom. I kept her shaky hand in mine as we walked that short distance together.

The light in there was blindingly bright compared to the lamps in the room. Jenny blinked, standing beside the toilet as she let go of my hand. She drew in a deep breath before reaching for the roll of paper and tearing off a few squares.

I glanced away as she moved to check, not sure if I could handle the answer any more than her. Heartbeats passed. Then the toilet flushed.

"It's okay," she said. "Corabelle was right."

I pulled her into me. She buried her face in my chest. I wrapped my arms around her back and held her close. She breathed, in and out, shuddering occasionally.

Eventually I led her back into the room and the bed. When I had her tucked back in, I adjusted the thermostat and killed all but one of the small lights on a side table.

I slid in next to her between the cool sheets. She didn't move into me, and I knew I was supposed to say something now. I tried to figure out the words, that it'd be okay, we'd figure things out. But I didn't know her, not really, and I couldn't make any assurances. We had a lot to sort out.

Finally, I said, "We'll figure things out tomorrow."

She didn't say anything to that. I reached for her and brought her in close. That's the best I could do for now.

# 44

---

## JENNY

I've had a lot of awkward morning-afters, but this one was the worst.

I woke up to Chance sitting on a chair by the window, showered and dressed, waiting for me to come around. I was embarrassed by my laziness and not sure where we stood.

I stepped gingerly to the bathroom, and checked again for blood, a compulsion I was sure would plague me for a while. Still clear. I sighed in relief and leaned my head against the wall.

I felt too naked, too vulnerable, so I wrapped myself in a big towel and headed back out to the room.

Chance stood up when I appeared. "Feeling okay?" he asked.

"Mostly. I could eat a pizza, though. The whole thing." It wasn't true, but it broke the tension.

He laughed. "Kid is definitely mine, then."

I sank onto the bed. If he could joke about it, then maybe things would be all right.

He rubbed his eyes for a minute like he was tired. "So were you not on the pill after all?"

Blame. I could see it coming like a freight train. "I was. I just…hadn't been with anyone in a long time. And I guess…I missed a few."

I gripped the towel with an iron fist. If he wanted to get mad at me, I'd take it. I deserved whatever he could dish out about this. I had messed up and dragged him right into my disaster.

"I don't reckon there's any point in worrying about what's past," he said. "Just figure out where to go from here."

I loosened my death grip on the towel. "Last night you acted like you might be interested in going back to California. Is that still true?" My pulse hammered in my throat.

"My biggest concern is getting a job at this point," he said. "The kid'll need health insurance and some stability."

So things had changed. I swallowed around the giant lump in my throat. "Are you going to stay here in Tennessee, then?"

He moved closer, to the other corner of the bed. But not next to me. "What were you planning on doing?" he asked.

"I may have a job. I'm going in to talk to them next week."

"Are they going to be all right with you being pregnant?"

I shrugged. "Not planning to tell them. I don't have to. My mom is going to help with the baby."

"So you've got a few pieces figured out."

"Not really. It's only been a few days. I'm making it up as I go along."

"This is a hell of a thing," he said.

"I'm sorry. I didn't mean for it to happen." My eyes burned, and now that I knew the grain of sand was okay, I told it to lay off the waterworks, please.

"When are you going back?" Chance asked.

"Classes start again Monday," I said. "I'll fly back Sunday unless I need to be here."

"So we have a few days."

"We do."

He stood up. "Well, let's get you fed, although I'm not sure we can rustle up a pizza at 9 a.m."

I managed a smile at that. I stood up and headed to my suitcase. "Toast and juice are fine."

I snatched up another set of jeans and a shirt. He hadn't run off, and he hadn't gotten mad. I had to hope that things were going to work out all right.

Chance and I headed for breakfast at a little diner up the street, walking along the sunny street with flowers blooming in the open circles around every tree.

"Chattanooga really is beautiful," I said.

"Yeah, I actually started realizing that on my way back yesterday," Chance said. "I've seen a lot of places now. I did like LA, though. The beach there was different than the one in Virginia."

"I haven't been to the Atlantic," I said. "I've been a West Coast girl all my life."

"The air smells different," Chance said. "It wasn't the same."

His face darkened when he said it, and I wondered what had happened on the beach in Virginia.

"I liked your mom," I said. "She seemed real old-fashioned."

He laughed. "Well, she's definitely not a modern woman. She does look after people, though. She did all right by me and Hannah after my dad left."

I reached out to squeeze his hand. "Your mother mentioned that."

"We did okay, me and Mom and Hannah." But his face darkened again, and I knew he was thinking about his sister.

"I met her, you know," I said quietly. "Hannah."

"Charlie told me you got dragged to her room."

"It was all right. She's a very pretty girl."

His jaw twitched. "She's never going to wake up. My mother keeps her on life support."

"The doctors said that?"

"Long time ago. I never thought it would go on this long. When I left—"

He stopped talking abruptly and dropped my hand. "I don't want to talk about this."

"It's okay," I said quickly. "We don't have to."

We continued along the sidewalk in silence until we came up to a hole-in-the-wall diner with a glass front. "This is the place," he said.

"Looks fine," I said, although just the thought of bacon grease and fried eggs made me queasy.

When he opened the door, the smell turned my stomach upside down. I refused to let it get to me, though, and ducked beneath his arm to go inside.

Booths filled the windows and a row of stools lined a long counter.

"Seat yourself!" a lady with a puff of cotton candy gray hair told us, a coffeepot in one hand and a plate in the other. The waitresses here all wore pink-striped uniforms. The youngest couldn't have been a day under sixty.

We slid into opposite sides of a booth. "A place like this would be super trendy in LA," I said. "You'd probably find the most high-dollar actors in it."

"Actually, I went to one while I was there, the morning after the party. With Dylan Wolf."

"Seriously? Dylan Wolf?" I couldn't hold back my surprise.

"Yeah, apparently he's the one who got the Sonic Kings that gig. I guess I owe him one."

I guessed we both did.

One of the waitresses dropped two coffee cups on the table and filled them without asking a single question. I looked at the mug, frowning.

"What, no coffee for the kid?" he asked, a lazy smile breaking across his face.

"I honestly have no idea," I said. "But I have a feeling it's out."

Chance waved the waitress back over. "We got a pregnant lady over here," he said, and grinned when the woman looked me over with a motherly gesture. "Bring her something good for the baby."

"You still feeling sick, honey?" she asked. "You don't look like you have an extra ounce on you."

"Pretty much," I said. "Just the smell of bacon is making me never want to eat again."

"Poor little mite," she said, and patted my shoulder. "I'll bring you some plain toast and jelly, a soft-scrambled egg, and some juice."

She took off without even asking Chance what he wanted.

"I see where I stand in the picture," he said.

I relaxed again. This roller coaster was making me crazy, but I would hold on to the good moments with both hands.

"So tell me about your family," Chance said. "Sounds like your mother is close by."

I nodded. "I was born in San Diego, and she still lives there. My dad moved to Florida. They divorced when I was fairly young." I, too, hesitated on the hard part. "After my little brother died."

Chance's eyes snapped to meet mine. "What happened?"

"He had seizures all his life. They couldn't control them. It was pretty scary as a kid, watching him have them all the time. Then when he was eight, he had a big one, a bad one. They got him breathing and all again, but his brain was shot. Mom and Dad had to take him off life support. I think that's what got to them. It's not an easy thing to recover from."

Chance pulled one of the mugs of coffee close to him and stared into the steam. "How old were you?"

"About ten." I took in a deep breath. "I don't really talk about this; not even my friends know about Bryan. It's not easy for me to talk about."

"Were you close to him?"

"When we were little. Then I got scared a lot. It wasn't easy to see him struggle." I picked up the napkin rolled around the silverware and fiddled with the paper band.

"Must have been hard."

"It was. And I have a lot of regrets. So I don't talk about him."

Chance looked up again then and met my gaze. "Why would you have any regrets?"

"My parents wanted me to be there when they…when they turned off the machines. They thought it would be good for me to say good-bye when it was time. For closure. But I wouldn't do it. I threw a tantrum. I refused."

"You were just a kid."

"I know." I plucked the paper ribbon off the silverware, no longer able to hold Chance's intense gaze. "But I should have been there. I should have been more brave."

The waitress returned and slid a plate in front of me. "Take it slow," she said. "Let me know if you need anything else." She took off again, still not taking Chance's order.

We both gave a nervous laugh. "I can spare a triangle of toast," I said.

"Stealing food from my own baby," he said. "Now what kind of man would I be?"

I picked up a piece, simultaneously starving and queasy, and took a timid bite. When it seemed okay, I added a sip of juice.

"I guess I could bring her back and order a full breakfast and just turn it over to you," I said.

He shrugged. "She'll figure it out." Then his face got serious. He looked out the window, watching people walk by.

My heart squeezed. Something was going on with him. I wasn't sure if it was about the baby, or my brother, or his sister.

His voice was scratchy when he spoke again. "I think maybe I left town so that I wouldn't have to be here when it happened."

My appetite fled. I knew he meant Hannah. I reached across the table for his hand. "It's okay. I get it."

He shook his head. "It's not okay. I'm a grown man. I should be able to deal with this."

I squeezed his fingers. "What do you think is getting you about it? Letting her go?"

He looked up at me, and his face was so haunted that my sympathy surged, and I couldn't stand it, but slid out of my side of the booth and moved over to his. I laid my head on his shoulder and wrapped my arms around his waist. "Tell me, Chance. I'll get it. I'll know exactly what you mean."

He hesitated. And I knew this was our moment. It was time to do all the things couples do way before they ended up where we were. Time to learn about each other.

# 45

---

## CHANCE

I didn't imagine ever telling this story to a soul. The only people who needed to know it had been there, and I hadn't really intended on having them in my life ever again.

But here I was, in a diner with this girl I barely knew but who already carried my kid. And I was going to tell her.

Her hair tickled my neck. She had a death grip on me, like she alone could hold me up. Maybe she could. She'd already found out about a baby all on her own, and gone on a wild-hair trip to find the man who'd done it, with no idea what she'd find on the other end. She had spunk.

"It was six months ago," I said. "And everybody was doing their typical stupid redneck shit, drinking beer and having pissing contests over every subject imaginable."

We had all sat on the dropped-down tailgates of our trucks. It rained a lot that week, and the fields behind the old stadium were a mud pit.

Me and Redmond and about six others were all out there. My then-girlfriend Barbie was with us, and a couple other girls. Carl was cutting donuts and whooping it up. He'd already clipped the lowered tailgate of Redmond's pickup and they'd come to blows over it.

Charlie had stopped by and yelled at us for being reckless and stupid. When she left, everybody laughed at the old lady, even though she was barely thirty to our mid-twenties. But she felt older, and certainly acted older. It was harmless fun, mostly.

Things took a turn when somebody showed up with two bottles of Canadian whiskey. We passed cups around and soon nobody was really sober enough to even get their key in the ignition.

"We're gonna have to sleep out here," Carl had said, falling back in the bed of his pickup. "I can't find my own dick."

"There's reasons for that," Barbie had said, all serious, and I'd snapped to attention, even as drunk as I was.

"How'd you know that, darlin'?" I asked her, still thinking we were joking.

Instead of dissolving in a fit of giggles, the way she would have if she was ribbing, she shrugged and took a long drink, looking pissed.

My blood boiled, realizing she'd slept with that asshole. Carl was newish in town, so it hadn't been that long ago.

I jumped down into the mud and stumbled my way over to Carl, aiming to punch his goddamn lights out. But Pete had gotten between us, saying we ought to settle this like civilized folks and have a race in the mud.

"Let's see who can hold on to the wheel long enough in a

360," he said.

So Carl and I got in our trucks and trundled farther out in the field.

I didn't even notice my sister, Hannah, had showed up in her little yellow Beetle as I rolled down the window and listened for the shout from Pete to get started.

The world spun even harder as I revved the engine and hauled ass across the ground, building up enough speed to start spinning.

As I moved into the first turn, the world slowed down. The wheel was solid beneath my hands. The truck made a perfect circle, dragging through the wet dirt smoothly, like the way my mother used to stir frosting in a bowl.

Both our engines were roaring. I could vaguely hear the shouting of our friends across the field. I couldn't see much of anything with the mud slinging across the windshields. I could only see out the driver's side, since that one was down. I hoped Carl had thought to keep his open, or else we'd slam into each other if he was totally blind.

A cold slice of fear almost made me take my foot off the accelerator. I was slamming the gas and the brake simultaneously to keep the hard turn in the spin, jerking the wheel based on experience and feel, since I couldn't see anything but the occasional flash of headlights from the cluster of cars up near the road, where our friends waited. The glimpse through the open window was brief, and enough mud was slinging across me that I had to resist the urge to roll it up.

During one of the spins, I saw a bright spot of yellow as my headlights crossed it. My mind didn't register what it was until much too late.

I heard screams and a sickening crunch. I thought maybe I'd hit Carl after all, but my truck didn't stop, didn't change position. I kept my spin going, thinking maybe it was some sort of ploy, but then it happened again, a terrible crash and the sound of glass breaking. Somebody was hitting somebody else. Had Carl spun into one of the buildings?

I let off the gas and eased the brake, letting the truck roll to a stop. I turned on my wipers, but they just smeared everything. I didn't want to get out if Carl was still spinning. He could run my ass right over.

I was facing the wrong way to see anything, my driver-side window looking out on the bank of trees at the far end of the lot. There was a lot of screaming and shouting, though, so I unbuckled and hoisted myself up to sit on the ledge of the open window.

And I saw it.

My sister's little yellow car, battered on both sides. Carl's truck, smashed in from front tire to back bumper.

People were running, slipping, falling in the mud. Redmond was on his cell phone, shouting.

Carl was still in his truck, holding his face, but moving.

I couldn't see my sister in her car.

My head cleared instantly, and I slid through the window and out into the mud. I slid and stumbled, almost crawling through the deep trenches we'd made in our spins.

The driver-side door of Hannah's car wouldn't open. I kicked at it, but it was crumpled and locked into place. I scrambled to the other side, and when it wouldn't open either, I started kicking the window. It was already cracked.

It was too dark to see into the car and the webbing in the glass blocked my view, but Hannah had to be in there. And she wasn't coming out. My ears roared with the slamming of my heart.

"I've got a crowbar," Redmond yelled at me and pushed me out of the way. About that time, somebody managed to drive their car close up and shine headlights on the scene. I wanted to peer in, but backed away as Redmond lifted the crowbar over the rear window.

The first blow cracked the glass into a brilliant web. The second made a hole, and he knocked the rest out.

"Careful going in," somebody said as he crawled in the back.

"Jesus," I heard him say, and I was about to follow him in when I heard the locks pop. I jerked open the passenger door.

Hannah lay crumpled against her door, sagging like a rag doll. I turned her head to me, but her eyes were closed. She didn't move at all. Blood trickled out her ears.

"Wake up, Hannah! Talk to me!" I shouted just inches from her face.

"I've called for an ambulance," Redmond said. He was kneeling in the backseat.

I frantically felt her throat for a pulse, but couldn't feel anything. I leaned down, pressing my head against her chest.

I straight-out cried when I felt the slow steady drum of her heart. "She's alive," I choked out.

Her hand was limp and cool when I took it in mine. "You'll be all right, baby sister. You'll be fine."

"Don't move her," Redmond said. "Let them figure out how to get her out the best way."

I nodded, clutching her hand. A couple bits of glass were stuck in her hair and I picked them out. Everything around us was shattered, all the windows webbed with cracks, a few chinks out and scattered on the dash.

"Did Carl hit her?" I asked.

"Yeah," Redmond said. "She drove straight out there for some reason. I guess he couldn't see her. He slammed right into her, knocked her sideways, then hit her again on the turn."

The airbag was deployed and hanging limp. "Only works once," I said.

He nodded grimly.

The air burst with color as the first responders approached, their sirens a brutal whine. Redmond climbed back out the window, but I didn't move, waiting for them to arrive.

"Take it easy," I said when a man opened the driver's door, jostling her.

"Is she conscious?" he asked.

"No," I said. "But she has a pulse."

He checked her himself and motioned for another guy to come forward with a stretcher. They took a board from it and slid part of it behind her. "Come on out so we can get her information," they said to me.

I obeyed, ducking out of the car and hurrying around. A third guy was over by Carl's truck, talking to him.

My vision went red then, and without even thinking, I mucked over to his door and pushed the guy out of the way.

"You motherfucker," I said, and punched his bloody face.

The uniformed man grabbed my arms and dragged me down. Headlights flashed into my eyes as I hit the mud. I fought him off, but he was trained and strong.

There were more shouts and people rushed from all around. I

saw more colored lights and felt the bite of something hard around my wrists. I managed to turn my head and saw a different uniform, dark blue, the police, I reckoned.

Shit.

"You're not doing your sister any good like this," a voice said, and after a minute, I recognized it and relaxed. Don Hopper had lived three doors down since I was born. He was a longtime police officer in Chattanooga.

"He…hit her," I said through gritted teeth, turning my face to keep it out of the slick ripples of mud.

"I know it," he said. "We'll sort it all out." His voice was soothing and calm. "Let him out of these cuffs," he told somebody else.

My hands were released. I pushed up to my knees. I was covered in a solid inch of mud from ankle to shoulder.

"I want to go with her," I said.

"Not the way you're looking right now," Don said. "Get yourself cleaned up. I'll call your mama and you can meet her up at Erlanger."

"Why are they taking her all the way there?"

"She's under eighteen. That's where pediatric cases go." He walked me over to his squad car. "Looks to me like you need a driver. You got somebody here to take you or you want to ride with me?"

I squinted my eyes in the glare of the headlights to find Barbie. I spotted her, over by Carl's truck, hanging on to his arm. Great. So that was going on right now, it seemed. I didn't have the time to even wonder why she hadn't bothered to break it off with me. It didn't matter. I was done with all of them.

"I'll take him," Redmond said.

Don sized him up for a second. "How much you had to drink?"

"I skipped the whiskey. I'm all right."

Don nodded. "Take him home, get him cleaned up. Then to Erlanger." He turned away.

The ambulance started bumping across the rough terrain of the muddy field. I winced with every bounce of the wheels. Hannah was in there, but at that moment, as bad as it seemed, I felt like she'd be okay. I thought I'd go and see her and find her lying in white sheets, a bandage on her head, complaining about how long it would be before she got home.

I was wrong.

# 46

## CHANCE

Jenny hadn't eaten much of anything, and now the food was all cold. I reached across and grabbed a bit of toast and showed it to her. "That waitress is gonna blame me if you don't eat this."

She turned her face toward my arm a moment, like she was going to refuse, then shifted away. She took the bread from me and took a bite.

There didn't seem to be much else to say. She knew the worst thing about me. Maybe now that she knew, she wouldn't want me around the baby at all.

"I'm kind of no good," I said. "You might be better off with nothing but a support check from cross country."

She set the crust of her toast on the plate. "Please don't say that. It's not your fault this happened."

"I was the one out there drinking and acting stupid. She came out there because of me."

"Why DID she go out there? For one, why did she show up at

all? For two, why did she drive into the field and not stay with the friends?"

These were questions that had bothered me for half a year. "She found out from my mother that we were out there. Mom sent her to save my soul from eternal damnation over the evils of drinking. She used to come herself. When Hannah got old enough to drive, she started sending her. Probably in hopes that Hannah wouldn't turn out just as wild."

"Was Hannah like her? Religious and stuff?"

"Yes and no. She was Mom's perfect little church girl. But she had her own life aside from that. She just wanted to please Mom in a way I never cared about."

"Sounds like she was a lovely girl."

"I don't know what to do about her. Lying there like that was just about her worst nightmare. I know this. Mother knows this. I don't know why she lets it go on and on."

"Maybe she's just like you," I said. "And me. Unable to let her go."

I hadn't realized this might be the thing Mom and I had in common. That she was just hiding it under the Bible.

The waitress stopped by and frowned at Jenny's plate. "Poor little mite."

She seemed to finally notice I hadn't ordered. "Two eggs, bacon, ham, and toast?" she asked me.

"That sounds fine. Over easy."

The waitress nodded. "I couldn't bring anything that might smell up the table and upset her stomach," she said.

Huh. That actually made sense.

Jenny laughed a little. "I don't know nothin' about birthin' no babies."

"I guess we'll figure it out together," I told her.

The waitress smiled. "That's all any of us do."

Jenny stayed close against me as we finished out the breakfast. I liked the feel of her next to me. Sometimes I thought about her belly, and what was swimming in there.

One thing I knew for sure. It was time to grow the hell up.

# 47

---

## JENNY

Chance drove me around Chattanooga for the day, showing me the river running through the city and some of the parks along the shore. We had lunch at a sandwich shop, much easier for me to manage without all the intense smells of a restaurant with hot food, and talked about our pasts.

I learned he had gone to junior college and hated it, then worked in construction. All along, he'd played guitar, sometimes being part of one temporary band or another. They didn't play a lot of gigs, and things always fell apart when somebody wouldn't practice, or somebody got a girlfriend who took too much time. But something else always came along.

He found out I had started coloring my hair in high school because some fool boy called my eyes "the most boring color ever stuck on a girl." My nickname became BW for black and white.

My mother, worried because I had become this sulky sad girl who holed up in her room with punk music, moved across town to a more liberal school without a dress code so I could change my hair and wear whatever I wanted.

He was impressed that she was willing to do that for me.

We wound up at the house where he'd lived before he left town that night. Redmond was there, and Pete. The short guy, Ace, who clearly didn't care for Chance, took off to go drinking with friends.

Redmond and Pete brought a bunch of beer out and plunked it on the scratched-up coffee table. When Redmond tried to hand me one, I waved it away. Then when Chance did the same, Redmond shook his head. "What's happened to everybody?"

Pete popped the top off his bottle with his boot. "They decided not to go down our highway to hell," he said.

I could tell Chance used to talk and act just like these boys. But he'd changed. I tried to imagine leaving everything behind and striking out with nothing but your guitar and some songs in your head. I couldn't see it.

"So what's your plan, bro?" Redmond asked Chance. "You want me to kick out Pete so you can have your room back?"

"Nah," Chance said. "I haven't decided if I'm staying."

Redmond aimed his bottle at me. "You see what an indecisive loser this guy is? Run, girl. Run fast."

I smiled at them. I was waiting on Chance to decide things myself. I wasn't sure I wanted to move to Tennessee after graduation, since I had a job and help with the baby in San Diego. But I remembered what my mom told me before I left. Babies take a long time to arrive. I had time to figure it out.

"I'm going to grab some more of my things," Chance said. "You want to hang here with these delinquents a sec?"

"Sure," I said. I guessed this meant he was going to leave with me again. I tried to suppress my hope that we'd work something out together, but it wouldn't let go. This was no fairy-tale situation, but I could still see the pretty version of the picture, a baby in a pink crib with ruffles all around, me standing over, and Chance playing his guitar and singing her to sleep.

"So whatcha do over there in Cali?" Pete asked.

"I'm about to finish my degree," I said.

"Job market is crap for most things," Pete said.

"I have a few connections," I said. "I think I'll get by."

"Like that movie director dude?" Pete asked.

Redmond nudged him.

"What?" Pete elbowed him back. "I can't ask questions before this girl runs off with our sensitive boy again?" He laughed.

I didn't really want to tell anybody else about Frankie, so I just kept quiet. If these guys thought I was some sort of Hollywood whore, so be it.

"Have you met a lot of famous people?" Redmond asked.

"Sure," I said. I rattled off a long list of names.

"Whooee," Pete said. "If I went to Cali, you think you could get me into one of those parties?"

I didn't bother to answer that. People dragging in gawkers was a source of annoyance for the industry people who attended the premieres and after-parties.

Chance popped back in the living room, and I couldn't be more relieved to see him. He had a duffel bag that looked to be pretty stuffed. This also made me feel better.

"Ready?" he asked.

I could not jump up from my chair fast enough.

"Aww, man, you just got here," Pete said. "I was worming my way into an invitation to a Hollywood party."

"In your dreams, man," Chance said. He took my hand. "Let's go."

"Hey, before you go," Redmond said. "You might want to check your messages. You haven't answered any of mine since last night." He looked at Chance pointedly. "But Charlie's been trying to get you. She finally bit the bullet and wrote me to track you down."

Chance frowned. "Is something going on?"

"Wouldn't say. Probably just wants to bitch at you some more."

Chance tugged me toward the door. "Thanks."

"Your funeral," he said, then realized what he'd said and frowned.

We went outside and loaded into Chance's truck. He pulled his phone out. "I didn't want to talk to anybody, so I ignored it all," he said.

I hadn't paid a lot of attention to mine either, although I had sent a message to Corabelle that I was okay and one to Mom saying I had found Chance. Whatever follow-up questions they might have had, I ignored.

"What is it?" I asked, a hollow feeling in my chest.

"Apparently some infection is going around the facility where Hannah is," he said.

"Charlie mentioned that yesterday. She made us wash our hands and put on masks."

Chance's face was grim in the glow of the light of his screen. "Hannah is spiking fevers. They think she has it."

"They can give her medicine, right?"

"For the fever, I'm sure. But Charlie always warned us that this would happen. When you're on a ventilator, this is bad. Real bad."

He fired up his truck. "We're going."

I held on to the seat belt as we roared out into the night.

# 48

---

## CHANCE

The entrance to the facility was locked, and I tapped my boot impatiently as I waited for someone inside to buzz me in.

Charlie met me at the door. She glanced briefly over at Jenny, then walked behind us as I hurried across the visitors' area. I wanted to kick myself for not visiting Hannah the minute I got in town. I should have done that.

"She's in the same wing, but a different room," Charlie said. "We moved her about three months ago."

Her words made me feel worse. All this time I hadn't been here for my sister. Now we had a crisis.

Jenny snagged my wildly swinging hand and squeezed, like she knew what I was thinking.

When we got to the hall, Hannah's door was open.

An aide stood just inside. "Scrub up," she said, pointing toward a sink. Then she looked at Jenny. "Family only."

Jenny stayed out in the hall as I walked in to wash my hands.

I accepted the blue mask she handed me after. I stuck it on, turning to take in the scene.

My mother was there, holding Hannah's hand. A nurse in gray scrubs was pushing buttons on a monitor by the head of the bed.

Hannah looked so much different than she had when I left. Her arms were thinner, but her neck was wide, like it had swelled. Her hair was thin and clung to her head. I had a hard time connecting this person with the girl before the accident, both serious and silly, always dashing around in a hurry.

Nobody talked. We watched the nurse write on a clipboard. Finally I asked, "Why aren't we taking her to a hospital?"

She turned around. "You must be Chance." She jotted something else down and set the clipboard back on top of the monitor. "Let's go out in the hall."

I followed her out. Jenny and Charlie were still out there. The corridor was dim for nighttime.

"I don't think you all can handle this here," I said.

"Chance," the woman said. "I was led to believe you were not in agreement with your mother about your sister's continued use of life support."

My eyes bored into hers, but she held the gaze, unflinching. She was right.

I looked past her at the wall, my jaw tight. "I don't know anything anymore," I said. "Why isn't she someplace with real docs?"

We moved a little farther away from the door. "We will not transport her to an acute care hospital until we know what the wishes of the family are."

"My mom is her guardian," I said. "That's why Hannah is still hooked up to begin with."

"We can file a motion in the courts. If there is a conflict in the family, and the new therapies we have to introduce due to the illness reduce her quality of life even further, we can probably get a judge to issue an order."

My eyes met Jenny's, then Charlie's. "My mother will never speak to me again."

The nurse nodded. "All right, then. I'll go ahead and get the doctor on call to order treatment."

She headed off down the hall. I turned to Charlie. "What happens if they don't treat her?"

"She gets pneumonia and dies," she said. "It would be over."

"Will she be in pain?" I asked.

Charlie drew in a deep breath. "We got that brain death certification within days of the accident, Chance. She can't feel anything."

I remembered being sick as a kid, having a fever and feeling like hell. Shivering and miserable, half out of it. How could Hannah not be feeling something?

I went back to the room. My mother had pulled a chair close to the bed and was humming some little song.

My rage started to peak. This was totally wrong, all of it. This was not the way it was supposed to be.

"Chance, be a dear and wet a towel for your sister. I'm going to put it on her forehead until they can get her something for the fever."

I didn't move. "We're not at home, and she doesn't just have a little cold."

Mom didn't look at me. "That's fine. I'll get it myself."

"Mother, look at me. She's gone. She's been gone for months. We can't just let her sit here and be sick."

Mom continued to look at Hannah's face. "It is not to us to question God's timeline."

I wanted to punch the wall. "It wasn't exactly God who sent her out there to find me, now, was it?"

She reached over and tucked a stray corner of the sheet beneath Hannah's arm. "I've asked forgiveness for my part in this," she said quietly. "Have you?"

That's when I realized I didn't care at all if she hated me. I was going to end this. For Hannah. For me. For all of us to move on with our lives. I spun around and hurried out the door.

# 49

## JENNY

I sat on the bed of the hotel room while Chance showered. We hadn't really slept, getting updates on Hannah from Charlie. The doctor had ordered a fever reducer and an antibiotic and both had been administered. It seemed like her condition was going to settle.

Chance came out, and my breath caught. He wore dark jeans, a button-down shirt, and a sports jacket. It was a huge difference from the T-shirts, and I couldn't help but admire the fit.

"I'm sorry all this is happening now," Chance said. "Sometimes I don't understand the laws of the universe."

I stood up and brushed along the sleeves of his jacket, just to touch him. "I'm glad I could be here."

"I hate deserting you," he said. "You want me to take you somewhere? The aquarium is a nice place to visit."

I shook my head. "I don't think I could focus on something like that right now."

He stepped forward and kissed the top of my head. We had

already begun to feel like a couple somehow, maybe through the tough experiences we'd been flung into so quickly. This all made my old life of hooking up with college boys and going to parties seem ridiculously far away, like a whole different world.

"You can call on Redmond to pick you up if you need to go anywhere far. Otherwise, there's a fair amount within walking distance." He looked down at my belly and for a minute I thought he was going to put his hand there. "Take care of yourself," he said. "I don't think I'll be more than a couple hours."

"Good luck," I told him. "I hope the lawyer can help."

"He says he thinks he can," he said. "Even though I'll have to sell my truck to pay for him."

"Trucks are overrated," I said, trying to force a smile. "You can get a Smart Car in Cali, be environmentally friendly."

"God, a clown car." He almost smiled back. Then he bent down and brushed his lips against mine. "I'll be back soon."

I watched him leave the room and carefully close the door. I sank back onto the bed. Of all the things I expected to happen when we found each other, this hadn't even entered the equation.

I took time to call my mom and tell her about Chance, and his mother, and the situation with Hannah.

"Oh, baby, I don't wish that on any family. There's really no hope?"

"I don't think so." I wished I could be sitting at the counter in her house instead of thousands of miles away. Funny, up until a few days ago, she hadn't been anyone I would have confided in, and now she knew my most secret everythings.

We talked a while longer about what I should be eating and she said she'd make my first appointment for me with her ob-gyn. "He delivered you," she said. "He'll love delivering the next round."

"Mom?" I asked. "If it's a boy, do you think I should name him Bryan?"

She was quiet for a minute, then said, "I think that's for you and Chance to work out."

My phone beeped with a text, probably Corabelle or Tina wanting updates. "I gotta go, Mom. I think I'm still coming home Sunday, but I'll let you know."

"Okay, baby girl. Try to eat."

"I will."

I hung up and exchanged some easy texts with my friends about Chance. I told Corabelle she could tell Tina about the baby. I didn't want to do it from a long distance, and I wasn't sure if Tina would handle it as well as Corabelle. But they both had kids in their lives now, Corabelle with Gavin's four-year-old son, Manuel, and Tina with Darion's young sister.

After that, I must have fallen asleep, because my phone buzzing woke me. I glanced at the clock. It had been five hours since Chance left.

Panic sizzled through me. Had something gone wrong? I snatched up my phone to check the message. It was Redmond.

*Coming to fetch you. Hannah's taken a bad turn. Might be time.*

I scrambled to put on the maxi dress I'd worn the first day, the only thing that seemed fitting for going back up to the home. I glanced in the mirror. My pink hair was so bright. I picked up the enormous hat, but that seemed disrespectful somehow. Mrs. McKenzie hadn't seen me last night since I had to wait in the hall, but she was about to get an eyeful of my dreadlocks.

I guessed she'd have to get used to it.

Redmond was waiting out front when I managed to make it downstairs. His face was grim.

I shut the truck door. "What happened?"

"She already had pneumonia, apparently. Her lung collapsed."

"Is she still at the home?"

"Nope, they moved her to the hospital."

My heart thumped. This family had been through so much. But then, so had mine.

"Why is life so hard?" I asked.

"Beats the hell out of me," Redmond said. "But the big guy upstairs ought to cut these people a little bit of slack."

We sped through town, and I was glad, so relieved, that nothing had happened to the baby the other night. I couldn't imagine piling that on top of all these other things the McKenzies were going through.

# 50

## CHANCE

The ICU waiting room was quiet. My mother sat in one corner with her Bible in her lap, and two of her church lady friends on either side.

Charlie sat by me.

I hadn't answered the buzz of my phone while meeting with the lawyer. Only when I got out did I get the frantic message from Charlie that Hannah was being sent back to Erlanger with a collapsed lung.

She had gone into cardiac arrest twice in the ambulance. My mother was with her, and each time instructed them to resuscitate. Hearing this made my anger spike into the red zone. Nobody should have to go through all this. Her body was done. They had to let it rest.

The older women talked in hushed tones in their corner. Charlie wore her work scrubs, sitting stiffly by me like a guard. Funny who became your friend in situations like this. She was the one I had counted on all this time.

Jenny and Redmond walked in. Jenny immediately sat right beside me and took my hand. Her pink hair was wild and chaotic. I glanced over at my mother. She saw the hair, looked at me, and shrugged. At least she wasn't going to make a fuss.

"Sorry," Jenny whispered. "The hat didn't seem right."

"I don't think it's high on her priority list right now," I said.

"Is your sister stable?" Jenny asked.

"We don't know," I said. "We haven't been updated since she got here."

She laid her head on my shoulder, and I had to admit, it felt good having her here. I kissed the back of her hand. I caught my mom watching us, a calm pleased expression on her face. She resumed her hushed conversation with the women.

Redmond sat opposite us. "You want me to hang out here?" he asked.

"Nah," I said. "Thanks for bringing Jenny, though."

"No problem, man," he said. He nodded at the church ladies politely, jutted his chin at Charlie, and took off.

The room got quiet. Nobody else was in here but a woman knitting by the door.

"You feeling okay today?" I asked Jenny.

"Perfect," she said. "Just talked to my mom and hung out."

A woman in regular clothes came into the room but didn't sit down. "Hannah McKenzie's family?" she asked.

I stood up. "We're all here."

"Will everyone come with me?" She noticed the women with my mother. "They are welcome if it is all right with you."

Jenny and I followed the woman first. I guessed we were going somewhere for an update on Hannah's condition.

We turned down the hall and entered a conference room with a long table. We'd been here before, after the accident, when they told us about her EEGs and CAT scans. My mother had sat near the end, announcing that she was having her family physician come in to assess Hannah before any decisions were made. This had set off the whole chain of events that led to her staying on the machines.

The lawyer had told me that since we had the two signatures we needed about her brain death, getting a judge to order the machines off wouldn't be hard. I had the doctors on my side, and in cases like this, they tended to understand how a parent could have trouble letting go.

My big problem was how to tell my mother what I was doing before she was subpoenaed to court.

I was torn about it. None of it was good. None of it.

The woman stood at the front of the table. "My name is Regina. I'm a patient information specialist. I'm going to bring in Dr. Foster, who coordinated care for Hannah when she arrived."

She left the room.

The tension was palpable. I resented the presence of the church ladies, who I didn't recognize. Charlie had stayed behind, so I was outnumbered.

"I think this would be a good time for a prayer," one of the women said.

I banged my hand on the table. "Well, I don't," I said, a little harsher than I intended.

My mother laid a hand on each of the women. "Martha, Ellen, it might be best for you to wait for us back in the waiting room.

Thank you so much for being here for me."

The ladies stood. "Of course, Carol Ann," one said. "We'll be there." She gave me a withering look as she headed out the door.

When they were gone, my mother said, "I still don't think a prayer was a bad idea."

I didn't answer. Jenny laid her hand on my forearm and squeezed.

Regina returned with two doctors, one man and one woman. The woman had a surgical mask dropped down, still tied around her neck.

"I'm Dr. Foster," the man said, shaking all our hands. "This is Dr. Perkins. She is our pulmonary specialist."

The three of them sat down, and Regina opened a file folder and took out a pen to take notes.

"When Hannah arrived, she was in respiratory distress," Dr. Foster said. "She had gone into cardiac arrest twice en route, and significant measures were taken to restart her heart rhythms."

He paused. "Unfortunately, after six months on a ventilator, Hannah's lungs and diaphragm were not strong enough for this, even with the breathing assistance in place. One lung had already collapsed, and by the time our team arrived to assess her, the other one had collapsed also. We administered several measures to inflate her lungs and restore oxygen to her body, but those measures did not succeed."

His expression was grim. "Hannah died about thirty minutes ago. I am very sorry for your loss."

Silence blanketed the room. I stared at this man who had delivered these words. It didn't quite sink in. Then I heard a keening cry from the end of the room. My mother had her hands over her mouth and shook from her sobs.

Jenny nudged me, and I got up and walked over to her, standing behind her with my hands on her shoulders.

"I'm very sorry," the female doctor said. "Let us know if you have any questions."

"Thank you for what you did for Hannah," I said.

The two doctors left the room.

Regina passed a box of tissues to Jenny, who took one and sent the box down to my mother. Then Regina said, "They have moved Hannah to a private room. You can go see her now."

My mom made no move to get up, so I bent and helped her to her feet. She leaned on me, heavy, stumbling, as if she carried too much weight for her to bear.

We followed Regina down the hall, past the waiting area, and to a small room. Hannah lay on a hospital bed just slightly inclined. The tubes were out of her mouth now and her hair splayed all across the pillow.

"My baby!" Mom said, and left me to rush to her side. She clasped Hannah's hands between her own. "My sweet, sweet baby."

I stood at the foot of the bed. My head buzzed with so many things. My sister as a little girl, riding her scooter down the street. The way she hero-worshipped me, even though I was no role model for anybody.

We'd failed her, all of us. And now here we were.

My mom rocked and held her hand, crying softly. "You were the most beautiful girl in the world," she said. "My most beautiful perfect angel."

She smoothed back Hannah's hair. "Your father will never know what he missed."

Anger surged through me at that. Where was that asshole anyway? I knew Mom had tried to contact him yet again after the accident, finding some social media account that looked like him. But he never responded. Maybe I'd hire that lawyer anyway, track him down, make him suffer for deserting Hannah.

My mind went a million angry directions, wanting to blame everybody for all of this. Most of all me. I never should have been out there, mud running. Never should have lost my temper over a good-for-nothing woman who was screwing one of my friends.

I wanted out of Tennessee. I never wanted to come back.

Just like my father.

Shit.

My mother held out her hand. "Come here, my boy," she said.

I stepped around the bed and took her wet fingers in mine. I didn't have anything to say. Hannah seemed lit up from above from this angle. I looked up at the recessed lamp in the ceiling. I resented everything, even the damn light.

We sat there a while, Mom connecting us with her hands. "We'll have her favorite music at the funeral," she said. "'Amazing Grace,' for sure. Maybe 'A Mighty Fortress Is Our God.'"

She talked on about Bible verses and the color of the liner of the casket. I couldn't look at Hannah anymore, preferring to picture her as I knew her before, young and happy.

"He answered our prayer, you know," she said.

I let go of her hand. "What do you mean?"

She fingered Hannah's hair. "We didn't have to be the ones to do it. It isn't on our shoulders."

I turned to look at Jenny, who was wiping tears from her eyes. She watched me with quiet pain.

My mother reached down for her purse and handed it to me. "There's a piece of paper in there, in the side pocket. Can you get it for me?"

I rooted around and found a weathered sheet of lined paper, so old and worn as to be feathery soft. I unfolded it, taking care not to rip it.

I glanced at the words. They were arranged in short lines and seemed vaguely familiar. A couple simple chord strums were written in here and there.

It was a song.

"Will you sing this at her funeral?" Mom asked.

I looked up. "I don't think I know it."

"But you do," she said. She turned back to Hannah.

I read through the lines again. The melody started to come to me. Yes, I did know this song. It was about fathers and faith and love. A Christian song. "Did we used to sing it in church?"

"No," she said. "As far as I know, nobody's ever heard it but me and Hannah."

I didn't remember them having any friends who played guitar. "Who wrote it?"

She turned to me, an incredulous look on her face. "Baby, *you* did. You had this amazing faith back then. You wrote this song."

The memory thundered back at me. I stared at the paper, realizing that this was the handwriting of my youth. I'd written this after my father left, not long after. It was the last of its kind, as I moved into other kinds of music after, blues and classic rock.

"You remember it now?" she asked gently.

I nodded.

She reached out for me again, restoring the bridge between me and Hannah. "Hannah loved that song. When you turned away from the church, we would pray you would come back, that you would find your faith again."

I held the paper in my hands. I could remember those days. We had a little band at the church, and that was where I first got interested in guitar. The first song I ever plucked out was "This Little Light of Mine."

What a long hard fall it had been.

# 51

## JENNY

I thought about the funeral as I sat on the plane, looking out the window. The church ladies, Chance's song, and the way so many people came to pay tribute to the sweet, silly girl I would only know from pictures and cell phone videos.

Chance ducked beneath the overhead bins. He'd sold his truck after all and boxed up his essentials. He said he was ready to try out California. He'd promised his mother to come back in a month to see her and sort Hannah's belongings and decide what to keep and what to donate.

She also gave him a box of Grateful Dead posters and the things she'd taken from his room.

Chance was still angry at his father for not showing up, not responding to anything anyone sent him about Hannah. I could tell he wasn't going to let it go, and somewhere down the line, we'd be dealing with this man who'd failed his family.

But we were heading home. Chance was going to live with

Jazz, the drummer for the Sonic Kings, at first. We were going to try dating like normal people, despite the grain of sand that was hanging around from our beach encounter. Get to know each other before making any big decisions about weddings or permanent locations.

My phone buzzed. I glanced at the flight attendants to see if I still had time to look at it before they asked us to power everything down. They wandered along the aisle, checking overhead bins.

I pulled up the message. It was just a notification from the pregnancy site I'd joined. Attached was a picture of a strange sea creature with a long tail. The text read "Congratulations! You are five weeks pregnant. Your baby has reached the embryo stage and now resembles a tadpole."

I looked at the picture again. Gross.

"What's that?" Chance asked, dropping into the seat next to me. "It looks like an alien."

"It's your kid," I said, bumping my shoulder against his. "It's supposed to be a tadpole."

"We're having a frog?"

I thumped him again. "It's got your good looks, then."

He laughed. "I can see how this relationship is going to go."

He bent down and nudged his nose into my jaw. "So when are we going to see the doctor to get the green light again?"

We hadn't been having sex since I was worried after the time I bled.

"Tuesday," I said.

"I can't wait for Tuesday," he said.

"You know what I can't wait for?" I asked him.

"What?" He pressed his lips against the hair over my ear.

"All the Tuesdays. This one and the next and the next, forever."

His arm came around me. "Let's take them one at a time."

# Epilogue

## JENNY

The wedding was undoubtedly the smash hit of the season.

The Sonic Kings blared from the canopied stage where the ceremony had taken place. With Chance's help, they were sounding better and their set list had a lot more punch.

Waiters carrying trays of champagne moved through the guests, nothing outlandish, maybe one hundred or so. There were a few hunky actors in the crowd, and certainly some bombshell-beautiful actresses. A few necessary industry types. But mostly, they were family and friends, ready for the big toast.

I felt bulky with my six-month belly preceding me as I moved between tables. Chance took my hand and waved away the waiters who approached. He still wasn't interested in drinking, not even for show.

I was definitely nervous. After going to work for Tellmund, I'd been managing two of his most problematic A-list actors' Twitter and Facebook accounts. Because I was back to going to premieres, often at movies way bigger than Frankie's were, the press had taken notice when my "bump" appeared.

Another set of stories erupted and I was the subject of the hashtag #guessthebabydaddy until finally Chance asked Dylan Wolf to congratulate us on *his* Twitter account, which went viral. And it all settled down.

Chance glanced back at me. "You ready for this?"

I nodded.

A photographer, this one hired and therefore controlled via a contract and non-disclosure agreement, aimed his lens at me. Chance helped me up the stairs of the stage, and we waited for Paul to strum the final chords of "Party in the USA."

Another waiter arrived with our glasses, these full of sparkling white grape juice.

"You'll be great," Chance said as the song ended. He passed me a glass.

Paul waved me over. "I believe we have just the perfect person to lead the toast," he said into the mike. "Put your hands together for the girl formerly known as Frankie's cotton candy tart, Jenny Gillespie!"

I gave Paul a light punch in the belly for that and he pretended to stumble back in pain. The crowd laughed as they turned to the stage.

I stepped up to the mike. It felt strange being up here when the last time I was here, I'd been standing down below. I felt this choice of location made sense. We were back to where everything had begun.

I searched until I found Frankie in the crowd. "You going to come up here or am I going to have to drag you?" I asked.

More laughter.

He reached for the hand of Alec, the screenwriter I'd seen mentioned shortly after my girlfriend contract with Frankie ended. They had gone public a few weeks after the party. Since Alec wasn't an actor or the type to get in trouble, the publicity around them had been pretty quiet. Lucky them.

They came up to stand at the base of the stage. A waiter brought them fresh glasses of champagne. Then they smiled up at me.

I took a deep breath and began. "When I met Frankie, it was not love at first sight. It involved a sheet of paper, a pen, and an NDA."

The crowd tittered.

"One of the things I loved about being his public girlfriend was his savvy. He knows everything about you people." I pointed out in the crowd, then aimed squarely at Tellmund. "Especially you."

More laughter.

"Because of him, I got involved in an amazing industry full of beautiful people and smart business. And of course, Frankie too."

Frankie held up his champagne glass. "Absolutely accurate," he said.

I smiled down at him. "I knew something amazing was going on. Something he wanted to protect. Something wonderful that needed nurturing and care away from the glare of the spotlight." I paused. "And definitely out of the camera flash."

The photographer took that moment to snap a shot, the light blasting the stage. Everyone laughed.

"I was lucky to be that girl. When I finally learned I was right, that Frankie had found somebody worthy of all that effort — and by effort, I mean putting up with me" — I waited out the laughter — "I had never seen him so happy."

I held up my glass. "So here's to you, Alec, for putting that amazing smile on Frankie's face. And for the biggest happily ever after on any movie screen to be the one you have written for yourselves."

Glasses clinked as everyone sipped. I handed the mike back to Paul and returned to Chance.

"That was terrific," he said.

"Thank you."

We headed back down into the party. Several people approached and commented about the speech. I moved toward the food table. The second trimester was definitely all about the calories.

Chance tugged on my hand. "Let's go back to the gardens for a second," he said.

I stood there, torn between our little memory lane and the crab cakes. But I went with him a short ways down the path where I had noticed a photographer watching and kissed him for the first time.

"This is a great spot," I said. "Right where I sucked you into my evil plot."

He laughed. I took a second to really drink him in. His shoulders were strong and broad in a charcoal sports jacket. Beneath, he wore a silk T-shirt, perfectly on-trend for the music set. He was learning.

He'd let his beard grow out just enough to have that sexy scruffy look that worked so well on camera. He didn't have a lot of paparazzi chasing him down since he didn't have a record contract or much of a following, but I had a feeling that one day he would.

For now, he played with the Sonic Kings and sometimes opened for the band who opened for Dylan Wolf, when Dylan was close enough and had something available. Chance didn't mind being that far down the totem pole. It was something just to be on it at all.

I made enough money to support me and the baby anyway, and we were trying to decide if he was stay-at-home-dad material. We might not know until we got there. He'd moved in with me a month ago, though, and despite his complete and utter disrespect for pastels, it was going all right.

"Come here," he said, pulling me close. "I have a question for you."

"Does it involve ordering pizza? Because Brannah needs some nourishment." We'd decided not to find out what gender the baby was, and had taken to calling him/her a combination of Bryan and Hannah's names.

Chance stepped back and pulled out his cell phone. "Your wish is my command. Pepperoni or veggie?"

"All of the above." I hung on to the lapels of his jacket.

"I'm going to have to work out more to be able to carry you at this rate," he said.

I jerked on the lapels. "Don't make me hurt you."

He laughed. "Okay, okay. But I do have a question for you."

Chance plucked my hand off his jacket and slipped a ring on my finger. "How's this one?"

I pulled my hand away to look at it. The stone glittered in the lamplight, brighter and bigger than it should have been.

"How did you afford this? I know what you make!" I couldn't stop staring at it.

"Mom sent me hers to trade in for something new. She wanted you to have the best."

Tears pricked my eyes. "Is she still asking if I've fixed my hair?"

"Nope," he said. "She knows you're kind of stuck until the baby's born."

It was true. It turned out that hair dye was bad for babies, so I'd been chalking my roots with various colors. I looked like a Rainbow Brite doll.

"You said you had a question," I said. "I can't answer until you ask it."

He smiled down at me, his lazy grin warming me up like it always did.

"Jenny Gillespie, mother of my grain-of-sand, alien-tadpole, Brannah-baby, are you going to marry me after all this?"

I gazed up into the night sky. "I think I might like to negotiate some bullet points in the contract."

He scooped me up in his arms. "You better just answer me." He pretended to stagger. "And fast, before I can't hold you any longer."

I grabbed his lapels again. "Yes, Chance McKenzie, father of my accidental dropped-condom failed-pill-taking grain-of-sand Brannah-baby, I will marry you."

He leaned in to kiss me, but I put my fingers on his lips. "I would like to negotiate that pizza now."

Chance snapped at my fingers with his teeth. When I moved them aside, he caught me, his mouth on mine, warm and tender.

A flash fired, lighting up the night.

I pulled away and looked over. It was the hired photographer.

He gave Chance a thumbs up and headed back to the party.

"You're sneaky, Chance McKenzie," I said to him.

"Oh, you just wait," he said with another of those lazy grins that I adored. "You're going to love the headlines about us in the morning."

"What can they say about us now? Hunky singer sweeps pregnant nobody off her swollen feet?"

"The baby could still be an alien love child."

He walked back up the path, carrying my bulky body in his arms, until we were in sight of the party. A great cheer went up in the crowd, and Paul stopped the song onstage. "Did she turn your sorry ass down?" he asked into the mike.

Chance shook his head, and they began a new song, one I'd never heard before. Chance set me carefully down on the ground and headed up onstage. I knew he'd been writing some new material. But I had no idea there was going to be one about me.

As he took the mike from Paul and looked down, I made my way to my spot at the stage, at his feet, just like the first time he'd sung for me.

And when he gave us the words to the opening line, I knew that so much more than fate had a hand in everything that happened to us, good, bad, amazing, or tragic. And people like Chance were here to capture those feelings, however they came, and let us feel them, figure them out, and always sing along.

**THE END**

~*´♥`*~

## FOREVER

*There ain't nothing you can say*
*To make me turn away*
*There ain't nothing you can do*
*To make me take my love away from you*
*Because I said forever*
*And that's just what I'm gonna to do*

*There ain't nowhere you can go*
*That I won't get my walking shoes and follow*
*There ain't nowhere you can hide*
*That I won't find you with the love inside me*
*Because I said forever*
*And that's just what I'm gonna to do*

*How could you believe that I*
*Would ever have the need to say goodbye*
*All those years ago*
*I said the words that should have let you know*
*Because I said forever*
*And that's just what I'm gonna do*

*There ain't nothing you can say*
*There ain't nothing you can do*
*There ain't nowhere you can go*
*And there ain't nowhere you can hide*

The FOREVER song is a real song! Hear it at
www.bradwhittington.com/forever.

Lyrics throughout this novel by Deanna's author friend,
singer-songwriter Brad Whittington.

# Also by Deanna Roy

Don't miss the other books in the Forever Series

 ***Stella & Dane***: Stella is ready to blow out of her honky tonk town when a hot stranger rolls in on a Harley, leading to a dangerous romance that upsets the locals and sparks a tragedy that will change everyone's lives. (Romance)

 ***Baby Dust***. Abandoned by friends and haunted by what they've lost, five women forge friendships to survive the death of their babies. (Women's Fiction)

# About Deanna Roy

 Deanna is a passionate advocate for women who have lost babies. She founded the web site www.pregnancyloss.info in 1998 after the loss of her first baby and continues to run both online and in-person support groups for women who have endured this impossible loss. Find her on Facebook, Twitter, Instagram, Google+, and Goodreads.

Learn more about the author at
www.deannaroy.com

Your review on Amazon is appreciated—it makes a huge difference to authors when readers provide their reactions to a work.

# Dedications to Our Moms
# and Mother Figures

♥ Janice Roy ~ Crafter extraordinaire, woman of God. ♥

♥ Jan Korfmacher ~ Fun-loving, classic, loved by all. ♥

♥ Pat Prouty ~ Extraordinary mom, aunt, and classy feisty lady. ♥

♥ Vivian ~ best mom ever! ♥

♥ Brenda O. ~ Forever my Mom, Forever my Friend ♥

♥ Brenda S. Grant ~ October 24, 1961- December 28, 2010 ♥

♥ RMG ~ For all that I am, and all that I will be is because of you...love you! ♥

♥ Mari E Silvestri ~ 06/06/50-03/03/06. To the best mother and Nani anyone could ask for. You will never be forgotten ♥

♥ Patti C. ~ May she always know what a hero she is, in my eyes, and in the eyes of my children. Love, AK ♥

♥ Debbie Tucci ~ Thank-you for making me the person I am today...loving, strong and independent. You are also a wonderful grandmother. ♥

♥ Bing Ying Jang ~ Best mom to us three kids and wonderful grandmother to her grandson, Janzen ♥

♥ Dorothy Rice ~ You made me who I am today I Love You Mom! - Jodi ♥

♥ Claudia Isenhour ~ The best mom anyone could ask for. I miss you every single day. Love you. ♥

♥ Sue Preston ~ My mom is the most loving person that I know. I am who I am today because of her kind heart and beautiful soul. I Love You Mom ♥

♥ Lucille C ~ always and forever my mom ♥

♥ Jennie Etling Holcombe ~ For all the love, help, and advice I thank you, mom. ♥

♥ Winnie ~ Love you mum, thanks for being my strength! ♥

♥ Melissa P. ~ Thank you for being the best mom in the world. I love you! ♥

♥ Marie Lahep ~ Kind heart, loving, caring, creative. Wonderful loving person ♥

♥ Aunt Meim ~ Thank you very much for being my Aunt, my best friend and my "Mom." I love you so very much. ♥

♥ Verna "Jeanie" Brown-Buckley ~ Thank you, for your love and knowledge. ♥

♥ Linda Yow ~ My mom, my biggest supporter, my best friend! ♥

Joann Weber ~ This is to my mother the women that gave birth to me. She been my rock when I needed a hard shoulder when my child died at birth and when my son and daughter came into this world. She is my world.

Lourdes Rodriguez ~ Without her I don't know where I'd be! Love her!

Cindy J ~ For your never ending support you have shown me. You are my family when I didn't have one to turn to.

Audrey C ~ Love you with all my heart Mum

Janice Quinn ~ Love you so much mom. Thank you for loving me and always being there.

Clara Nell ~ We love & miss you!!

Mandy Matthews ~ Thanks for being there for me and my babies when we needed u. Love you mum, love Lisa

Jackie ~ You are missed! 10/2/02

Eula Faye Torbett ~ Our Mother: remembered on Earth; living eternally in Heaven.

Audra Lee ~ My precious Grandma, may she rest in peace

Angeline C ~ Our family anchor!

Sharon S. ~ My best friend, always in my heart

Sheila Everson ~ So blessed to have had you as our Mam, Chrissie & Julie

Vira W ~ 08/05/2004 Gone, but not forgotten. I love you.

R.A.T. ~ Mama Llama

My mom Gabrielle ~ Simply because she loves me no matter what and she's awesome.

Ruth Lessard ~ My Mom, My Best Friend!

Pat Claffey - Best Foster Mom ~ Thanks for loving me like your own child

Stacey L. ~ Mommy, you may be 1000mi away, thought you are never far away!

Rose-Marie W. ~ Grammy- You raised us, we love you so much!!

Milani T. ~ Mom- thank you for being my best friend. I was blessed to have you as my mom. It's been 2 1/2 years since you have passed away and I just want to let you know that I miss you everyday. <3 Michelle

Judy C ~ Love you Mom!

Susan ~ Love you Mom!

Lois Ahlson ~ to my mom who is watching over me from above.

My mom Anna P. ~ I love and miss you every day. Until we meet in heaven I know your always watching over me.

Becky Quintana ~ thanks for everything you do. Love you!

♥ Darla Jean ~ We love you! ♥

♥ Aunt Rita ~ Thanks for taking me under your wing after my mom passed! ♥

♥ Sue Card ~ My Grammy, <3 Lyndsi ♥

♥ Brenda Patterson Hayman ~ My wonderful step-mom. I love you so much! ♥

♥ Dorothy W. ~ Handicapped from birth but led a long life full of love ♥

♥ Vickie L ~ Love you Mom! ♥

♥ Terry S. ~ For always supporting my Forever. ♥

♥ Marilyn Davis ~ Miss you ♥

♥ Dorothy (Dotty) Adams ~ I love and miss you every day ♥

♥ Linda H. ~ Thank you for always supporting me through thick and thin! Love you Mom! ♥

♥ Margaret Madeline ~ 7/3/1928 ♥

♥ Sharon Schumacher ~ Mom you are the greatest roll model of how to be strong, loving woman. I love you. ♥

♥ Sandy Gray ~ You're the mother and best friend a girl could ever ask for. I love you always! <3 ♥

♥ Doris Jillette ~ Thank you for being my rock. I love you more! * Cynthia ♥

♥ Walli Oesterreicher ~ In my heart forever, love always ♥

♥ Delores M. (Inky) ~ My mom is the best. ♥

♥ Eleanor Macedon ~ A woman whose values, morality, and integrity sets a high bar to pass. Love you always. ♥

♥ My mom, Gertrude Evelyn Ballard, the most wonderful mom ever. Would love to visit her just one hour. Miss her terribly. ♥

♥ Mom/Mamaw ~ Rest in Peace 4/9/42-5/18/13 ♥

♥ Joyce Macielag ~ Thanks for all you do. I love you, Mom! ♥

♥ Dlrunge ~ To my mom, my friend, confident , my everything. Thank you for all you showed us how to be. We Will love you forever and always . ♥

♥ Marsha Harbour ~ Even though you're my sister, you stepped up and took the lead to help with my girls. I am FOREVER GRATEFUL I love you ♥

♥ Marly R. ~ Thank you for being you and being there for me <3 ♥

♥ Charlane Carlson ~ My Mom, my hero I admire your strength everyday. ♥

♥ To my mom Esther G ~ Thank you for all you've done for your children and your community. You do not realize how loved you really are! ♥

♥ Wilma G. Roush ~ She raised us to be strong faithful adults. She is always there for us when we need her and even when we think we don't. I love you Mom forever, Gayla ♥

Gayla Roush Miller

ERGE ~ Wish everyone had a mother as wonderful as mine

Gwendolyn Mae Hamilton ~ Love & miss you! I think of you daily!

Rachella Baker ~ My mom is my best friend, when I am sad, I call just to hear her voice to cheer me up. (lots more)

Nancy T ~ To the BEST mom ever! I love you!

Katy Rakel ~ A thousand thank you's could never be enough. I love you bunches mama

Anita "Nana" Bixler ~ You taught me how a mother's love for her children knows no bounds and the type of mother I strive to be every day.

Iola F ~ I can still feel your love and encouragement

Elizabeth Swift ~ I lost the best mother in law, friend on March 27, 1999. Loved and missed daily.

Jamelah Aishah Ambor Tago ~ Because you're you, and I wouldn't change that.

Mae Huggins ~ I love you mom!

Francis Morgan Johnson ~ "Gone but not Forgotten" A very brave, strong, & courageous woman! I miss you and love you mamaw!

Ellie Mae Lewis ~ I'll always remember you and the strength and courage you had!! I love you and miss you!

Susan G. Pittmann ~ Your love and example light the way before me as I try to make a difference in our world.

Donna E. ~ Thx for your love and support

Lynn H ~ You will be a survivor Mom!! I love you

Gloria Aleman ~ You make my heart happy. Love always.

Cindy J ~ U r the best, thank U 4 all u have ever done for me. I love u.

Patricia V ~ My hero, my mom. Forever in my heart.

Momma Gail ~ Always putting us first an loving us conditionally.

Frankie Gibbs ~ For being my Mom when you didn't have to be.. Love an miss u so much.

Bobbi Lindsey ~ I love you, Mom!

Brenda S. Grant ~ I miss you always and I'll love you forever! October 24, 1961- December 28, 2010